THE SECRET OF THE

KING'S TOMB

THE SECRET OF THE KING'S TOMB

A RICHARD HALLIBURTON ADVENTURE

BOOK 1

GARRETT DRAKE

The Secret of the King's Tomb
© Copyright 2019 Garrett Drake

First Edition 2019

Published in the United States of America

Green E-Books
PO Box 140654
Boise, ID 83714

For Faith, Julia, Elijah, and Sarabeth,
my four little adventurers

"Those who live in the even tenor of their way simply exist until death ends their monotonous tranquility. No, there's going to be no even tenor with me. The more uneven it is, the happier I shall be."
— *Richard Halliburton, 1919*

PROLOGUE

Fall 1912
Memphis, Tennessee

THE EARLY MORNING SUN BEAMED THROUGH THE thinning foliage overhead as the truck came to a halt. Mr. Wesley Halliburton adjusted his hat before addressing his sons.

"Boys, I need you to entertain yourselves for a few minutes while I talk to Mr. Jackson about purchasing this land," Wesley said. "Do you think you can do that?"

Richard and Wesley Jr. both nodded before racing out of their father's automobile and dashing across the wooded acreage.

Within two minutes, a game of Patriots and Redcoats had broken out, a favorite of Wesley Jr.'s. The two boys selected their weapons from the broken limbs lying on the forest floor before staking out their forts.

Richard crouched near the base of an oak tree and waited for the right moment to strike. He scanned the area in search of his younger brother. Wesley Jr. had scrambled down the side of a hill about twenty yards away and disappeared. As a gentle breeze swept by, crisp leaves rustled, adding to the serene sounds of nature. A bubbling brook at the bottom of a short ravine and constant birdcalls provided a symphony that struck the right chords with Richard. It also provided the cover he needed to launch an assault on Wesley Jr. the second his movements surrendered his hiding spot.

When a woodpecker began hammering away on a nearby pine tree, Wesley Jr. rolled onto his back and stared upward with a smile on his face as he watched the show. Clutching a stick in one hand and a fistful of acorns in the other, Richard seized the opportunity to attack. He stormed down the hill and unleashed a barrage on his unsuspecting brother.

"Back to England with you," Richard said as he watched Wesley Jr. twisting and turning to escape.

Richard grinned, admiring his stealthy move for a moment longer than he should have.

"Never, you traitor!" Wesley Jr. said.

Wesley Jr. spun around and kicked his legs out, catching Richard in the back of his knees and toppling him. Richard fell down, crashing face first into the moist Tennessee earth amidst a sea of leaves. In a deft move, Wesley Jr. pounced on top of Richard, securing him with a bear hug. The two boys tumbled down the hill, coming to a stop just a few feet short of the water.

Richard broke free from his brother's grasp and took up a new position behind him. With Wesley Jr.'s face pressed flat against the dirt, he struggled, thrashing his arms and legs in an attempt to buck Richard off. But after several failed attempts to shred Richard, the fight left Wesley Jr.

"I'm not falling for it again," Richard said.

Wesley Jr. grunted. "I'm not trying to trick you. I promise. I see something."

"You see something?" Richard asked. "I don't care what it is. I'm not letting you get up until you surrender."

"I see an arrowhead," Wesley Jr. said.

"Where?" Richard said as he stood, hoping to be the first to put his hands on it.

Wesley Jr. darted toward the water and scooped up the artifact before Richard could snatch it.

"Haha!" Wesley Jr. said, dancing back and forth in triumph. "This looks like one from the Choctaws that Dad showed us a few weeks ago."

Wesley Jr. kept talking, but Richard wasn't listening.

"Yeah, yeah," Richard said as he knelt next to the edge of the brook.

"I'm gonna go tell Dad," Wesley Jr. said as he jumped to his feet and raced off.

Richard didn't even consider joining. He plunged his hand into the freezing water and retrieved a shiny object. After studying it for a few seconds, he dipped it back into the stream and cleaned off the edges. When he was finished, he used his shirt to dry the piece off and then held it up to inspect it further.

Spanish gold!

Richard could hardly contain himself as he mulled over the possibilities of how the coin arrived at this point.

Perhaps this belonged to DeSoto when he led the conquistadors through here. Or maybe it belonged to some Choctaws who robbed a few Spaniards.

Whatever the gold's true origin didn't really matter to Richard. He was confident he could spin a tale interesting enough to lure his classmates into forking over a penny for the privilege to see the ancient artifact.

CHAPTER 1

The Hermitage Hotel
Monte-Carlo, Monaco
January 29, 1922, 9:45 p.m.

RICHARD HALLIBURTON KNOCKED ON THE DOOR AND then tugged on the bottom of his bellhop jacket while waiting for someone to answer. Smoothing out the wrinkles around the breast pockets, he wondered if anyone would notice that his uniform was about one size too small. Had there been more time, he would've scrounged up a proper-fitting uniform from the hotel's washroom. But Richard had been sent to rescue Dr. Thurston Miller in the most urgent of missions.

Richard dug into his pocket before pulling out his dagger. Hiding it behind his back, he waited for someone to open the door. Nearly thirty seconds had passed, and he hadn't heard a sound. He knocked again. Thirty more seconds. Still nothing.

Using his left hand, he turned the knob and opened the door. Much to Richard's surprise, the door wasn't locked.

"Hello, Dr. Miller?" Richard called as he entered.

He turned on the light and scanned the room. Papers were strewn across the floor. Drawers were haphazardly placed near the dresser. A briefcase and its contents covered the bed.

That's when Richard noticed a man sitting in a chair

facing the wall in the far corner.

"Dr. Miller?" Richard called again before shutting the door behind him.

Again, there was no response.

As Richard drew near, he noticed the man's hand dangling over the chair's arm with a gun just below his fingertips. Upon closer inspection, Richard realized that the drapes were now decorated with blood splatters.

He gasped as his eyes widened.

What have I gotten myself into?

According to Hank Foster from U.S. Army Intelligence, the assignment was allegedly a simple one: Warn the famous British anthropologist about the impending danger of meeting with his guests and urge him not to give up any information. Then Richard just had to listen in on the conversation and report back what he heard.

Such a task seemed simple enough from the fast-talking Texan who Richard had met just hours earlier in the Monte-Carlo Casino. The recent Princeton graduate needed something to help him forget that a few short hours earlier he was on his way to amassing a small fortune at the roulette table before losing it all. But it was the reward that ultimately lured him to accept—a fully funded trip to explore Egypt.

Richard shoved his hand into his pocket and fished out the small replica of the Sphinx given to him by his grandfather J.W. While he was a prisoner during the Civil War, he said there were only two things that kept him alive. The first was hope that he would be reunited again with his beloved Juliet. The second was that he would one day travel the world and visit the ancient sands of Egypt. While Richard never met his grandfather, the story was passed down along with the Sphinx. J.W. never laid eyes on Egypt, and neither had Richard's father. But Richard vowed to see it for them all.

He pocketed the item and continued to scour the room. On top of the desk, he found a sloppily written letter begging the world to forgive him for taking his own life. Richard found another document with Dr. Miller's signature and compared it with the signed note. They appeared similar but not in the exact manner one would expect from a scientist known for his fastidiousness.

After five minutes, Richard had seen enough and decided to report back what he had observed. But as he strode toward the door, he heard footsteps clattering down the hallway and men shouting.

Richard knew he couldn't be caught in the room, especially if it was the Germans who were headed here for the meeting. Ripping his knife out of his pocket, he darted out onto the balcony. He pulled the doors shut behind him and plastered his back against the wall. A stiff breeze whipped across his face, which was assaulted by the driving rain. The drops pelted the window and resulted in a high-pitched tinkle.

"We must have missed something," one of the men said in German. "Check the room again."

Richard had picked up enough of the language while traveling through Europe for the past six months that he understood the conversation.

"Wilhelm, look at this," one of the other men said.

After a long pause, the man referred to as Wilhelm spoke. "I don't remember seeing this earlier," he said. "A little model of the Sphinx. Interesting."

Richard patted the outside of his pants pockets, feeling for the replica.

It must've fallen out.

"Someone has been here," Wilhelm said. "Search this room again in case they're still here. If we don't find the document, we must go search his holiday home."

Footsteps thundered around the room—and then they stormed toward the balcony.

Richard was on the third floor and contemplated a jump. However, he knew he was sure to break his leg or ankle in the fall.

Better than being dead.

The door swung open, and he didn't wait around for the man to make eye contact. Aside from getting murdered, the last thing Richard wanted was for the man to see his face. Richard hurdled over the railing toward the diagonal balcony.

"*Stopp ihn!*" the soldier yelled.

Richard didn't even pause as he leaped over the railing again, this time landing on the sidewalk. Despite staggering as he hit the ground, he regained his balance and stayed upright. With his face drenched, he brushed away some of the rain with the back of his hand before breaking into a sprint.

Richard weaved in and out of the foot traffic clogging up the sidewalks on Monte-Carlo Avenue. Above the spatter of rain on the concrete and shouts of umbrella-bearing pedestrians miffed with his clumsy navigational skills, he heard rapid footsteps behind him. Around him, the street lamps flickered as the wind picked up.

Hustling toward the Monte-Carlo Casino, Richard searched for a place to hide. Entering the hotel would likely enable the Germans to hone in on his location. With the crowd thinning along one area of the street, he sought a nook to hunker down while the Reichswehr soldier stormed past was vital for survival.

He identified a possible spot across the street, a small park with trees and a structure that he figured could at least provide an opportunity to escape once and for all. Dodging a horse-drawn carriage and two motor vehicles, Richard crouched down against the base of the tree and peered around the edge to see if he could find his pursuer.

Seconds later, a man stormed into the park and stopped, putting his hands on his hips as he peered in every direction. Richard leaned back, shielding himself from being recognized. His palms started to sweat, his heart racing.

When he leaned forward to see if the man was there, Richard let out a sigh of relief. The man was gone.

Richard wanted to head for the casino but needed to make sure he just missed the Reichswehr agent. When he attempted to lean forward a second time, he felt two large hands clamp down on his shoulders and yank him backward.

CHAPTER 2

W HAT ARE YOU DOING OUT HERE?" DEMANDED THE man clutching Richard's shoulder. Turning around, Richard was relieved to see Hank Foster. "I was followed," Richard said.

"Let's get inside now," Hank said. "You need to tell me everything."

Richard hustled up the steps after Hank before the two men found a table near the back wall and collapsed into a pair of chairs. A waiter stopped and asked the two men if they wanted towels. After they said yes, the waiter disappeared and a recounting of the event began.

"What did you find out?" Hank asked.

Richard glanced around the room before leaning in close. "They killed him."

"Dr. Miller?" Hank asked, his eyes widening.

Richard nodded. "Shot him in the head and then staged it to look like a suicide."

Hank cursed as he clenched his fist. "Dr. Miller was a good man."

"Well, the Reichswehr were looking for something. The main German leader—I believe he went by the name Wilhelm—mentioned something about looking for it at Dr. Miller's holiday home."

"He winters in Marseille, a relatively short train ride

away," Hank said. "We need to know what the Reichswehr is after there."

Richard cocked his head to one side. "You mean, this isn't over? I have to do more for you?"

"Probably not much more," Hank said. "Look, all you need to do is get on that train in the morning for Marseille. Then just slip some money to some of the house staff after the Germans leave to find out what the Reichswehr soldiers were asking about or looking for. Then just report back to me."

Richard scowled. "Earlier, my simple task was to eavesdrop on the meeting and tell you what I heard—and you agreed to pay for my trip to Egypt."

"That was all before Dr. Miller was murdered."

"And that's exactly why I don't think I should be compelled to continue on this foolish expedition for you."

Hank chuckled. "Come on, Richard. This shouldn't be difficult for you. Heck, you usually tempt fate at least twice before breakfast. Remember, I've been following you across two continents. I know you aren't genuinely fearful of something as benign as making new friends at a dead archeologist's winter home and snooping around a bit."

Richard felt his heart still thumping in his chest, which wasn't unusual given his past history. As a young teenager, he spent a few months in the hospital while doctors tried to figure out why he had such a rapid heartbeat. And while it eventually subsided, he wasn't sure he'd ever experienced this amount of pounding.

"If I jump off a cliff and drown, I've got no one to blame but myself for my own stupidity," Richard said. "But secret German soldiers creeping around in the shadows and murdering innocent people? No, this not the same thing as what I do."

"Sure it is," Hank said. "They're both exciting and adventurous. You could die in either one of these scenarios."

"But if the Reichswehr kills me, it won't be on my terms."

"If you think you always get to dictate the terms of adventure, you haven't been on enough journeys," Hank said.

Richard knew Hank was right. Aside from a short trip to Europe that ignited the unquenchable wanderlust raging within, Richard hadn't seen much of the world. If the Great War had continued, maybe he would have. He looked forward to serving his country in battle. But lurking in the shadows to spy on an elite team of German soldiers? Even to Richard that seemed like a dangerous venture—and one he now knew could have fatal consequences.

"Can't you find another one of your spies to do the job? If this job is as simple as you claim it is, practically anyone could do it."

"I don't trust just anyone."

Richard eyed Hank cautiously. "And you trust me?"

"I'm an expert at discerning the character of a man. My job depends on it."

"In that case, I'm still baffled why you've chosen me," Richard said. "When you approached, I was barely a little more than a down-on-his-luck gambler who tossed away the wealth I'd amassed because of my greed."

"You're still young," Hank said. "It's an excusable offense."

"Yet you think you know what kind of man I am? I *still* don't know what kind of man I am, nor am I convinced that my decisions are always the best ones."

"You run toward danger without blinking an eye—and you love your country," Hank said. "Those are two traits that make you an exceptional candidate for this line of work."

"Perhaps you're a skilled recruiter because you have to continually fill new openings."

Hank chuckled. "I'll admit that there's a high turnover rate, but that's the nature of the business."

"And that doesn't sound like any kind of business I want to be involved with."

"Aren't you the least bit curious why a group of German soldiers would murder a British archeologist in a Monte-Carlo hotel?"

"All I'm thinking about is that I might be next," Richard said. "Besides, if this job in Marseille is so simple, you could probably do it yourself."

Hank looked down and sighed.

In an instant, Richard saw through the ploy. "You already know what's going on here, don't you?"

Hank shrugged. "I have a hunch, but I need it confirmed—and by someone other than me."

"Where are they going?"

"We believe they're headed somewhere in Egypt."

"You offered to pay my way there because you want me to follow them, don't you?"

Hank nodded. "It's not a crime to ask."

"You have an underhanded way of asking."

"Look, I don't want you to kill anyone or confront them," Hank said. "I just want you to keep an eye on them and report it back to me. We have teams of highly trained soldiers that could handle the messier duties of this mission if the situation called for it."

"I don't know," Richard said before taking a deep breath and then exhaling. "I'm not sure this is the kind of adventure I'm after, even if it is just spying on someone."

"You think you'll be satisfied with taking pictures of famous sites around the world? Trotting the globe isn't enough for you, and you know it."

Richard scratched under his shirt collar. He gazed off

in the distance, mulling over the best way to respond. Ultimately, Hank was right in one respect. Richard craved something beyond being just another travel writer, taking pictures of himself pointing at monuments and regurgitating the information that everyone else already knew. Such activities felt self-important and aggrandizing. He was sure to get plenty of pats on the back from fellow Princeton alum, but would it truly be satisfying work? What Richard feared the most was navigating listlessly through life without making his mark on the world, a world he desperately wanted to explore. And he couldn't help but wonder if that's where he was headed if he turned down Hank's offer. However, the twisted path that led to this offer were still befuddling.

Earlier in the afternoon, he had left his hotel a few miles across the border in Nice, France, with Pauline, a young woman he'd met by randomly when the clerk assigned them the same room by mistake. Richard viewed the chance meeting as the fates bringing together two like-minded free spirits. When she agreed to accompany him to the Monte-Carlo Casino, he was pleased—but not as much as when he converted their fifty francs into more than eight hundred. However, it was all just a dream, thrown away when Richard let visions of yachts and mansions dance in his head. In a matter of minutes, they'd lost everything, including their joy. That's the state Richard was in when Hank approached—and also the moment Pauline struck off for another roulette table in an effort to build her own fortune apart from Richard, who had mistakenly given her bad strategy advice. Without Pauline to keep him company, what could it hurt to take up Hank on his offer? Now, a few hours later, Richard wondered if he would even live long enough to regret it.

"Richard?" Hank asked, snapping his fingers. "Are you still with me?"

Richard emerged from his contemplative state. "Yeah, I'm still here."

"But are you *with* me?" Hank asked again.

Before Richard could respond, he noticed Pauline trudging across the floor toward him with a sour look on her face.

She stopped in front of him. "You're back."

He nodded. "Got here maybe ten minutes ago. What's the matter?"

"I lost it all," she said.

"How much?"

"Everything I brought with me, except enough money to get back to the hotel tonight."

"I'm sorry," Richard said. "This was all my fault. We should've quit while we were ahead earlier."

"This night has been most forgettable," she said. "But you did make an agreement with me earlier this evening. You promised that if it wasn't memorable, you'd do something fun with me."

"Are you sure it hasn't been memorable?" Richard asked. "I doubt you'll ever forget the night you won a small fortune and then lost it in Monte-Carlo."

"I'll remember it only if you make good on your promise."

Richard smiled. "Want to go cliff diving?"

She nodded. "I just checked outside. The clouds are gone and the moon is out again. It's better than staying miserable in here."

"I can't disagree with that," Richard said.

He turned toward Hank. "Thank you for the offer, sir. But I'm going to have to decline."

"What about Egypt?" Hank asked.

"What about it?" Richard replied. "I'm not going to let

a little thing like a lack of means prevent me from reaching my next destination. Farewell, Mr. Foster."

Richard turned toward Pauline and offered his arm. "Shall we?"

A wide grin spread across her face.

"What was that all about?" she asked. "What did he want you to do?"

"Nothing I'm interested in. Now, let's go find a cliff."

CHAPTER 3

Nice, France

HUNCHED OVER THE TABLE, KARL WILHELM adjusted the magnification on his jeweler glasses while studying his bonsai tree. Approaching one of the upper branches slowly, he snipped off a leaf with his trimmer. He leaned back in his chair to examine his work again. A slight upward curl formed at the corners of his mouth.

Footsteps thundered down the hall toward his room before the door to his hotel room flung open. Wilhelm didn't take his gaze off his plant. His men surrounded him, trained to remain silent until spoken to.

"Did you get the tickets?" Wilhelm asked as he moved in steadily to snip another leaf from the tree.

"Our train leaves for Marseille in the morning at seven o'clock," answered Hans Reinhard, Wilhelm's second in command.

"Excellent," Wilhelm said. He made a precise cut before setting the trimmed piece over to the side in a neat pile.

The men remained quiet as he continued to work. After a long pause, one of the men, Felix Ludwig, spoke up.

"Sir, when are you ever going to be finished with that tree?" he asked.

Wilhelm maintained his stare on the bush. "In horticulture, your work is never truly finished, even for those who reap a harvest. There is always another crop to produce or seeds to plant."

"Don't you ever grow tired of such a tedious hobby?" Ludwig pressed.

Wilhelm turned in his chair toward the inquiring young soldier, lifting up the magnifying lenses and peering over the top of his glasses.

"The only thing that would make this hobby tedious was if I ever expected it to be finished," Wilhelm said. "There's always a leaf to be cut or a branch to be trimmed. If I wanted to admire my creations, I would work with dead wood, not living things. Such artistry requires a ruthless commitment to perfection, much like our mission."

"But one day our mission will be completed," Ludwig countered.

"A good soldier knows that he will always have a homeland to defend or an enemy to squelch," Wilhelm said. "Our mission is not just one thing. We're here because we all want to see Germany restored to its rightful place in this world, which is an unmatched power. And for the time being, we must lie in wait. But when we flex our might, we will avenge all these unjust sanctions that have crippled our empire."

"In that case, we should be training with our fellow soldiers," Ludwig said. "When the moment comes for us to rise up, we need to be the most prepared force in the world. I can hardly see how these types of missions will prepare us for that."

Wilhelm stood and removed his gloves before slamming them onto the table. None of the soldiers flinched, all of them accustomed to their leader's physical outbursts. After methodically moving around the table, Wilhelm came nose-to-nose with Ludwig before replying.

"Perhaps you're too young to appreciate all that we had before the war," Wilhelm said. "You missed all the privilege and prestige of what accompanied being from our incredible empire. Yet our leaders thought there was more for us, and rightly so. But it took nearly the entire world to stop us. Our leaders have promised that we will never succumb to such a fate again. That is why we're on this mission. We already have excellent forces, but we want to possess all the resources winning a war against the rest of the world would require. And we're going to do it by stripping the world of its richest resources—every country's treasures from their heritage. We will stuff our coffers so full that it will be impossible to stop us from ruling every corner of the earth."

"Wouldn't we be better thieves than treasure hunters?" Ludwig asked, unfazed by Wilhelm's diatribe.

"Our motives would be exposed, leaving us subject to the heavy-handed sanctions from those monsters who have sought to destroy us through monetary means," Wilhelm said. "That's why you have all been selected, an elite group of men who can each mask your nationality while all possessing the other skills necessary to capture the treasures of ancient civilizations."

Ludwig nodded. "I understand, sir. I hope you don't regard my questions as if I was viewing your direction of our team as anything less than ideal."

"Great leaders aren't afraid of questions," Wilhelm said as he started pacing around the room. "They're only afraid of failure. Now, go get some sleep. We have a long day ahead of us tomorrow."

All of the men scurried out of Wilhelm's room and to their own quarters down the hall, everyone except Hans Reinhard. Once the last soldier filed out, Reinhard closed the door behind them and locked it.

"Ludwig can be a little tempestuous," Reinhard said.

"He's very skilled, but he is naive. I don't take offense to his questions. I will take offense if he questions my leadership. We need him for this mission."

"Who will you send into Dr. Miller's house tomorrow?"

Wilhelm shrugged. "As long as Ludwig is one of the two men, does it really matter?"

Reinhard settled into the chair across from Wilhelm, who donned his jeweler glasses again and resumed trimming his bonsai tree.

"Did you have something you wanted to talk about?" Wilhelm asked as he focused his attention on the plant.

"Sir, I know that you may not know the answer to this question, but I need to ask it."

"Go ahead."

Reinhard sighed for continuing. "If we secure this treasure—"

"*When* we secure this treasure," Wilhelm corrected.

"When we secure this treasure, how much longer will we be on this particular mission?"

Wilhelm chuckled. "Do you have somewhere else you need to be?"

"No, it's just that I—I miss my wife and daughter and—"

"Your sacrifice isn't unique," Wilhelm said. "Everyone on this special team is leaving friends and family behind, people we love and cherish. But it's for those people that we're all here."

"But my daughter, sir, she's—"

"I have daughters, too. I have three of them, to be exact. But you won't hear me bemoaning the fact that I won't be able to see them for a while. Now, I chose you to be my second in command because I thought you had the fortitude to handle leading these men with me. But now that you're coming to me with these mundane excuses, I'm starting to wonder."

"No, sir, it's not like that," Reinhard said, waving his hands. "I just want to know how far along this particular treasure could advance our goals."

"Don't waste your time on such conjecture," Wilhelm said as he placed his tools on the table. "We're going to be traversing every continent until the Reichswehr has enough resources to put Germany's boot on the throat of the world."

"But you're certain that Dr. Miller was lying?"

"Without a doubt. Now, go check on the men before curfew. We must ensure that everyone has a good night of sleep. Tomorrow is critical for gathering the information we need to move forward."

Reinhard stood and saluted Wilhelm before exiting the room. Left alone, he snipped off one final leaf before leaning back to admire his work. For the moment, everything was perfect. But it wouldn't stay that way nor could Wilhelm do anything to prevent the tree from requiring any more tending. Such was the nature of his hobby, which was not much different than his work.

He prepared for bed, mulling over how he would handle the next day. All he needed were the documents to identify the exact location of Dr. Miller's findings while working on some ancient Egyptian texts and his team could begin the excavation process of one of the richest treasures in the world.

* * *

HANS REINHARD RAN HIS FINGER ACROSS THE SMALL portrait of his daughter as a tear trickled down his face. While rushing to get to Monte-Carlo for the meeting with Dr. Miller, Reinhard never had the opportunity to tell Wilhelm about his little Emilia, his precious *schatzi*.

Reinhard stared at the photograph until his eyes blurred

with tears, wondering if he'd ever see her again. Two days before the team deployed, he took her to the doctor where he received gut-wrenching news. Emilia was dying from cancer. The doctor who treated her was hesitant to say how long she might have to live, but he estimated around a year based on the history of his previous patients with the disease.

"Maybe more, maybe less," was as definitive of an answer as Reinhard could get from the doctor.

With the weight of that news, Reinhard wanted to back out of the mission, but his wife encouraged him to go. She rubbed her stomach, which was bulging from her long-awaited second pregnancy.

"Your mission is important," said his wife, Annemaria, who was the daughter of General Paul von Hindenburg. Her loyalty to her country was difficult to match, even for a patriot such as Reinhard. He suspected it was one of the traits that made him so attractive to her. Growing up in General Hindenburg's house, she couldn't have merely just married a loyal countryman—he had to be a soldier, and one who was committed to the nation above all else.

And if Reinhard had been asked just days before learning of Emilia's fatal illness if he would have put anything above his devotion to his country, he would have emphatically said no. One fifteen-minute visit in a doctor's office changed all that. This was his *schatzi*, the girl who had managed to wrap him around her finger for the past decade, the girl who he knew was waiting for him to return from the Great War. The thought of not seeing her again terrified him. Never to hear her singing to her dolls as she twirled them around her room was an unbearable thought.

I'll see you before you can even miss me, schatzi.

Reinhard clutched the picture before drifting to sleep on a damp pillow.

CHAPTER 4

RICHARD AWOKE THE NEXT MORNING WITH A THUD, hitting the wooden floor hard. The jarring introduction to his morning left him in a disoriented state as he attempted to regain his bearings. Glancing down at his attire, he noticed he was wearing only a pair of boxers. He pulled the blanket off the couch just above him and covered his waist.

A woman wrapped in a housecoat squinted as she stood over him.

"Are you all right?" she asked.

Her face came into focus. It was Pauline. Then the events of the previous evening rushed back—the wispy clouds zipping in front of the pale moon, the jagged cliff, the numbing cold when his body hit the water, and the frigid walk home while soaking wet. He remembered enough to realize that hitting the water from such a tall height accounted for his throbbing headache and his hazy memory.

"I think so, but there are gaps in my recollection," he said as he sat up.

"Don't worry," she said. "You were a perfect gentleman and refused to let me stay alone after those men tried to snatch my purse on the way home."

"Perhaps I overstayed my welcome."

She flashed a smile. "You were fine. Not that my purse

contained any money for them to steal. But it was rather chivalrous."

"My head hurts, and now you're reminding me of everything that went wrong earlier in the evening," he deadpanned.

"Well, you didn't promise the night would be memorable specifically for you. But it appears as though you haven't forgotten what made it forgettable."

"The ebb and flow of gambling has a way of making you want to erase everything from your memory, at least when you end up on the negative side of things."

She chuckled. "Believe it or not, the most memorable thing you said all night was in your sleep."

Richard froze, unsure if he wanted to ask her what he said.

"My, how quickly you've turned red," Pauline said as a faint smile spread across her face. "Don't worry. I already told you that you were the perfect gentleman. You didn't say anything that you should regret."

"That's a relief."

Pauline held up her index finger. "However, you did say some strange things regarding some people you encountered in your dream. You kept telling them to leave you alone and pleaded with them not to kill you."

Richard swallowed hard and dismissed her concerns with a logical explanation.

"I had quite a bit of childhood trauma," he said. While he considered himself an honest person, he understood the foundation of selling a lie: base it on the truth and you'll never get caught spinning a blatant tale.

"What happened?" she asked.

Richard took a deep breath and was about to launch into a long story when a knock at the door interrupted them.

"Expecting someone?" he asked.

She furrowed her brow and then shook her head.

"I'll answer it," he said as he got up and draped a blanket over his shoulders. As he neared the door, Richard said, "No one requested a bellhop here."

"I'm not a bellhop," came the familiar voice.

He glanced over his shoulder at Pauline.

"It's Hank Foster," he said softly. "I'll handle it."

She nodded before retreating to the bathroom.

Richard opened the door and scowled. "How on Earth did you find me?"

"Have you forgotten what I do for a living?" Hank asked.

Richard shook his head. "No. But what are you doing here at this time of the morning? I'm only awake because I fell off the couch a few minutes ago."

"You're an even better spy than I thought."

"What's that supposed to mean?"

Hank looked down at the floor. "Too many good men succumb to the allure of a woman's warm bed and divulge costly secrets, but not you. You sleep on the couch."

"Can you just get to your reason for being here?" Richard asked. "I'd really like to go back to sleep."

"So would I, but I can't help but wonder if you're thumbing your nose at your destiny."

"I already told you that the adventure you've promised me isn't the kind I'm interested in," Richard said. "Now, if you'll please see yourself out."

Hank didn't budge. "I need a smoke. Join me on the balcony, will you?"

Richard sighed and shook his head, realizing that Hank's relentless ways were battle tested. Resisting would've only prolonged the conversation.

"Might as well get your rejection over with," Richard said as he marched over toward the French doors and flung them open. He gestured for Hank to go outside. Hank nodded approvingly as he sauntered into the cool morning air. Richard joined him before settling into one of the two chairs outside.

Richard pulled the doors shut before igniting a cigarette. He blew a couple large plumes of smoke skyward, standing firm in silence.

"What are you doing here, Hank?" Richard finally asked.

"I came to apologize."

"For what?"

Hank took another long drag before answering. "I should've been more straightforward with you about my intentions."

"That's quite an understatement."

"Look, you're not the typical recruit, and I can't expect you to respond in the same way as the others I pursue."

"Most of the men you coerce into doing your bidding are easily manipulated?" Richard asked.

Hank shrugged. "I guess that's a fair criticism, though I've never really perceived that what I do is cajoling others into doing my bidding. There's always a greater purpose to what I do."

"Any purpose that involves me putting my life on the line needs to come with a greater reward than what you offered me, though I'm not sure there's any compensation worth that."

Hank blew another plume of smoke into the air before leaning on the railing. He settled into one of the chairs outside and then flicked some ashes onto the concrete floor.

"I'm not going to beat around the bush anymore," he

said. "I need you, Richard. And I don't care what it takes to get you. Maybe my compensation offer wasn't on level terms with what I asked you to do, but I'll do whatever you ask to make things fair."

Richard sighed and looked down. The sun was peeking over the horizon in the east and the city street below was beginning to come to life.

"It's not that I don't want to help, especially since this concerns my country," Richard said. "It's just that I find it difficult to justify doing anything that could result in my death that doesn't include me slinging a rifle over my shoulder and going to war."

"You wanted to do that, didn't you?" Hank asked.

Richard nodded. "While I was at Princeton, I certainly imagined myself going off to war and fighting for my country. But that time has come and gone."

"War isn't limited to trenches and foxholes. Sometimes the fight can look vastly different."

"I appreciate your persistence, but I think you need to find someone else. Besides, you've been blunt about your ability to recruit. Why not find another person for the job? I'm sure there are plenty of willing young Americans who would love to serve their country on a mission such as this."

"There's no time for that," Hank said. "Assigning an untrained agent to a task of this magnitude would likely result in death."

Richard cocked his head to one side and watched Hank send another puff of smoke billowing upward.

"Do I need to remind you that I'm not trained either?" Richard asked.

"I haven't forgotten that fact, not that it's relevant in your case."

"What do you mean?"

"Richard, you're a natural. And I'm not just flattering you with that statement. I've never seen anyone as gifted as you when it comes to turning a dire situation into a favorable one. I've observed you, in essence, making apple pie out of mud."

"Earlier, you made it sound as if any lackey could handle this job. You even said there were special troops who could come in and do the dirty work."

"Both exaggerated statements as well," Hank said. "Despite the adventure, I didn't want you to feel as if your life was in danger on both accounts."

Richard eyed Hank cautiously. "I quickly figured out my life was in danger, but you mean to tell me that there are no troops waiting to attack the Germans?"

Hank shook his head. "Not in Egypt, at least. The British are rumored to be pulling out of the country soon, and the Egyptians are clamoring for their independence again. The last thing they want to do is allow American troops into their country while trying to expel the Brits."

"So if I were to agree to do this for you, I'd be doing it on my own?" Richard asked.

"I'd provide support where possible, but that's the only promise I can make, though I understand it's a tenuous one."

Richard drew in a deep breath and then exhaled slowly. "Just for a moment, let's say that I'm interested in helping you. What exactly could you do for me to make the compensation fair?"

"I know that traveling to Egypt with your expenses all paid was an attractive proposition for you, but I have a feeling that you'd like to do more than simply visit these places and write a few magazine articles here and there. So, I'm prepared to not only compensate you handsomely for your efforts but also can arrange a meeting for you with the director of a prominent speaker's bureau, William Feakins."

"*The* William Feakins?" Richard asked, his eyes widening.

Hank nodded. "I'm sure with an introduction like that, you'll be more than capable of sealing any kind of deal you desire."

Richard gazed onto the street below, which had slowly been coming to life with each passing minute. This was the kind of deal he knew he'd only get once in life. And it was just one mission—spy on the special Reichswehr unit and prevent it from stealing back to Germany with the mystery treasure. Richard didn't need to take long to weigh the proposal.

"When do I start?" Richard said as he offered his hand to Hank.

"There's a seven o'clock train to Marseille," Hank said as he slapped three hundred dollars into Richard's palm along with an envelope containing contact protocol. "If you hurry, you can make it."

CHAPTER 5

RICHARD LEFT A NOTE FOR PAULINE ON THE BED before scrambling back to his room and cramming his personal effects into his bag. He hustled to the train station, purchasing a ticket just as the conductor shouted, "*En voiture!*" The engine chugged forward, and Richard raced for the rear passenger car, grabbing the railing and pulling himself up.

With his head down, he shuffled his way through the narrow aisle in search of an empty seat. He identified one near the front next to a window and sat down.

Behind him, two men held a short conversation in French. From what Richard understood, it sounded like a rather benign discussion about the weather. However, there was a tinge of German in the voice of one of the men—and the tone sounded vaguely familiar.

As Richard settled in for the three-hour ride, he read over Foster's detailed notes about how to contact him at the Army Intelligence outpost in Langres, France. It didn't promise to be a quick process, but at least there was a way to reach out and issue a report. Richard dug out a novel he'd been reading periodically during his trip. E.M. Hull's desert romance *The Sheik* wasn't exactly his favorite genre, but it did give him a glimpse into the life of those in the region of North Africa. Eventually, he drifted off to sleep only to be awakened by squealing brakes and a hissing engine as the train came to a stop at the Marseille/St. Charles station.

Richard rubbed his eyes and tried to regain his bearings. He turned around and noticed the two men who'd been carrying on about the weather were gone along with about half of the car. After easing outside, Richard scanned the platform area for a group of men who might resemble the German soldiers he'd seen the night before. When he didn't see any group forming, he concluded that the men were likely going to meet elsewhere to avoid standing out. He hustled inside and checked his luggage with a porter before walking outside to the front of the station. Without any sign of the man he suspected to be a German soldier, Richard decided to identify the Reichswehr members in another manner—his hunches.

Being around plenty of soldiers for the past few years, Richard noticed that the German variety, in particular, had a stilted gait. They never glided casually across the floor, instead moving in a jerky action that would've earned them compliments from commanding officers. When two men distinguished themselves in this manner, Richard followed them discreetly. He maintained a healthy distance, giving them plenty of space to go toward their ultimate destination without the slightest hint that they were being followed.

As the two men stood on a street corner, another man joined them and then another. Before Richard could prove his hunch based on his deductive skills, the group swelled to ten, dismissing the need to make any further assessment. The men trudged inside a nearby pub and surrounded a long table. Richard quickly followed, settling onto a seat at the bar near their table and opening up the abandoned newspaper he'd snatched off a bus stop bench.

While Richard was competent enough in German, it

didn't matter since most of the men spoke French. Their accents impressed Richard, but he knew better. The conversation drifted from the mundane to their impending voyage to Alexandria, Egypt, later tonight. However, Richard's attention was arrested when two of the men announced they needed to take care of some business.

Richard promptly paid his bill in an effort to beat the men to the door. He slid onto the bench outside and watched as the two men eased down the street. Moments later, the bus arrived. Richard stood and followed them, navigating through the steady stream of customers jostling for position to board. Less than a block ahead, the two men maintained a swift pace, keeping their heads down aside from an occasional polite nod at a passerby.

The brisk stroll lasted a half hour before the men approached a home overlooking the water. Richard saw the name "Miller" emblazoned on a sign above the front steps and decided to take up a less conspicuous position. A hundred meters past the house was a small park that included a bench looking back down the street. Deciding that was the best place to wait out the Germans, Richard walked to the location and sat down.

While Richard could hardly wait to experience the sands of Egypt and all her ancient treasures, he wondered if the free trip would be worth the monotony of sitting in silence and staring blankly at a French newspaper. A few feet away, he watched a mother dote over her two boys, who were engaged in a lively game of chase. It reminded Richard of what things were like with Wesley Jr. when they were youngsters. And he found himself pining for the simplicity of such times, though Richard dismissed the thought—and the pain that accompanied it—when he considered how close he was to reaching Egypt.

Wesley would be so proud of me right now.

Less than fifteen minutes later, the two men emerged from the house and began walking back toward the city center.

Richard folded up his newspaper and tucked it beneath his arm as he strode up toward Dr. Miller's house. When he knocked on the door, a woman answered. Her voice quivered as she spoke, trails of dried tears stretching down her cheeks.

"I'm sorry if this is a bad time," Richard said. "I only found out the new about Dr. Miller's death this morning."

The woman sniffled and then nodded.

"Before he died, Dr. Miller had asked me to pick up some documents from his private collection for an expedition we were planning on taking soon to Egypt together."

She eyed him carefully. "And what's your name, sir?"

"Thomas Baker," Richard said.

"But you're American," she said, the uncertainty in her voice making Richard wonder if she was stating a fact or asking a question.

"Guilty as charged," he said.

"Dr. Miller hated working with Americans," she said. "He always said their techniques were antiquated and not very adept at preserving the integrity of artifacts."

"Perhaps that's why he said I was his favorite American during our last dig," Richard said in an attempt to dispel any notions that he was a fraud.

She didn't budge. "What exactly did he send you here to retrieve? I handle his house cleaning duties as well as his scheduling when he's wintering here—and I don't recall him ever mentioning your name. I especially don't remember him saying that anyone would be stopping by to collect some of his papers."

"I saw him last night in Monte-Carlo before his untimely demise," Richard said.

"And you came here this morning? All the way from Monte-Carlo?"

"I was staying in Nice," Richard said. "But when I heard about his death last night while gambling late into the night at a casino, I wanted to rush here to ensure that any ne'er-do-wells wouldn't try to take advantage of a grieving house staff. Dr. Miller was a man with plenty of secrets."

"Thank you for concern," she said. "However, the only people who have stopped by so far have been a pair of detectives. In fact, you must've just missed them."

"What did they want?" Richard asked.

"They don't seem convinced that Dr. Miller would shoot himself in the head on his own volition."

"And what do you think since you know what kind of man he really is?"

"He was a good man, and I know he wouldn't ever shoot himself in the head."

"It doesn't seem right, does it?" Richard said, drifting into a sincere sympathetic state. "He was such a good man with so much left to give."

She nodded. "He was a real gentleman, an increasingly rare breed in this day and age."

"Did the detectives find anything that might give them a clue about why this may have happened?" he asked.

"They took a few things from his study," she said. "Most of it was just a bunch of papers. But I did notice a map that he had supposedly created about a treasure he believed to be in Egypt. But he wrote it in some type of code."

"What type of code?"

She shrugged. "I only saw it once, and it looked like a bunch of gibberish to me, though that's not entirely unusual. I don't understand much of the relics that passed through this house over the years."

Richard stroked his chin as he studied the woman. "I have one last question before I leave you alone."

"Go ahead."

"The detectives you mentioned—they weren't the two men who just left a few minutes ago, were they?"

She nodded. "That was them."

Richard sighed. "Those men weren't detectives. They were German soldiers."

"That can't be," she said. "They showed me their credentials."

He shook his head. "I saw them in Monte-Carlo yesterday speaking German. In fact, I saw them with Dr. Miller before he died."

"But I—" she said before pausing as her face went pale. "I should've known. It all makes sense now."

"What did they say?"

"I heard one of them say something in German, which I thought was odd at the time, but maybe they were discussing an object Dr. Miller discovered and it was only known by that name. It was so brief, I hardly gave it a second thought until now."

"But you still don't know all the documents they took?"

She shook her head. "I know he kept his most precious papers behind a secret bookshelf in his study. But I didn't open it for them."

"Where is his study?" Richard asked.

"Follow me," she said, spinning on her heels and racing up the stairs. Richard stayed close behind her, afraid of what they might find.

"It's right here," she said before hanging her head.

Richard peered inside and noticed what stopped the woman in her tracks. The bookshelf was slightly ajar. He rushed over to inspect it, pushing it until it latched.

"They found it," she said. "I rarely went in there except to dust on occasion when Dr. Miller asked me to. And the shelf was never left unlatched. I feel like such a fool."

She sobbed softly, burying her head in her hands.

"Don't worry," Richard said. "They won't get away with this."

* * *

LATER THAT EVENING, RICHARD VENTURED OUT FOR A MEAL. He contemplated the best way to stay out of sight while keeping his eyes focused on the activities of the Reichswehr unit. With a ticket in hand for a midnight departure to Alexandria, Egypt, he felt a little spring in his step. Egypt was about to become demystified for him through a personal visit. No longer would it be a historic land populated with ancient civilizations; rather, it would be a thriving experience, one waiting to be shared with those unfortunate souls who would never have the privilege to sink their toes in Egyptian sand.

He meandered along a vacant alleyway in an attempt to explore more of Marseille. The main street façade only told the tale that the city wanted you to know. Richard preferred to see everything for himself for a story that was grounded in reality. However, he never imagined what he would find.

A few meters away from emerging back onto the lighted street, a handful of men jumped out of the shadows and attacked Richard. He dished out several vicious punches, but he was quickly overwhelmed. There were just too many men for him to escape or ward away. With Richard teetering from exhaustion and pain, the ringleader nodded at two men. They seized Richard's arms in an effort to hold him still, and then the man delivered a flurry of punches to Richard's midsection. Before releasing their hold, the two gang members tightened their grip on him as the other man searched through Richard's pockets. They confiscated his ticket as well as all his money, save the fifty dollars he'd stuffed into a compartment in the bottom of his bag still safely in his hotel room. Once they were finished looting Richard's trousers and jacket, they darted down the alley, disappearing into the darkness.

Richard crawled on his hands and knees to the main street before collapsing against a storefront window. He moaned as he felt his side. Picking up his shirt, he inspected the wounds, which were bruised but not bloody.

He looked up in time to see the two Germans he'd followed earlier in the day stroll past. One of the men flipped a coin at Richard that landed on his chest.

Richard staggered to his feet and stumbled back to the hotel before rushing toward the port. When he arrived, he attempted to purchase a ticket. The man at the window informed Richard that only first class tickets remained for the voyage.

"But I have to be on that ship," Richard said.

"If you don't have enough money, I'm afraid *that* ship will have to wait."

"When does the next one leave for Alexandria?"

"When this one comes back to port in two weeks."

Two weeks wasn't an option—but neither was forking over the $150 necessary to purchase a first class ticket.

CHAPTER 6

WITH HIS HANDS SPREAD WIDE, KARL WILHELM leaned on the table, his gaze bouncing all around the map splayed out in front of him. He tried to resist the urge to laugh, but he couldn't help himself. Dr. Miller wouldn't talk but ultimately didn't stop the Reichswehr unit's mission. And Wilhelm enjoyed a nice glass of French wine while two of his men managed to snatch the document right from under the nose of the naïve housekeeper.

"Men," Wilhelm began as he stood upright, "you were chosen because you are the most elite soldiers the Reichswehr has among its ranks for your particular talents. And with the stunning results you have already produced, I can no longer refer to you simply as a unit. No, there is only one name suited for the way you have handled task after task on this mission, and from now on I will call you my *wolfsrudel.*"

Once, as a young boy on a camping expedition,, Wilhelm witnessed a pack of wolves devour a crippled lamb with unfathomable precision and efficiency. Within five minutes, the animals had hardly left any bones for the vultures to pick over. And so began Wilhelm's obsession with the ferocious hunters. But now he had a pack of his own— and one worthy to be called as such.

"Does anyone have questions before we board our ship tonight?" he asked.

Felix Ludwig nodded. "Sir, I wanted to let you know that I believe we're being followed and watched."

Wilhelm's eyebrows shot upward. "By whom?"

"I noticed a man in Monte-Carlo at the hotel as well as today in the restaurant while we were eating. He appears to keep to himself, but I saw him studying our team."

"Our *wolfsrudel*," Wilhelm corrected. "Have you spoken with him?"

"No, but I believe he's spying on us and it would be in our best interest if we disposed of him before he became a problem."

"Then make it happen."

"Yes, sir," Ludwig said before saluting.

"Please, don't salute me, not even in private," Wilhelm said. "All it would take it someone to catch you doing that and suddenly international police are cracking down on us again, claiming we're violating the treaty."

Ludwig put his hand down and nodded knowingly.

"Well, what are you waiting for?" Wilhelm said. "I want to see this man suffer for his sheer arrogance. Anyone who thinks they can spy on us without experiencing great consequences is mistaken. Let's ensure he meets a violent end as a lesson for all those who might dare to track us."

Ludwig leaked a wry smile before exiting the room first with the other men right behind him. Wilhelm took up his position at the rear along with Hans Reinhard.

"Are you sure this is a wise move?" Reinhard asked.

"Did Ludwig yield his position as chief questioner to you this evening?" Wilhelm replied.

"No, sir, it's just that—I thought we wanted to handle our business as quietly as possible. Murdering a spy doesn't exactly seem to fit our preferred operational procedure."

"What's preferred is that we send a message to deter this type of behavior from ever happening again."

"Our enemies may not see it that way," Reinhard said. "They may seize upon this as a chance to exert more pressure."

"And by the time their bureaucratic ways grind through their antiquated system, Germany will have all the resources necessary to launch an offensive and sustain it until the allies yield."

"Isn't it possible to get the same result but without attracting such attention?"

Wilhelm shrugged. "Anything is possible. Besides, we'll be gone before anyone can trace the death back to us, even if a host of people witnessed it."

"As you wish," Reinhard said, refusing to press the matter any more as they both continued on in silence.

Wilhelm appreciated that about Reinhard, a second-in-command officer who wasn't afraid to challenge a decision but would ultimately respect it regardless of how the discussion concluded. When left alone, Wilhelm would often contemplate his men's alternative suggestions, discarding them more often than not. But sometimes he took their ideas seriously and on the rare occasion would reverse course. Just not this time.

If someone was following his *wolfsrudel*, that person needed to be eliminated.

"I know my response might seem harsh to you," Wilhelm said, breaking the quiet between them. "But I can explain."

Reinhard held up his hand. "There's no need, sir. I trust your judgment."

"I feel I must."

"Then by all means, please continue."

Wilhelm took a deep breath and then exhaled slowly. "My father was nearly sixty years old, but he refused to quit, volunteering to pilot a Gotha for the Imperial German Air Service. Navigating one of the airships was often viewed as a suicide mission, but my father didn't care. After a successful bombing run over London just before Christmas four years ago, he crashed on an attempted landing in Rochford. His entire crew survived, but he got caught and was quickly scuttled away to a British prisoner of war camp. We never saw him again. The official report was that he died of a heart attack while being interrogated, but we knew better. My father was in outstanding health. I can only imagine what they did to him to break his body down to the point that he couldn't survive their torture."

"I'm sorry to hear that, sir," Reinhard said. "I never knew what happened to him."

"Thank you," Wilhelm said, fighting back tears. "What they did to him was barbaric according to some of the other soldiers who were there. He never stood a chance. And as a result, they refused to send his body home."

"I cannot imagine such tragedy."

"And then there's my grandfather, the owner of a ball bearing factory, whose fortunes have been squelched by the suffocating sanctions handed down as a result of the Treaty of Versailles. He used to have a very profitable business, exporting his manufactured items all over the world. But no longer. He's limited to selling his wares to his countrymen, who are all too poor to afford his products. He had to shutter his business two weeks ago, and I fear there is no one who will be able to take care of him properly. He barely has enough to eat these days."

"We will change all of this."

Wilhelm nodded knowingly. "For my widowed mother, for my grandfather, for your Annemaria, for your Emilia."

"For all of them," Reinhard said. "They all deserve better."

"They deserve the best. Let's give it to them."

Once they reached the street, Ludwig needed only a few minutes to round up the suspected spy.

"I swear, I'm not a spy," the man said, his eyes wide with fear.

"No one ever admits to being a spy," Ludwig said. He turned and looked at Wilhelm, who gave the signal.

* * *

POSITIONED NEAR THE RAILROAD TRACKS, A TRAIN CAME roaring toward them.

"I'm just a poor college student," the man said, his voice quaking. "Please don't hurt me. I don't even know who you are."

As the train bore down on their position, several of Wilhelm's *wolfsrudel* surrounded the young man.

"Now," Ludwig said.

Acting in concert, the *wolfsrudel* snatched the man off the ground and hurled him toward the tracks. The lead engine shredded his body, leaving a grotesque mess.

A tinge of blood landed on Wilhelm's nose. Using his index finger, he scraped off the fluid and looked at it before wiping it off on his pants. He smiled in satisfaction at the gruesome execution of a spy who dared to follow them.

That was for you, Father.

"To the docks," Wilhelm said. "We have a ship to catch."

The world will respect us now. No, they will fear *us again.*

CHAPTER 7

RICHARD SLUNG HIS BAG OVER HIS SHOULDER AND clutched the strap. Crouching down behind a stack of pallets, he waited in the shadows for the *Harvraise* steamship to finish loading. Once the last passenger was ushered aboard, several deck hands retracted the platform and began untying the ropes from the dock.

He waited until the ship shoved off before making a move.

Securing his pack by cinching it tight to his back, he took a deep breath before breaking into a sprint. With his eyes focused on the rope dangling over the side of the deck, Richard gauged his jump to perfection. He hit the metal on the edge of the dock and leaped toward the hull. Before he crashed into the ship, he secured both hands around the rope. However, he slid down a few meters, dipping the bottom half of his body into the water before shimmying his way to the top. The darkness provided all the cover he needed to sneak aboard without getting detected.

However, he wasn't expecting to be questioned less than a minute after climbing over the railing. A man wearing a uniform eyed Richard closely for a moment before asking to see his ticket.

Richard placed both hands on his chest and then dug into his trouser pockets before shrugging.

"I guess it's in my bag," he said. "If you'll give me a minute, I can probably find it."

Richard hoped the gentleman would dismissively wave him away and move on to the next traveler who appeared suspect. But the man didn't. Instead, he crossed his arms and tapped his foot.

"I'll wait," he said.

Richard rooted through his bag, knowing that he would never be able to produce the required document. He only hoped the delay would frustrate the man and drive him to move along.

After a few minutes, Richard was disappointed to look up and see the man still standing there.

"I've been around long enough to know a stowaway when I see one," the man finally said.

Richard shot a glance at the ship's orchestra gathering on the deck to perform a few songs as the vessel headed for the open seas.

"Perhaps I could earn my keep by playing the violin for you?" Richard said.

The man smirked and then furrowed his brow. "Can you actually play—or is this another ruse?"

Richard decided to let his skills speak for themselves. He snatched the nearby instrument and started to saw away. Within seconds, the man's countenance transformed from a scowl to a look of surprise.

"You actually do know how to play," the man said. "And I think you'd give my first chair quite the challenge."

Richard forced a smile before halting the tune. "I wouldn't tease you with such a thing. However, I did buy a ticket—it's just that I was mugged on my way through the streets of Marseille, and my boarding document was stolen as well. I intend to find out who used it, if anyone at all."

"Well, if you play like that, you can have first chair in my orchestra until we get to Alexandria," the man said. "I'll even make sure you get a cabin in first class."

Richard flashed a wide grin. "Thank you, sir. I promise you won't regret this decision."

"Then make sure that I don't," the man said. "I'm Francis Gerard. Welcome to my orchestra."

Richard introduced himself as Frederick Powers before shaking the man's hand. Fortunately, the *Harvraise* didn't have an orchestra comprised of elite musicians. The performers were merely sufficient, at least that's how Richard assessed the situation based on his ability to land a spot as first chair among the orchestra's violinists. To make a more proper judgment, Richard would have to wait and hear how everyone sounded together, but in the moment, he was grateful to his mother for forcing him to take violin lessons from a demanding instructor.

Francis ushered Richard back to the sleeping quarters where he was paired with a tall, thin man named Antoine Pavard who played the French horn. Antoine was still unpacking his clothes when Richard entered the room. Despite a kind welcome, Richard perceived that Antoine was rather miffed that he wasn't going to spend the next few days with a room to himself.

"Don't worry," Richard said. "I don't snore."

Antoine chuckled. "Well, I do. You might want to find something to plug your ears before you go to sleep."

Richard used the warning as a good opportunity to venture around the ship for a pair of earplugs all while covertly searching for the Reichswehr unit. Ten men traveling in the first class cabins was a surefire way to attract attention, just as it would be in third class. Based on the group's desire to move stealthily around Monaco and France, Richard speculated that they would be scattered throughout various classes.

Hustling down to the laundry room, Richard found a fresh shirt and pair of linen pants that fit him. After changing, he began exploring the rest of the ship. His search for the Reichswehr team wasn't five minutes old when he strode into the dining hall and identified the man he believed to be the group's leader. His voice was distinct, one filled with bass— and unforgettable. Richard closed his eyes and could hear a man speaking in the same tone as he gave the order to search Dr. Miller's hotel room again. It was the man referred to as Wilhelm.

Richard poured hot water into a cup at a self-serve station and dropped a teabag inside to let it steep. He then meandered over to a table near the men, taking a seat next to a couple who were canoodling, uninterested in engaging him in conversation. Staring at his drink, he strained to hear the Reichswehr commander speaking with one of his subordinates. For ten minutes, they droned on about benign subjects—family, the arts, the challenges of sleeping on a boat while tossing about at sea. Eventually, they got up and retreated outside.

Casually following them, Richard circled the deck, catching snippets of the two men's discussion. And while he didn't hear much, he heard enough to know what he would eventually be doing once they arrived in Egypt.

"When you say this map will lead us to one of the richest treasures in the world, how rich are we talking?" the subordinate asked in French.

"As it was related to me, this would be enough to change the fortunes of an entire country," the leader responded.

Richard's eyes widened. The fact that the Germans

were chasing treasure wasn't news to him. But this didn't sound like just any treasure. This was the secretive type, perhaps the kind of fortune Dr. Miller was preparing to excavate once he received permission from the proper authorities. Without knowing anything else, Richard let his imagination run wild with just how much money such a discovery could bring. Maybe his pursuit of being a travel writer was misguided as was his moonlighting venture as a spy. Treasure hunting was starting to sound more his speed.

"All we need is a guide and someone to help us interpret this map," the commander said as he tapped his breast pocket.

All I need is to get my hands on that map.

CHAPTER 8

Somewhere in the
Mediterranean Sea

THE FOLLOWING EVENING AFTER AN EARLY CONCERT performance, Richard roamed around the ship in an attempt to gain a better understanding of what he was up against. Hank Foster's information on the Reichswehr soldiers had been scant, forcing Richard to do some of his own reconnaissance work. While he was still attempting to identify where all ten men were on the ship, he found the leader engrossed in a game of poker with several other gentlemen. Richard lingered nearby long enough to notice a document tucked inside Wilhelm's jacket pocket. And then Richard hatched a plan.

Hustling back to his room, Richard found Antoine slipping into his pajamas, signaling that he was retiring for the evening. However, it was what Antoine took off that made Richard's jaw go slack.

"Your mustache is fake?" Richard asked in disbelief as Antoine placed it delicately into a small case on top of the desk in the corner of their quarters.

"I stopped growing hair a long time ago," Antoine said, pointing to the top of his bald head.

"You can't grow any facial hair? I've never heard of such a thing," Richard said, shaking his head. "What I wouldn't give to have a life without shaving so often."

"Just grow a beard, and you won't," Antoine said with a cheeky grin.

Richard sighed. "You know what I mean."

Antoine chuckled before easing beneath the covers and pulling them taut.

"Can I borrow your mustache?" Richard asked boldly.

"Borrow it? It's not a piece of property to be bandied about."

Richard wasn't flustered. "Do you have an extra?"

Antoine sighed before flinging the covers off and then stomping across the room to the closet. He removed a small box from the top shelf to place it on the desk. Opening the top drawer, he produced a mustache and handed it to Richard along with an adhesive.

"You'll want to slather the glue on the back because it doesn't hold as well for some reason," Antoine said. "If you really want to walk around the deck with a mustache, this one should hold up for you."

Richard thanked Antoine before promptly slathering the back of the mustache with the sticky substance. After several adjustments, Richard studied his upper lip in the mirror, satisfied that no one would be able to identify his prop as such. Richard palmed a pair of reading glasses Antoine had left sitting out as well as his hat. Once Richard was in the hallway, he situated the spectacles near the end of his nose, straightened the bowler on his head, and marched back toward the card game.

As soon as Richard arrived, several men were pushing back from Wilhelm's table. The men stood to leave, ignoring the large pile of money sitting in the center. Richard sat down and chuckled as Wilhelm raked the money toward him with a sly smile on his face.

"Did you leave the poor fools penniless?" Richard asked.

Wilhelm grinned. "You're the poor fool who's next if you take that chair."

"Ah," Richard said. "You're German?"

Wilhelm scowled and shook his head. "What makes you think that?"

"Your accent. I never forget one of those. Not to mention that I always defeat Germans in poker."

"Good thing I'm French," Wilhelm said.

Two other gentlemen sat down, and the game began. Wilhelm gestured to the dealer to begin.

Five minutes into the game, Richard figured out the scam. The other two players, who barely mumbled a word, were German soldiers. Their job was to drive the bids up and apply pressure on the one player who wasn't in on the bed. Once it was clear that they needed to fold, they did. It didn't take long before Richard was digging into his empty pockets and producing the last crisp twenty-dollar bill he owned other than an emergency fund he stashed in his sock.

"Your money isn't long for this table," Wilhelm said. "I believe I hear it begging to be swept off the table and into my pockets."

Richard maintained his composure, refusing to back down from Wilhelm even after he gained a significant advantage by winning a large pot.

"It's not over yet," Richard declared.

"You would do well to walk away from the table unless you want to get up empty handed."

Richard shook his head. "I never back down."

"It's difficult to accept submission, but that's where you are going to end up—and you're going to end up there in a hurry."

Richard stared at the card in his hand from the latest deal. Without hesitating, he pushed all his chips toward the center.

"All in," he said. "And you?"

Wilhelm responded by doing the same.

"Let's up the ante," Richard said. "I have a gold watch in my room. I'll go fetch it for you if I lose. Do you have any other object you might be willing to include in this wager? Perhaps that document you keep clutching next to your chest?"

Glaring at Richard, Wilhelm removed his watch and dropped it on top of the pile of chips in the center.

Richard looked at his card. Four nines and the ace of spades. The hand was a winner, no doubt. He laid down his cards and smiled in satisfaction.

Wilhelm didn't flinch, laying down a royal flush in hearts. "I'll need you to go get that watch for me now."

Richard sighed before standing up. There was no watch in his room—only a sleeping Antoine who wouldn't be happy about such an intrusion.

"If you'll excuse me," Richard said as he stood.

"I think I'll accompany you," Wilhelm said.

Several minutes later, Richard was opening the door to his room, which was received by Antoine with much disdain. He grunted and moaned when the desk lamp pierced the darkness.

"What are you doing?" Antoine asked, shielding his eyes as he turned in the direction of the desk. "I'm trying to sleep."

"I'm looking for my gold watch," Richard said. "I placed it right here on the desk before I left."

"I haven't seen your gold watch," Antoine said as he turned over and buried his head beneath his pillow. "Now get out so I can get some sleep."

Richard rooted around the room for less than a minute on a mission he knew would be fruitless. He finally exited the room and put his hands on his hips.

"Someone must've stolen it," Richard said. "I left it right there."

Wilhelm narrowed his eyes. "You're lying."

"I swear, I'm telling the truth."

"Swear away, but I know a liar when I see one," Wilhelm said. "You need to accompany me to see the captain."

Richard refused to budge, but Wilhelm wasn't having it. He gestured toward two other men to grab Richard. They complied with the direction, while Richard surrendered his fight.

Wilhelm led them to the captain's quarters. The man was enjoying a glass of wine over dinner with his wife.

"Sorry for the intrusion, sir," Wilhelm began, "but I'm afraid we need you to render a decision on what to do with this rascal."

"What offense did he commit?" the captain asked, peering over the top of his glasses.

"Refusing to pay his gambling debt," Wilhelm said. "He claimed to have a gold watch in his room that he offered to add to the pot. Yet when he lost, we went back to his room to retrieve the promised item and it wasn't there."

"Someone must've stolen it," Richard said. "There's a real thief running around on this ship somewhere."

The captain scowled as he studied Richard. "You're lying. Take him to the brig. We'll keep him there until we reach port and then decide what to do with him."

"You can't throw me in the brig," Richard said, his eyes wide with disbelief. "This is all a big misunderstanding. If you'll just let me explain, I—"

The captain waved dismissively at Richard. "I don't need another explanation. I know a lying thief when I see one. Now, if you'll excuse me, gentlemen, I need to finish my meal."

The door slammed shut, mere inches from Richard's face, the sound reverberating down the hall. However, it wasn't nearly as sickening of a sound when the brig door clanked shut.

Richard grabbed the bars with both hands and looked down at his feet. A rat scurried across the floor, weaving in and out of the cell as he appeared to be searching for food. A steady leak dripped from the ceiling, pooling in the far corner.

"What's your name?" asked a guard as he settled onto a stool outside the prison door.

Richard hesitated, lost in thought over his ill-fated bid at the poker table.

I shouldn't have been so confident.

The guard snapped his fingers several times. "Sir, I asked you what your name is. Do you not speak English?"

"My name is Fredrick Powers the Third," Richard said with an air of pretentiousness.

The guard scribbled something down on his clipboard. "Well, Mr. Powers, I would tell you to get comfortable, but there's nothing comfortable about that room in there. Just don't let the rats nibble on your nose."

Richard lay on the bed and pulled the sheets taut around him. He covered his face with his hands and prayed that he wouldn't have to encounter any rats in the middle of the night.

Then he began to plot his escape.

CHAPTER 9

SITTING IN PRISON WASN'T A NEW EXPERIENCE FOR Richard, though spending time in a ship's brig was. While sailing across the Mediterranean Sea, the *Harvraise* was a floating jail cell in some manner of speaking. Even if Richard could get beyond the bars that held him, he was still limited in where he could go to elude capture. However, he received the break he needed when Francis Gerard visited Richard just over twenty-four hours since first being incarcerated.

The orchestra conductor strode up to the gate and looked at Richard for a few seconds before speaking.

"I hardly recognized you in that disguise," Francis said. "And I would've been down here sooner had I recognized your name on the brig roster."

"One can never be too cautious while gambling with a ruthless opponent."

"Well, *Mr. Powers*, I'm sure you've had time to contemplate the seriousness of your actions."

"The only thing I've contemplated was my arrogance in thinking that the man I was playing poker with couldn't be holding a royal flush."

Francis sighed. "Why would I even be remotely surprised that you're down here? What else should I have expected from a stowaway?"

"I'm not a stowaway," Richard said. "I already told you that someone mugged me and stole my ticket a few hours before the ship was preparing to leave."

"I remember," Francis said. "But the funny thing is I went and looked at the ship's manifest and couldn't find a single Frederick Powers listed. Now how do you explain that?"

Richard shrugged. "Perhaps I wasn't added because I purchased my ticket too close to the departure time. The manifest may have been recorded already."

"That's not how the manifest works."

"In that case, maybe it was an oversight."

Francis sighed. "None of your excuses sound very convincing to me."

"Did you come here just to mock me?"

Francis shook his head. "I must admit that the reason for my visit is self-serving, though I certainly didn't intend to come down here and needle you about your imprisonment."

"What do you want?"

"I want my top violinist back."

Richard huffed a soft laugh through his nose. "Isn't he out there already, roaming the ship freely?"

"Actually, my previous top violinist is indisposed right now, suffering from a nasty bout with the flu."

"I'm sure I'll contract something soon enough down here. These aren't exactly the best conditions to be living in."

Francis shook his head. "Unfortunately, he's not the only one who's contracted something. With the Captain's Ball scheduled for tomorrow night, which is our last performance before we reach port, I have eight of my musicians unable to perform due to sickness, including two of the other three violinists. As I'm sure you can attest to, a serious orchestra needs more than just one violin."

"I will help you on one condition," Richard said as he stood and started to pace around his cell. "You must get the charges against me dropped."

"I'm sorry, but I can't do that," Francis said. "I already spoke with the captain about this, and he's fearful of what might happen if a first-class passenger is wronged and there are no reparations made. He must hold you accountable for your actions."

"In that case, I'm not sure I can help you."

"Here's what I can do for you," Francis said. "I already spoke with the captain about this, and he's agreed to let you go free on the ship provided that you perform at the ball tomorrow night. After the dance, you'll be escorted back to your cell by one of the guards. I know it's not much of a concession, but you must understand the position the captain is in. I'm sure you'll be able to work something out to avoid staying in an Egyptian prison for very long."

"Let me think about it," Richard said.

"You have one hour. After that, I'll begin to make other plans."

Left alone to ponder the proposition, Richard only needed five minutes to agree to it. He would've agreed to Francis's deal the moment it was offered, but Richard didn't want to seem too eager for fear that the orchestra conductor might suspect a scheme had already been hatched, even if only in Richard's mind.

When Francis returned, Richard agreed to the terms with one caveat—that he would remove his disguise in an effort to avoid embarrassing the captain over allowing an accused criminal to roam free on the ship.

"Why were you even wearing a disguise in the first place?" Francis asked. "Never mind. I probably don't want to know the answer to that."

"So, we're agreed?" Richard asked.

Francis nodded. "I'm sticking my neck out for you. You better not let me down."

"Don't worry," Richard said. "I wouldn't miss tomorrow night's gala for the world."

* * *

RICHARD AWOKE THE NEXT MORNING IN HIS BED WITH Antoine looming over him. Before Richard could get his bearings, he sat up and scrambled back against the wall.

"I was beginning to wonder if you'd absconded with my bowler," Antoine said as he straightened his hat.

"Just a little detour yesterday," Richard said, forcing a nervous laugh.

"It didn't have anything to do with the fact that you were scrounging around the room, looking for a gold watch, did it?"

"Now why would you think something like that?"

Antoine shrugged. "Perhaps your curious behavior makes me wonder about what kind of man you are."

"All you need to know is that I'm the kind of man who keeps his word—and I told Francis I would be playing with the orchestra at the Captain's Ball tonight."

"I guess I'll believe it when I see it, though I prefer you not skip the dance. Francis made me play violin yesterday, and let's just say that it's not my preferred instrument."

"Just like I brought your bowler back as well as your fake mustache and glasses as promised, I guarantee you'll be bellowing on your French horn tonight."

Antoine was already exiting the room as he shouted back. "You better not disappoint me."

Richard moaned as he got out of bed and staggered over to the sink. He stared into the mirror and inspected his eyes, underscored by sagging pockets from the lack of sleep.

After splashing water on his face, he looked again at his reflection and smiled. As dire as his circumstances felt, he remained optimistic that he would evade any further consequences, legal or otherwise, for his actions. Yet his confidence in the matter wasn't the only reason he felt somewhat giddy: In less than a twenty-four hours, he would be in Egypt.

He stayed out of sight for most of the day, venturing out of his room only to eat. The fear of being recognized by Wilhelm or any of the other Reichswehr members was a valid concern, one that could best be abated by refusing to tempt fate. And while abandoning his target may have been unconventional behavior for a spy, Richard concluded that it wasn't endangering his mission since the Germans were trapped on the same boat he was until they reached Alexandria.

A half hour before the musicians were scheduled to arrive to warm up and review the song list, Antoine returned to the room to get ready. He scowled when he found Richard napping.

"What on Earth is wrong with you?" Antoine asked. "Please tell me you're not sick. You promised that I would be playing my French horn tonight."

"And that's what you will be doing," Richard said as he sat up. "I was just catching up on my sleep, that's all. No need to panic."

Richard stretched before standing. He plodded across the room in an effort to make sure Antoine left first.

"You better be there," Antoine said before exiting and disappearing down the hall.

Richard rushed around the room, gathering his belongings and stuffing them into a bag. He also snatched Antoine's bowler hat as well as his spare spectacles and mustache. After a brief pit stop in the restroom near the dance hall, Richard ducked out onto the main deck and scanned the area. When he was confident no one was looking, he slid his bag into one of the lifeboats.

Upon joining all the other musicians, he took a seat in the first chair and tuned up his violin.

"Glad you could make it tonight, Mr. Powers," Francis said.

Richard forced a smile as he situated his notes. "Just doing my part."

Despite the absence of several key instrumentalists, the Captain's Ball went off without a hitch. The orchestra performed so well that Francis couldn't stop raving about it afterward, heaping plenty of praise on Richard. After Francis dismissed everyone, Richard remained behind as instructed until one of the guards appeared in the doorway, waiting to escort the accused criminal back to his cell.

Richard strode across the floor toward Francis, who was packing up his materials into a briefcase.

"The captain seemed to appreciate the show tonight," Richard said as he leaned down and spoke softly. "Any chance you might be able to convince him to reconsider his position and show me some leniency?"

Francis clasped his attaché case shut. "I already told you that he must act in the interest of justice or else have his reputation sullied."

"Showing a person mercy should boost one's reputation, not taint it."

"Says the guilty man in desperate need of a pardon."

Richard exhaled slowly. "If what I've heard about Egypt is true, their punishments often don't fit the crime. And quite frankly, what is my crime here?"

"You lost a wager, and you must make good on it. It's simple fraud."

"Exactly. *Simple fraud.* It's more like I got caught up in the moment while playing a competitive game of poker and spoke more confidently than I should have."

Francis shook his head. "You should know better than that. Besides, nothing good ever really comes out of gambling."

"I recognize that now, but I shouldn't have to pay a steep price simply because we were sailing in the open waters."

Francis patted Richard on the shoulder. "I'm sorry, son. You're a slippery one, but I'm sure you'll find your bearings soon enough, even if you have to waste a little time working in an Egyptian labor camp."

"Labor camp? What are you talking about?" Richard asked as his eyes widened.

Francis glanced at his watch. "Would you look at the time. We're going to be docking within the next half hour. And I need to get back to my room. Good luck."

Richard watched Francis walk away, though his departure felt more like abandonment. Their symbiotic relationship worked, but in the end it was hollow for Richard, leaving him with the stark realization that they were simply using each other and were never actually friends. A friend would have fought for Richard's freedom by standing up to the captain. But Francis refused to do such a thing.

"It's time to go, Mr. Powers," the guard said as he tapped his watch.

Richard shuffled toward the doorway and then asked if he could use the restroom. Once inside, he located the hat, glasses, and mustache he'd stowed beneath the sink and donned his disguise again. He removed his coat and placed it across his arm before exiting. The guard who remained outside didn't even flinch when Richard walked by.

Richard didn't turn around, afraid that a second glance might awaken the guard to the fact that he'd just lost his captive. Once outside on the deck, Richard scanned the area again. Passengers and crewmembers alike scurried back and forth in anticipation of finally reaching the *Harvraise's* intended destination. Not a soul was paying him any attention.

Richard lifted up the tarp and slid into the boat. It rocked back and forth for a few seconds before it sat still. He barely moved for the next two hours as he heard the bustling sounds of unloading and excited chatter.

When he was sure that only the workers were left, Richard rolled over the edge and headed straight down to the hull, where workers were unloading goods and supplies shipped by French merchants. He found a nearby dolly and hoisted a barrel of wine onto it before guiding it across the narrow plank leading to the dock. A man barked directions at Richard, telling him where to leave his item. After following directions, Richard stole off into the shadows and surveyed the scene around the *Harvraise* one final time.

The passengers congregated nearby before slowly beginning to disperse. Many of the seafarers had made new friends and wanted to stay in touch through writing letters. Others wanted to travel together and were planning how they could merge itineraries. And then there was a large group from Thomas Cook & Son, the world's premier tour agency. With organized excursions all across Europe and Asia, Richard found it impossible not to cross paths with their customers.

But there was only one conversation on the deck that mattered to Richard—the one occurring between the captain and Wilhelm. The longer the two men chatted, the more animated Wilhelm got. Just as he prepared to turn and walk away, the guard from the brig rushed over to them and said something. Whatever message was passed set Wilhelm off, as he stomped twice, angrily shaking his fists as he did. He then spun around and walked away, leaving an exasperated captain with nothing to do but throw his hands in the air.

"I wonder what that was all about," Richard asked with a chuckle.

Upon regaining his freedom with his secret identity still intact, Richard resumed following the Reichswehr, who appeared to have no plans to spend the night in Alexandria. They all headed straight toward the train station and purchased tickets for the midnight train from Alexandria to Cairo.

Richard dipped into his scant reserves and purchased a ticket as well. He was finally in Egypt, but he still had a job.

CHAPTER 10

Cairo, Egypt

THE RICKETY RIDE FROM ALEXANDRIA TO CAIRO didn't provide Richard with an opportunity to get quality sleep. Between the crowded second-class cabins stuffed with unruly children and screaming babies who seemed to spur one another on in a contest of ear-splitting cries, Richard caught a few winks between the chaos. There were several stops along the route, which led him to carefully watch the platform for any Germans exiting. The Reichswehr had purchased tickets for Cairo, but Richard wouldn't have been surprised if that was simply a precautionary measure to throw anyone off their trail. But apparently, they didn't think such extreme measures were necessary, remaining on the train until it reached the end of the line in Cairo.

With the sun already peeking over the horizon as the conductor bid the passengers to unload, Richard kept an eye out for Wilhelm, following him through the crowd. Richard sat in the lobby of the Shepard's Hotel where the Reichswehr chose to stay, checking in individually to maintain a low profile. He poured himself a complimentary cup of coffee from the concierge's desk and then pondered his next move. A few hours of sleep would've done him wonders, but he instead decided to explore the sights and sounds of Cairo before resuming his reconnaissance. However, he needed to wire Hank Foster an update.

Richard navigated his way through the markets in search of a telegram station. He was accosted in several open-air markets and almost got sidetracked while winding up in a hashish den before finding a location that would send a note. While he didn't have room for many words, he explained how he'd become virtually penniless and needed more funds—and that the Reichswehr were in Cairo with plans to hunt for treasure.

Venturing to see the pyramids, Richard did so with nothing but his bag, a few coins, and a dagger. If someone considered mugging him again, he would be more than prepared to ward off the attacker. When Richard reached the ancient architectural wonders rising out of the Egyptian sands, he couldn't stop staring. He was so overtaken by the view that he wrote a letter to his parents describing the grandeur of the structures.

For a fleeting moment, he considered remaining there all evening and watching the moon rise over the Sphinx, but he wasn't so free. The Reichswehr was calling.

Upon returning to the Shephard's Hotel, Richard marveled at the curbside scene, a confluence of the old and the new—motorized vehicles parked near horse-drawn carriages. He watched as a beautiful young woman stepped delicately out of a car and was ushered inside by a host of hotel staff. With keen interest, he monitored her movements through the lobby, determining that he must make her acquaintance.

Later that evening, many of the hotel's guests had finished their sightseeing adventures and were gathering over meals in the dining hall. Richard found a quiet table at the back where he could observe Wilhelm and several other Reichswehr members who had taken up seats at various empty tables around the room.

Moments later, the woman who caught Richard's eye

paraded past on a search for a place to sit, eventually circling back toward him.

"Is this seat taken?" she asked in a strong American accent.

Richard stood and gestured toward the chair across from him. "I wasn't expecting anyone, but I'd be delighted for you to join me."

After wanting to meet the woman, Richard was pleasantly surprised that she chose his table. Her company also gave him sufficient cover from the Reichswehr if they happened to suspect he was following them.

"I'm Sara Catherine Holbrook," she said, offering the back of her gloved hand to him.

"Richard Halliburton," he said before kissing her on her outstretched wrist. "It's a pleasure to meet you."

"And you as well," she said as she sat down.

Richard marveled at the brunette beauty. Sporting a bob haircut with a tapered back, she moved in a sophisticated manner. With effortless grace, she opened her clutch and dug out a cigarette along with a holder. She connected the two latter objects and handed her lighter to Richard. He ignited it and held it out for his dinner guest until her cigarette was sufficiently lit.

"What brings you to Egypt?" she asked.

"I was about to ask you the same thing, especially a woman traveling all alone like you are."

"I asked you first," she said with a wink.

"Adventure, wonder, an ancient civilization's incredible feat of architecture, the Nile, the opportunity to walk in Cleopatra's footsteps," he said before stopping abruptly. "I could go on, but I don't want to bore you."

She smirked. "I get the idea. You're a romantic."

"That's one way of looking at it," he said. "I've been

traveling all over Europe and now heading down into Africa. I feel like I'm on the royal road to romance."

"Romance is all around us. We just need to know where to look for it."

Richard's eyes sparkled. "I feel the same way. Is that why you're here? Are you on some search for romance, the kind we experience in the literary sense?"

She signaled for a waiter and ordered a drink, offering to buy Richard one as well. He graciously accepted the offer.

"I'm sure I could come up with plenty of reasons why I came here, just like you," she said. "But I'm not going to mislead you. The main reasons I came to Cairo were to tour this grand country and to consume plenty of alcohol."

"This is a long way to come just for alcohol."

"Like I said, it's one of two main reasons I traveled this far, but not the only one."

The waiter returned with their drinks, resulting in Sara Catherine clapping her hands with excitement.

"What exactly do you do that affords you the means to travel so exorbitantly?" she asked after taking a long pull on her glass. "I know this hotel isn't cheap."

"I'm travel writer and explorer," Richard said. "However, this place is out of my budget for the time being."

"You must plan on making it big one day, Mr. Halliburton."

"I was doing fine on this trip until I was mugged on the streets of Marseille. I had to join a ship's orchestra just to pay my way here."

"Oh, you poor thing," she said as she reached across the table and patted him on the hand. "That must've been awful."

He nodded. "They nearly took all my money, and now I'm just trying to survive and see as much as I can before I return home."

"Well, why don't you stay with me tonight?" she asked. "I have a large room with a couch that you could sleep on until you acquire some more money. What do you say?"

"That's very generous of you, but I—"

She waved at him dismissively. "I won't take no for an answer. Understand?"

Richard wanted to argue but decided against it. He didn't want to sleep on the street.

"Thank you," he finally said.

"And you need to eat, too. It'll be my treat," she said, snapping her fingers to get the waiter's attention.

"Yes, madam?" he asked as he stopped by her table.

"We need another menu," she said.

He nodded knowingly and returned a few seconds later, presenting Richard with a list of the evening's offerings.

"You really have no idea how famished I am," Richard said, cracking a wry grin as he read the descriptions of the entrees.

"Might I suggest the *fattah* with lamb," she said before standing abruptly. "Now if you'll excuse me, I need to visit the ladies room."

Richard waited until she disappeared around the corner before he stood and sauntered over toward the bar. Wilhelm was engaged in a serious conversation with the bartender. Standing just far enough away to hear, Richard leaned against one of the stools and strained to listen in on the discussion.

"I'm looking for a good guide who can interpret Sanskrit," Wilhelm said. "Know anyone who fits the description?"

"Jabari Gamal is the best," the bartender said.

"Do you have an address for him?"

The bartender scribbled something down onto a napkin and then handed it to Wilhelm, who forked over a handsome tip.

Richard kept his head down as Wilhelm slid past and exited the restaurant. When a waiter showed up at Richard's table, he scowled and scanned the room.

"Sorry about making you wait," Richard said as he hustled over to order. "I was at the bar."

Richard placed his order and took a seat. A couple minutes later, Sara Catherine emerged from the restroom with a wry grin.

"What are you smiling about?" he asked.

"I just saw Carmel Myers," she said. "I even got her autograph."

Sara Catherine placed a napkin debossed with the Shepherd's Hotel logo on it along with a barely legible signature on the table.

"You never know who you'll run into halfway around the world," he said.

After Richard finished his meal, Sara Catherine ushered him up to her room and unlocked the door.

"Make yourself comfortable," she said. "I need to go back down to the front desk to get one of my bags that I left with the concierge."

"I can go get it for you," Richard said.

She waved him off dismissively. "It's no trouble. And you need to get settled."

He didn't want to be contentious due to her gracious hospitality, though he might have insisted on fetching the extra item if the situation had been different. After removing his toiletries and hanging up one of his coats, he strode out onto the balcony and stared down at the bustling city. Cairo had quickly grown into one of the premier destinations for both Europeans and wealthy Americans. The city's grandeur still had otherworldly charm about it, charm that Richard felt was enchanting. With incredible architectural feats from an ancient civilization dotting the landscape in the distance, Cairo was making a mark in the modern era through its reputation as a place for arts and entertainment as well as a place to relax. And as much as Richard wanted to bask in the city's opulence, he figured there would be time for that later. He still had a job to do for Hank Foster, one that was more important than first imagined.

After taking a deep breath, Richard re-entered the room. He was searching in the closet for a blanket when the door opened.

"Did you get it?" Richard asked.

"Get what?" answered a gruff, familiar voice.

Spinning around, Richard was eye to eye with Wilhelm, who had his gun drawn.

Richard threw his hands in the air. "I'm sorry. I thought you were someone else. Who are you?"

"I think you know who I am already," Wilhelm said, gesturing to a pair of his men who started to tie up Richard. "But what I want to know is who you are and why you've been following me."

"I don't know what you're talking about," Richard said. "I've never seen you before in my life."

Wilhelm chuckled. "You're a terrible liar—and you still owe me a gold watch."

CHAPTER 11

Two members of the Reichswehr unit marched Richard down the hall toward the back stairwell. He jerked in the opposite direction as if he was going to make a run for it, but a firm hand on his chest stopped him. The soldier wagged his index finger and then revealed a gun holstered on his belt, glancing at it as if to emphasize the warning. Foregoing the idea of escape, Richard turned forward and kept walking.

When they reached the street, a truck was waiting for them. Several soldiers hoisted Richard over the tailgate and inside where two more armed soldiers sat. Wilhelm sat in the passenger's seat and banged on the side of the door once everyone was inside the vehicle. The driver understood the signal and stepped on the accelerator, navigating the streets crowded with people drifting from one pub to another with deft skill.

Once they reached more open space, the driver turned off the main road and headed straight toward the banks of the Nile River. Skidding to a stop a few meters away from the water's edge, the men in the back with Richard slung him over the side and onto the ground. Richard hit the sand with a thud and groaned as he stretched out prone.

"Get up," one of the soldiers said with a growl before kicking Richard in his ribs. He staggered to his feet and stood upright. One of the guards shoved Richard toward the front of the truck, the headlights blinding him as the Reichswehr soldiers appeared little more than silhouettes.

"I'm going to ask you again, and this time I want the truth," Wilhelm said. "Do you understand?"

Richard nodded, immediately regretting his acceptance of Hank Foster's proposal.

"Who are you? And what are you doing here?" Wilhelm asked.

"My name is Frederick Powers, and I'm an American journalist," Richard said, sticking with his cover.

"What publication do you write for?"

"Whichever ones will pay me for my stories," Richard said.

"I don't believe you," Wilhelm said. "You're lying."

"That's not what I do. I'm a truth teller."

"Then where is my gold watch?" Wilhelm said.

"Someone stole it from my room," Richard said. "Perhaps I can make this up to you some other way."

Wilhelm shook his head. "I've found that people aren't very honest with me, but they will tell me the truth if I apply just the right amount of pressure."

One of the other soldiers fished Richard's passport out of his coat pocket and handed the document to Wilhelm.

"Frederick Powers? That's certainly not the name listed here," Wilhelm said. "Is it, Mr. Halliburton?"

"I can explain," Richard said. "You see—"

"Silence. Enough of your lies."

"Please, sir. There's no need to do anything rash. I'm afraid I got caught up in something here and I'd just as soon walk away than press the matter any more. I can leave you alone. You don't need to kill me."

"No, I'm not going to kill you," Wilhelm said. "But you are going to die."

Richard furrowed his brow, unsure of what exactly Wilhelm meant by his riddled response.

Two men stepped forward, each taking Richard by an arm and escorting him toward the water where a small fishing boat was beached. One man was already seated in the center of the boat, gripping the oars. He leaned to the side to let Richard and one of the guards past. Two other men shoved the boat out into the water.

"What's going on?" Richard asked.

Wilhelm stood on the shore, his arms crossed and a smirk on his face. "You're going to tell my men the truth about who you really are and what you're doing here."

"I already did," Richard said with a snarl.

"You will pay your debt, one way or another," Wilhelm said before he waved.

The soldier at the front of the boat held a lantern out over the water as the man in the center strained at the oars. After a few minutes, Richard saw the light glint off a pair of eyes hovering just above the surface.

The soldier up front signaled for the oarsman to stop.

"This is your last chance," the guard next to Richard said. "Tell us who you really, are or else I will throw you in the river."

Richard glanced around and saw that the eyes had vanished. And while great danger lurked somewhere below the surface, he had seen what the Reichswehr was capable of, the image of Dr. Miller still seared in mind. Richard decided to take his chances with the crocodiles. With the Nile predators, Richard at least stood a chance of survival. But a bullet to the head wasn't something he could overcome.

"I already told your commander everything," Richard said.

"It's your choice," the man said before he lugged his prisoner off his seat and tossed him into the water.

"May you rest in peace," the soldier said.

The boat turned toward the banks and began to disappear into the darkness. Overhead, the clouds danced in front of the moon, giving Richard occasional glimpses of his surroundings. He kicked his feet furiously, treading water without the help of his hands. After a minute, he wondered how long he could keep his head above water before he grew too tired.

A thick fog rolled across the surface of the river, decreasing visibility. As Richard struggled to stay afloat, he spun around in different directions. The width of the river was surprising as it flowed swiftly. Without being able to see either shore, he wondered if he had the stamina necessary to make it ashore, much less side was the closest.

He drifted along with the current and considered his options. Crying out for help seemed to be about his only shot at safety. With a deep breath, he prepared to scream when he bumped into something bobbing in the water. Richard's instinct was to get away from it, but the object seemed to be rather inanimate.

He realized it was a channel marker. Grabbing ahold of the frame, he felt his way around in an attempt to find any sharp edge to free him from his bindings. Despite his background as an accomplished swimmer, his legs were starting to tire. If he could use his arms, he'd be able to reach shore quickly despite the Nile's strong flow.

After a few seconds, he happened across a jagged piece of metal. Working quickly, Richard placed his bindings on the edge and started to saw away. Within a couple minutes, his hands were free.

Using the marker to orient himself, Richard decided to swim to his left in an attempt to reach the banks of the river. Slashing through the water with his arms and legs, he glided toward what he believed to be the shore. However, the first thing he ran into wasn't the ground but a pair of night fishermen.

"Please," Richard said. "Will you help me?"

Instead of offering a hand, the two men began to beat back Richard with their oars.

Maybe I'm bad luck.

Undeterred, Richard reversed course, waiting until the boat was out of sight before he swung back around. Swimming toward the shore, he hit the water furiously, splashing everywhere with each stroke. However, he slowed for a moment to take a peek over his shoulder. What he saw terrified him.

Two beady eyes illuminated by the moon reflected off the river's surface and glided straight toward him. Richard tried to remain calm while doubling his pace.

When he looked back, he saw the crocodile lunge out of the water toward him. Richard darted to his right, avoiding the snapping jaws. He didn't think it was possible to swim any faster, but he did.

Moments later, he glanced back to see if the crocodile was in pursuit, but the waters were still. Then he heard a splash and looked over his shoulder again. The beast was making another pass, honing in on Richard's position and speeding up.

CHAPTER 12

RICHARD HAD ONLY SEEN PICTURES OF CROCODILES until this moment, though he'd read enough about them to know that he wouldn't survive a tussle with one in the river. With adrenaline coursing through him, he continued to rip through the water and looked for any sign that he was nearing the shore. Just a few meters ahead, a small light flickered, and Richard swam toward it.

After a couple more strokes, the silhouetted outline of a boat came into view. Reaching over the edge was a man, offering his hand. Richard lunged upward and grabbed it. He tried to wriggle his way over the side as the man yanked Richard inside the vessel. Collapsing in an exhausted state, Richard looked up and realized his troubles weren't over.

The fisherman who'd saved him was now engaged in a battle with the crocodile, which rammed the side and rocked the boat back and forth. Richard sat up and saw the man warding off the reptile with a paddle before wasting no time in joining him. The two men slapped furiously at the animal. The sounds of water splashing and a jaw snapping interrupted an otherwise serene night along the Nile.

At one point, the crocodile wrapped his jaw around the side of the boat and pulled down, but Richard turned his paddle on its edge and cracked the beast on its snout, causing it to let go. After a minute of intense battling, the animal retreated.

"Are you okay?" the fisherman asked.

"Yeah," Richard said, shocked by the question in his own language. "You speak English?"

The man chuckled. "I'm a fishing guide for tourists during the day—and no local would be foolish enough to wade into this section of the Nile at night."

"Well, it wasn't by choice," Richard said. "Someone threw me in the river."

"You need new friends."

"They weren't my friends."

The fisherman shook his head. "Either way, you're fortunate to have learned a valuable lesson about swimming in the Nile at night. Most people never survive."

"I promise not to squander my good fortune then."

The fisherman rowed the boat toward a nearby dock and let Richard out. He thanked the man profusely for his courage and decency before heading back toward the hotel.

While Richard wasn't keen on returning to the Shepherd's Hotel, he needed to gather his belongings and get a dry set of clothes. He considered sleeping in the back and waiting until morning to revisit Sara Catherine's room. However, he noticed the light to her room was still on and the balcony doors wide open.

As he started walking up the steps, he considered that maybe she was working with the Reichswehr unit. He also theorized that perhaps she was forced to let them into her room. After all, she was gone when they stormed inside.

He saw the light beneath her door and knocked gingerly. When she answered, she was wearing her housecoat and smoking a cigarette.

"What happened to you?" she asked, her brow furrowed. "I've been worried sick all night. When I got back, you were gone and had left all your things."

"It's a long story," Richard said.

"Come on in and tell me all about it while you dry off," she said. "You look like you've been keelhauled."

He stepped inside and locked the door behind him. "I might as well have been."

Richard thanked her again for her hospitality before toweling off. He then proceeded to recount what the Reichswehr unit had done to him before barely surviving a predatory crocodile in the Nile.

"The croc didn't follow you ashore, did he?" Sara Catherine asked.

"No need to worry. I locked the door."

She chuckled and bid him to join her on the balcony. Politely declining, he explained that he preferred to remain far out of sight for fear the Germans might see that he survived.

"It's probably best if you report to the authorities in the morning that an American journalist named Frederick Powers went missing last night," he said. "At least that will give off the impression that I was drowned or died in the jaws of one of those monsters."

"What exactly did you do to make these men so mad?" she asked.

"It's silly, to be honest. I told a little fib while I was playing a game of cards."

"What kind of fib?"

Richard sighed. "I told him that I had a gold watch in my room and that I would throw it into the pot to up the ante, confident that I wouldn't have to fetch it."

"And when you lost?"

"He demanded it. So, I feigned as if someone had stolen it."

"That's still quite vindictive over a lost bet," she said. "I hope you learned your lesson."

"I doubt I'm off the hook just yet. That's why I need you to promise me that you'll report me missing at daybreak."

"I promise," Sara Catherine said. "And what exactly are you going to do tomorrow?"

"I'm going to do what I came here to do," he said. "I'm going to explore Egypt."

"My offer to sleep on the couch still stands," she said as she closed the balcony behind her. She gestured toward the couch.

"I'll gratefully take you up on your offer again."

She smiled. "And this time, no intruders."

* * *

JUST BEFORE DAYBREAK, RICHARD WOKE UP AND SCRIBBLED a quick thank you note to Sara Catherine. He gathered his belongings and crept out of her room. Sneaking out through the back stairwell, he found an empty alleyway and curled up in a doorstep before falling asleep again.

Richard didn't wake up again until early in the afternoon. He bought a piece of bread off a street vendor to momentarily squelch his hunger pangs and then donned a hat and costume mustache he'd pocketed while on the *Harvraise*.

Upon re-entering the Shepherd's Hotel dining hall, he strode over to the same bartender he'd seen talking with the Germans.

"Excuse me, sir," Richard said. "I was wondering if you could tell me how to find Jabari Gamal. I hear he's one of the best guides around for us English-speaking people."

The bartender shook his head. "No, he's the best around for anyone. You won't find a more knowledgeable man in all of Egypt if you intend to explore any of our country's great monuments and tombs. It's as if he actually lived through all the dynasties."

"He sounds like the kind of man I'd like to escort me there then," Richard said.

The bartender ripped off a piece of paper from a pad behind him and then scratched down an address. He handed the note to Richard.

"Give this to one of the concierges in the lobby," the bartender said. "They'll be able to get you there."

"Thank you."

"You're welcome. But you better hurry. I sent some other men over to him yesterday. I think they're supposed to leave later this afternoon. Maybe you can all go together."

Richard forced a smile and tipped his cap before spinning toward the door.

That's not gonna happen in this lifetime.

He quickened his pace. If he didn't hustle, he might lose the Germans for good.

CHAPTER 13

K ARL WILHELM KNOCKED ON THE DOOR OF THE address he'd been given. Only two of his men joined him, while the rest remained in the bed of the truck parked down the street, not visible from the front steps. Wilhelm didn't want to make a show of force if it wasn't necessary—and he was confident the handsome sum he was prepared to offer Jabari Gamal would make the Egyptian guide readily agree to assist the Reichswehr unit on its mission.

Jabari cracked the door just wide enough to fit his face through the opening. His gaze darted back and forth between Wilhelm and his two companions.

"Jabari Gamal?" Wilhelm said.

"Who's asking?" Jabari asked.

"My name is Karl Wilhelm, and I'm with the German Archeological Society from Berlin. I was hoping you would be able to assist us on a dig we plan to make at the Valley of the Kings this week."

"I'm sorry, but I'm afraid you've come to the wrong house," Jabari said. "I'm not a guide. How did you get my name?"

"We heard about you at the Shepherd's Hotel from one of the bartenders there," Wilhelm said. "He said you were the best in all of Egypt. Was he mistaken?"

"There was a time when I used to help certain tourists during their excursions in the Valley of the Kings, but that was a long time ago. I don't do that anymore."

A woman's voice rang out from behind Jabari.

"Who is it?" she asked in Arabic.

"It's no one," he replied in the same language as he shouted over his shoulder. "I'll be back in a minute."

Wilhelm narrowed his eyes and glared at Jabari, who withdrew when he noticed his visitor's angry demeanor.

"I'm not a nobody," Wilhelm said, placing his hand on the upper portion of the door and pushing.

Jabari staggered backward, apparently caught off guard by the bold move to enter his home without permission.

"You need to leave my home," Jabari said as he glared at Wilhelm.

Wilhelm shook his head. "I need the best guide, and I'm not leaving until I get him."

"Then you'll have to look elsewhere. I'm not a guide, and I'm not about to start now for a rude person like you."

"For some reason, I doubt the bartender at the Shepherd's Hotel was lying," Wilhelm said. "His name is Ahmed Gamal. Any chance he's related to you?"

"Get out now."

"We're not going anywhere," Wilhelm said as he pushed back the side of his coat, revealing his holstered gun. His two assistants followed his lead, also revealing their weapons.

As the men stood there in silence staring at one another, a young child shuffled into the room.

"Papa," he said, holding up a bag. "*Hadha lirahlatak.*"

Jabari scowled at the boy and gestured for him to leave, but he remained pat as he continued to hold up the pack.

"I know Arabic," Wilhelm said. "I know what he said. *This is for your trip.*"

Jabari's eyes widened. Wilhelm had the guide on the ropes. There was no more denying, no more lying. A little innocent boy had exposed his father's attempt at escaping a job he didn't want for some reason. But Wilhelm wasn't about to accept no for an answer.

"You're coming with us," Wilhelm said, breaking the silence.

"I don't have to do anything you say," Jabari said.

One of Wilhelm's men lunged for the boy, snatching him away from Jabari before he could react. The other soldier held up his hand and then pulled out his weapon.

"You come with us, or we will shoot your son right now," Wilhelm said.

Jabari threw his hands in the air in a gesture of surrender. "Okay, okay. Just let him go. He's done nothing wrong. I'll help you."

The boy's eyes welled with tears before a single drop streaked down his face. Jabari crouched down next to his son and gave him a hug.

"Everything is going to be all right," he said in Arabic. "Tell your mother I will be back in a few days."

Jabari took the pack from his son and strode toward the door. He turned around for a moment to bid his son farewell. He was sobbing, which attracted the attention of his mother. She rushed into the room in time to see her husband being led out of the door.

"I'll be back soon," he said in Arabic.

Wilhelm eyed the woman closely, wagging his index finger at her. "We will take care of him."

She let out a desperate scream as she rushed to the front steps. Wilhelm trained his gun on her and then shook his head. And she obeyed, freezing at the doorway yet continuing to cry out for her husband in agony.

"Don't turn around," Wilhelm said to Jabari. "Just keep walking. We don't have time for her theatrics."

Jabari did as commanded, keeping pace with the two guards until they reached the truck that was parked down the street. When Wilhelm shoved his prisoner—and guide—into the back, he grinned.

"Gentlemen, we have ourselves a guide," Wilhelm said.

The men cheered and smiled.

"Now let's go find ourselves a treasure," their leader said.

Wilhelm climbed into the passenger's seat and then slammed the door shut. He slapped the seat hard as the driver turned the ignition key, bidding the truck to roar to life. The vehicle sputtered for a moment before the engine came alive and started to chug.

"Are you ready, sir?" the driver asked.

Wilhelm nodded. "Full speed ahead to the docks. We're going to Luxor as unsuspecting tourists."

The man eased onto the gas as the vehicle lurched forward. In an instant, the journey started toward the last stop aboard one of the Cairo luxury steamboats that ferried rich Europeans up and down the Nile River.

CHAPTER 14

RICHARD KNOCKED ON THE DOOR AND WAITED FOR someone to answer. After a long minute with no one coming, he looked with raised eyebrows at the concierge who served as an escort to Jabari Gamal's house.

"Are you sure this is the address?" Richard asked the concierge, who went by the name of Amir.

He nodded. "I've been here several times. This is where Jabari lives."

"Then why isn't he answering?"

"Perhaps he isn't here."

"But his entire family?" Richard asked.

"It's possible that they all went to the market."

Richard had waited long enough without any response that he was about to spin around and walk away when he heard something. The voice of a child and accompanying footsteps shuffling across the floor.

"Someone is in there," Richard said to the concierge.

He shrugged. "I can't make them answer the door."

"What is his wife's name?"

Amir sighed. "Sagira? Are you there?"

A few seconds later, Richard heard footsteps shuffling toward the door followed by a woman's voice.

"She asked what you want," Amir said.

'Tell her I'm staying at the Shepherd Hotel and I want

to speak with Jabari."

Amir relayed the message.

"Well?" Richard asked.

Amir shook his head. "He's not here."

"Ask her when he'll be back," Richard said.

Amir and the woman spoke again briefly.

"She said she doesn't know if he's coming back," Amir said.

"Just tell her that I desperately need to speak to her."

Amir obliged and passed along the message.

A few seconds later, she unlocked the door and gestured for them to come inside before quickly locking the door behind them. Once they were all safely indoors, she collapsed onto the couch, tears streaming down her face.

"Sagira, what happened?" the concierge asked in English.

"These men came into our home and took my husband," she said. "They threatened to kill my son if Jabari didn't comply."

"I'm so sorry," Richard said. "I know who these men are, and they are dangerous."

"Can you help me get my husband back?" she asked. "I don't know what I'll do without him."

With a creased forehead, her little son climbed up into her lap.

"I might be able to help," Richard said. "I think I know what those men are up to, but I need to know where they were taking him."

Sagira shook her head. "They never said where they were going, but there's only one place my husband ever goes, the place he is known as the expert guide—and that's Luxor."

"The Valley of the Kings?" Richard asked.

She nodded. "He has been working there for a number

of years. His familiarity with the dig site as well as his knowledge of the English language has made our family a wealthy one—but not wealthy enough to stop a host of soldiers from storming our front door and stealing Jabari away from us."

"How long ago were they here?" Richard asked.

"Maybe an hour ago at the most," she said. "They weren't here long until they coerced Jabari into joining them. He didn't even tell me what he was doing or where he was going. But I knew."

"Do you think he would trust me if I approached him?"

"It might take some convincing, especially after what just happened."

"How does he usually travel to Luxor?" Richard asked.

"There's a steamboat that leaves several times a day," she said. "The next one should leave in about a half hour. If you hurry, you can make it. Otherwise, I don't know when I'll ever see my husband again."

Richard turned toward the concierge. "Do you think we can make it there in time?"

"It's not likely, but it isn't impossible. Can we borrow Jabari's motorcycle?" the concierge asked.

Sagira nodded. "Take whatever you need. Just bring my husband back to me."

"I'll do my best, ma'am," Richard said.

She ushered them toward a shed in the back and then unlocked the door. When it was flung open, Richard spied various tools tacked to the wall and scattered about the shed. In the center of the room, a motorcycle leaned to the side, secured only by the kickstand.

Richard was taken aback by the age of the vehicle, which looked as if it hadn't been driven in several months, maybe even years. Amir checked the gas and then kick-started the bike. Richard would've preferred to drive, but he didn't want to quibble about it. Instead, he wasted no time in saddling up behind Amir and clutching him around the midsection. It wasn't exactly what Richard imagined when he first set out for adventure on the continent of Africa, but he wasn't about to complain. Striking off across the Egyptian sands provided a certain level of adventure all unto itself.

"Hold on tight," Amir said as the engine rumbled. Within seconds, the motor whined as they tore along a winding road leading away from Jabari's home. They descended into the valley in a matter of minutes before getting halted by a train huffing and puffing its way along the tracks.

Richard stared, his mouth agape, at the long number of cars stretching out behind the engine. "We're never going to make it out of here."

Amir twisted the accelerator handle and tore off in a different direction. Less than a minute later, they were parked on the top of a nearby plateau.

"What are we doing?" Richard asked.

"We're going to leap over the train so we can make it to the docks in time."

"Have you done this before?"

The concierge ignored the question as he glanced over his shoulder. He then revved his engine and flew down the road. Near the bottom of the hill was a small berm that ran parallel to the tracks. Richard could tell they had sufficient speed to get airborne once they hit the natural ramp, but the lingering question remained: Would it be high enough?

"Lean forward when we jump," Amir said. "I'll lean back into you."

Richard nodded and looked for the end of the train,

which still wasn't in sight. The cars huffed along as they neared the moment of truth.

When the bike hit the berm, they were launched into the air. But Richard could immediately tell they weren't high enough to clear the top of the train. However, he hadn't sees the genius in the timing at first. Amir had them poised to leap over a flatcar, which was the first in a long sequence stacked with logs and only about half the height of a boxcar.

Richard gripped Amir tighter and leaned forward as instructed. Glancing down as they passed over the train, Richard guessed they cleared it by a few inches. When they hit the ground, the motorcycle couldn't absorb all the force, sending them bouncing along for a few meters before Amir lost control. The bike slid out from underneath them as they skidded along the sand, stopping a few feet shy of the Nile.

A woman who stood nearby washing her clothes along the riverbank stared wide-eyed at them. She grabbed her two children, clutching them against her legs before shouting at the two daredevils in Arabic.

Richard staggered to his feet and smiled at the woman before giving her a friendly wave. Amir dusted himself off and snatched Richard by the back of his collar, dragging him toward the bike.

"We must keep going if we're going to make it," Amir said.

Richard glanced down at Amir's shirt, which was covered in blood. "Your arm doesn't look so good. Are you sure you can continue?"

"Don't worry about me," Amir said as he picked the bike up and started it. "I can still drive. Now get on."

Richard saddled up, wrapping his arms around Amir. "Why do you care so much about what happens to Jabari?"

"When I was a young boy, I lost my father. He was

forced into working at a mine without a choice. Six months later, he died when one of the tunnels collapsed and trapped him inside. I know what it's like to grow up without a father and watch your mother do all she can to help you barely survive. No child deserves that."

The back wheel flung dirt in the air as they sped toward the dock, which didn't look much farther than a couple kilometers away. With arms spread wide, Amir hunched over the handlebars, focused on making it to the dock in time.

"You're going to need to hurry," Amir said over his shoulder.

Richard nodded as he watched the crew begin to remove the ropes from the pylons. They were less than half a kilometer away.

Come on, come on.

As soon as Amir skidded to a stop, Richard leapt off the back of the bike and sprinted down the dock. The plank connecting the ship to the deck had already been removed, while the workers methodically put away all the gear and supplies utilized when keeping a ship the size of the steamer close to the shore.

The boat slowly churned through the water, giving Richard hope that he could reach the edge and leap onto the deck. But as he neared and prepared to leap, a man stuck his arm out, clotheslining Richard and knocking him to the ground. Undaunted by the setback, he scrambled to his feet and backed up a few steps before making another run at reaching the boat, ignoring the man who impeded the attempt. Richard realized he was unlikely to make a successful jump but figured he could swim up to edge and pull himself aboard without much trouble.

As he neared the edge of the dock, the same man grabbed a fistful of Richard's collar and pulled him to the ground.

I'll just swim for it.

Richard leaned over the water and was about to dive in when the man grabbed him a third time. As Richard shuffled backward from the river's edge, the man broke into a deep hearty laugh. With wide eyes, Richard shook his head, grateful that he'd been stopped.

Swirling around the dock was a trio of crocodiles, a couple of them snapping up at the workers.

Richard turned toward the man. "Thank you."

The man shook his head. "You would be dead by now if I hadn't stopped you."

"I now understand that," Richard said. "Thank you for being persistent in stopping me."

And while Richard was grateful that he hadn't been captured or devoured by three reptiles, it didn't change the fact that he had lost the steamboat and with it the chance to keep track of Wilhelm and his Reichswehr unit.

Richard walked back toward the shore, honing in on Amir.

"That was bad luck," Amir said as he shrugged. "And you'll need some good luck if you expect to find Jabari."

Richard shook his head. "More than luck, I need a way to get down the river."

CHAPTER 15

WILHELM LEANED BACK IN HIS CHAIR POSITIONED against the wall of his first-class cabin and took a long pull on his glass of scotch. The trip down the Nile to Luxor was anything but a pleasure cruise, yet he felt like his men needed to rest a little before the difficult task ahead. It also gave them the opportunity to plan in peace without some foreign spy meddling in their affairs.

Hans Reinhard paced around the room before stopping to stare out the window.

"Pour yourself a drink," Wilhelm said to his second in command. "You look like you could use one."

"I'd trade it all to be able to share this moment with my family," Reinhard said.

"Just don't forget they are who you are doing this for. What this team is doing is important work not only for our country but also for the rest of the world. It's pretty clear that people everywhere are adrift at sea and need someone to help steady their ship and steer it in the right direction."

"And you're sure Germany is the one to do that?" Reinhard asked.

"Have you forgotten what the rest of the world has done to us? In their arrogance, these world leaders have forced a yoke around our necks that we can barely breathe, let alone thrive. We must show them that we see through their guises and don't need their help."

"Is this really possible? Can Germany be that force in the world?"

Wilhelm smiled. "You must never underestimate the power of money—or mankind's greed for it. If you possess enough riches, you can change even the most defiant minds. And when you have enough power, people will see things the way you want them to. Obviously, we didn't have a sufficient amount of either of those two things during the Great War. But when we strike again, we'll have both—and we'll have our way with the world."

"I hope so," Reinhard said. "If there's one thing I don't want, it's for my children to grow up in a country so ravished by war that hope is in short supply."

"Your daughters will not only have hope, they will have prestige and privilege as citizens of the greatest nation on earth. And you are one of the elite members of this Reichswehr unit who will help give it to them."

A hint of a smile appeared on Reinhard's face. "That's definitely something worth fighting for."

Wilhelm sighed. "But we have a long way to go before we get there, including a very important mission awaiting us. I think it's time we had a little talk with our guide."

"I'll go get him," Reinhard said before exiting the cabin.

A few minutes later, he returned with Jabari Gamal in tow.

"Mr. Gamal," Wilhelm said, gesturing toward the chair opposite of him, "why don't you take a seat. We need to have a conversation."

"About what? About how you threatened my family?" Jabari said as he narrowed his eyes.

Wilhelm held his hand up. "Would you like a drink?"

Jabari didn't flinch, refusing to answer Wilhelm's question.

"I find that a stiff drink relaxes me a little, especially when I'm in tense situations."

"I don't drink."

"Well, you're missing out. But let's discuss our objectives here on this dig."

Jabari crossed his arms and leaned back in his chair, remaining silent.

"Perhaps I should just tell you what you're going to do for us," Wilhelm said. "I hate making threats, but I've found that sometimes they are necessary to coerce stubborn people to comply with my demands. And trust me when I say this, you don't want to see me keep my word with a stubborn person. But you will if you don't become more compliant."

"What do you want?" Jabari asked.

"We want to dig in the Valley of the Kings."

Jabari burst into laughter. "Why not just ask for wings so you can soar above the Sahara? That might be more possible given my limited powers in such realms."

"Then make it possible."

"I'm afraid you don't understand how this works," Jabari said. "You can't just thrust your shovels into the ground and start sifting through the sand on your quest to find treasures. There are rules for how you can dig in this country, rules that are closely followed to avoid suffering severe consequences."

"What kind of rules?"

"You must receive the proper permits or else risk getting escorted out of the country, never to be allowed re-entry."

Wilhelm shrugged. "That shouldn't be a problem."

"The application process takes up to a year for approval from a committee at the Egyptian Archeological Society. They control everything, like who digs where and for how long. I'm sorry to deliver this disappointing news to you, but I won't be able to help in the way that you expect."

"What I expect, Mr. Gamal, is that we will be digging within twenty-four hours upon arrival at the Valley of the Kings. That is what you will do for me or else suffer a fate worse than death."

"Despite what you think about people who live in Egypt, I am not a genie. I cannot snap my fingers and make something appear out of thin air."

Wilhelm nodded at Reinhard, who walked over to the closet and dug out a large briefcase before handing it to his boss. After unlatching the locks, Wilhelm opened the top and spun it around so Jabari could see the contents—tight stacks of cash.

"Do you think this might help you become more genie-like? Wilhelm asked.

Jabari's eyes widened as he drew back. "I'm not sure that I can just walk into the Egyptian Archeological Society's office and throw money at them to get a permit to dig."

"Mr. Gamal, I don't know anyone at the society, but I do know people. And people respond to offers like this without questioning why or what you're doing, that much I can promise you. Now, do you think you can get us a permit?"

Jabari shrugged. "I guess with enough money anything is possible, but I won't make any promises."

"I don't want promises—I want results."

"I will do my best with whatever resources you give me."

Wilhelm grinned. "Good, because your family's life depends on it. Now, Mr. Reinhard will escort you back to your room."

For the next ten minutes, Wilhelm finished his drink

while inspecting the document he'd taken from Dr. Miller's home. He wasn't prepared to show it to his guide just yet, but Wilhelm knew he would have to eventually and then ensure that Jabari never left the team's sight.

A knock at the door jolted Wilhelm out of his brooding.

"Come in," he said.

Reinhard returned, clutching a small envelope.

"Did you get the guide settled back into his quarters?" Wilhelm asked.

"He was less than compliant this time around, but he eventually acquiesced," Reinhard said. "However, I passed a member of the ship's staff who said that a telegram arrived for you at our last stop."

"A telegram?" Wilhelm asked. "Who would—"

He stopped and took a deep breath. While getting contacted on a mission wasn't entirely abnormal, there was only one person who could trace the steps of the team closely enough to reach them with a message.

"It's from Seeckt, isn't it?" Wilhelm asked.

Reinhard shrugged. "I haven't opened it yet."

Wilhelm strode across the room and handed a decoder to Reinhard. "Use this to translate it for me, and then read it aloud."

Reinhard followed Wilhelm's instructions. While his second in command pored over the letters to make sense of the message, Wilhelm wondered what kind of fiery note he was about to read from the commander of the Germany army. If Seeckt was reacting in such a manner, one that endangered the entire mission, something had changed. Or maybe the mission was to be aborted altogether. Seeckt wasn't the kind of man to give up early. He was cold and calculating, just the kind of leader the military needed during rebuilding years. With Seeckt at the helm, the Reichswehr could find its footing—and its funding—far earlier than anyone ever expected. And Wilhelm knew sometimes a surprise attack could help a lesser group of soldiers defeat a more robust and better-trained troop. Seeckt didn't just want to level the playing field with surprise; he wanted to tilt it in his favor. The tactic was one Wilhelm appreciated and fully understood required exquisite precision. Yet he couldn't help but grow anxious about all his theories regarding Seeckt's surprising letter.

"Have you finished the decoding process?" Wilhelm asked as he wrung his hands and started to pace around the room.

"I almost have it," Reinhard said. "Give me one more minute."

Wilhelm found the suspense agonizing. One way or another, something was afoot. And he couldn't imagine any of the reasons being good.

"Here it is," Reinhard said, offering it to Wilhelm.

He waved away the letter dismissively. "You read it to me."

Reinhard cleared his throat and followed instructions.

Wilhelm,
The incident in Marseille has raised more inquiries. Proceed with caution. Do not leave a trail that will put us in danger. I am watching.
H.v.S.

Wilhelm stood and cursed. The veins in his neck bulged as he stormed around the room, muttering about the message. To conclude his tantrum, he stomped his foot before smashing his glass onto the floor.

Reinhard cocked his head and stared, mouth agape. "What exactly do you find so unsettling about this message?"

"How does Seeckt know what happened in Marseille? How did Seeckt find us here along the Nile in the middle of nowhere? He must have embedded a spy within our own troop. And I find that absolutely revolting. If he doesn't trust me to handle this mission, he shouldn't have asked me to do it."

"I'm sure Seeckt is confident you can get the job done," Reinhard said. "Maybe he just wants you to exercise more care since the fallout could be more stringent sanctions due to the terms of the Treaty of Versailles."

"Did you read the same letter I heard?" Wilhelm asked as he narrowed his eyes. "Seeckt is watching us. Someone is reporting our movements back to him, and he felt the need to warn me as if I'm some child who must be minded. Our mission is to bring back a treasure trove to Berlin, and I'll be damned if I'm going to fail. There are always casualties in war—and don't be fooled by that treaty. We are still at war."

"Regardless, we can't ignore what Seeckt has said, or else we will surely suffer the consequences," Reinhard said.

"We will only incur his wrath if we fail. Regardless of his veiled threat in that message, I know he's only interested in results."

"I think you should at least reconsider your plans for our guide."

Wilhelm grunted and shook his head. "Nothing has changed in that regard. When our mission is completed, we will deal with him as planned."

"But, sir, I'm not sure that is a wise idea?"

"Do not question me," Wilhelm said, wagging his finger, "or perhaps you can join him. Now get out."

Wilhelm turned his back and stared out the window as Reinhard hustled out the door.

"How dare he spy on me," Wilhelm said aloud as he returned to pacing around the room, broken glass crunching beneath his feet.

I will find out who it is and eliminate him.

CHAPTER 16

A S THE STEAMSHIP VANISHED AROUND THE BEND, Richard kicked at the dirt and threw his head back in frustration. He jammed his hands into his pockets and walked up the hill back toward the village. Everywhere he turned, the smell of delicious Egyptian delicacies wafted in front of his face. Deciding he needed to eat something to assuage both his hunger and help him think, Richard dug into his reserves and spent the equivalent of twenty cents on a meal. The cost quickly doubled when he offered to buy Amir lunch as well, which he readily accepted.

Richard and Amir found a spot against an alley wall and began eating.

"What do you think of our country?" Amir asked as they devoured hawawshi.

"From what I've seen so far, it's beautiful," Richard said. "I only hope I get to see more of it. But that will only happen if I'm able to catch up with those men who've taken Jabari."

Amir grinned. "In our country, anything is possible— as long as you have the money to pay for it."

"And that's the problem, Amir. The money I had was stolen by some vandals in France, and now I've barely got enough to get back to Alexandria."

Amir chuckled.

"What's so funny?" Richard asked.

"You thought you were going to get on that boat without any money, didn't you?"

"I was going to rescue Jabari. I'm sure they would've been gracious."

"My friend, you have not been here long enough to understand how this country works. You can thank the British for teaching us how to ensure that no one gets anything for free anymore."

"They do have a gift for that, don't they?"

Once they were finished eating, Richard stood and shook Amir's hand.

"I think from what you said, it's perfectly clear that we must part ways," Richard said. "I have nothing more to offer you—and I'm sure you're losing tips just by being with me."

"It has been my pleasure serving you, though I wish I could help you more."

"Maybe you can," Richard said. "I need to know if there's any other way to get to the Valley of the Kings before Jabari does on that steamer without spending my last dime."

Amir nodded. "There's a train that travels to Luxor every day, usually full of tourists. It doesn't stop here, but it will be along in about a half hour. However, it makes a stop in the town about five miles south of here. Perhaps you could get someone to take you there and you could buy a ticket. It's far cheaper than to travel in luxury on the Nile."

"How much cheaper?"

"Maybe about five of your dollars to travel in third class."

"That's still too rich for my blood at the moment," Richard said.

"Unless you find a kind soul who's willing to take you there, I would say you might find it hard to reach Luxor at all, especially before Jabari arrives."

"I will think of something."

"Good luck," Amir said with a wave before turning and straddling the motorcycle.

"Tell Jabari's wife that we tried," Richard said.

"I will."

Amir kicked down on the motorcycle, igniting the engine before spinning around and heading north.

Richard ambled up the hillside toward the railroad tracks, where he found five children playing nearby. While the children couldn't speak much English, he decided to engage with them, playing a simple game of chase. After a few minutes, Richard had an idea.

He dug into his pockets and offered each of the children a penny if they would play on the railroad tracks until they saw the train come along. Moments later, the train's whistle pierced the air as it chugged toward them. Richard stayed with the children, playing in and around the tracks for the next few minutes until the engine came into view as it rounded the bend.

The engineer tugged on the whistle's rope again, and then the hiss of brakes filled the air.

"Run," Richard said each time after depressing a penny into the palm of their hands. The children dashed away toward the village side of the tracks, giggling with delight as they stared at the shiny object given to them by the foreign man.

Meanwhile, Richard eased toward a tree that was situated near the tracks and waited for the right moment to pounce. Once the train's final car appeared, he took a deep breath and prepared to make a run for it. Richard scanned the train one final time to see if anyone was watching him. As he planned it, everyone on board was straining their necks to see what the conductor was screaming about on the other side.

Perfect.

Richard raced down the small hill in an attempt to grab on to the back of the final car. His stunt with the children had slowed the speed of the locomotive just enough for him to keep pace before gripping the rail and pulling himself up. After easing himself inside, he navigated down the aisles in search of a seat.

The train was packed with travelers and their belongings. Women jammed all their children onto one bench. Some men held large boxes in their laps. One man stroked a small goat, which nipped at Richard as he passed. Twisting and turning to escape the luggage strewn across the aisles, he made his way to the front of the car and surveyed it once more. There wasn't a seat to be had and barely space to stand. He decided to continue his search.

After opening the door, he took a long step between the connected cars and moved forward. While not as chaotic, he was unable to locate a free seat. Richard had almost concluded his hunt when a conductor stood and pointed a finger at him.

"*Marar alkitab, min fadlik,*" the man said.

Richard wasn't sure what the conductor meant until he held out his hand.

He narrowed his eyes. "Passbook, please," he said, switching to English.

Richard patted his breast pockets and then his pants. He feigned a panicked look before ripping his pack off his back and rifling through it.

"I'm afraid I don't have it," he said.

"You don't have it or never had one?" asked the conductor.

"Don't you remember checking it when I boarded?"

The conductor shook his head. "No, but you will be dealt with appropriately. Come with me."

Richard followed the man to the first class cabin where there were ample seats.

"Unfortunately, we don't have room available except in the first class cabin," the conductor said.

"I guess that all depends on your point of view," Richard said.

The conductor glared at Richard and pointed at a padded bench. "Sit down."

Richard had barely taken a seat when he had a pair of handcuffs slapped on him, chaining him to the handrail rising above the bench in front of him.

"I'll be back to check on you," the conductor said. "Don't go anywhere."

Richard shrugged and looked at his hands. "That's pretty much impossible at this point."

He looked over his shoulder, watching the conductor return to the other car. Richard sighed and looked at his attire, feeling self-conscious after glancing around at the rest of the passengers. Their pressed suits and sharp hats appeared in stark contrast to his dust-laden pants and white shirt smeared with stains on his sleeves. Then there was the woman seated alone across the aisle from him, who wore a black cloche hat with a beige blouse and a dark skirt. She was reading a book but cast a few sideways glances in his direction. After Richard received a third look from her, he decided to strike up a conversation.

"I'm Richard Halliburton," he said. "I would shake your hand, but that's a little difficult for me at the moment."

She furrowed her brow and looked away, ignoring him.

"I know, I know," he said. "You're probably thinking, 'What's a vagabond like him doing up here in first class?' Well, the truth is—"

"If you're going to prattle on, perhaps you should find

someone a little more interested," she said in a thick English accent before turning her attention back to her novel.

"I understand your reservations about speaking with me. After all, it's not often that some random handsome stranger sits next to you on a train while leisurely winding alongside the Nile. I'd probably be a little nervous myself."

The woman rolled her eyes, accompanied by the faintest of curls at the edge of her lips.

Richard persisted. "Don't let your prejudices in life prevent you from meeting new people. Some of the best people I've ever met were the ones I could've dismissed by their appearance if I had been so inclined."

A portly gentleman decked in a three-piece suit sitting in front of her turned around and glared at her.

"For goodness sake, ma'am, would you please stroke this man's ego so he'll shut up?" he said with a growl as he tapped his cane on the floor.

"This isn't about ego. It's about a friendly conversation with someone who is sadly wasting her time reading someone else's story instead of enjoying her own adventure," Richard said. "I mean, look around you. We're in Egypt! Egypt! A land of ancient sand and timeless wonders on a train full of people who are experiencing this grand moment in life with you. This is not the time to read. It's the time to take a deep breath and inhale the specter of this place."

The woman looked down at her book, closed it, and set it aside. "Well, Mr. Haliburton, I must say you made a convincing case. You're also far more interesting than the travel book I was reading."

Richard chuckled. "Anyone can point to the Taj Mahal and take a picture. But have you taken a dip in her pools? Or listened to the birds awaken in her trees?"

The woman turned toward him. "Have you been to India?"

"Not yet, but that's what I plan on doing when I get there," Richard said.

"You're quite the bold adventurer, those handcuffs there withstanding."

"As you are also," he said. "Just look at you, a single woman striking off for adventure all by herself in a foreign country halfway around the world."

"England is much closer than America," she said with a wink. "I'm Elizabeth Corbett, by the way, and it's a pleasure to meet you, Mr. Halliburton. I apologize for being so cold toward you in the first place. After all, you were—and still are—tethered to a bench and very much looking like a vagabond."

"Well, this vagabond went to Princeton."

She laughed. "Are you now trying to impress me with your education? If you didn't attend Oxford or Cambridge, I'm not sure I would be all that enamored with your schooling. But an American university? That is one of the funniest things I've heard in quite some time."

"Perhaps it isn't as well respected as one of your country's best schools, but it gave me quite the education. And for that, I'm very grateful."

"Apparently you still have much to learn about how to travel in an exotic place like Egypt."

"Miss Corbett, I won't take offense to your comment, but I swear it would be different if I hadn't been mugged by those nasty Frenchmen."

"Is there any other kind?" she asked with a giggle.

"My, you're feisty. We would get along famously in the Valley of the Kings."

"I doubt we would," she said, cutting her eyes toward his shackles. "I don't do very well when confined to one place for a long time. And as it stands, you're only going wherever this train takes you."

Richard looked out of the window and watched his train pass the Reichswehr's steamship cruising along the Nile. "You don't happen to know when we're scheduled to make the next stop, do you?"

"According to my passbook, we should be making a stop in less than five minutes if we've maintained our schedule," she said.

Richard craned his neck to see around the bend and caught a glimpse of a depot no more than a quarter of a mile down the tracks. He felt the train start to ease up and heard the first hiss of the brakes.

"Ah, what a gorgeous setting," he said, returning his attention to the nearby Nile. "You have to wonder why God created such beautiful scenery for us to enjoy, though I'm more inclined to get out in it myself."

Elizabeth stared out the window. "I feel the same way. It could be because I . . ."

Richard stopped listening to her when he looked down the center aisle and into the car behind them. He noticed the conductor was walking steadily back to first class. And Richard didn't have a second to waste.

He strained while forcing his wrists back through the handcuffs, freeing himself. Then he darted toward the front of his car and opened the door. Hustling down the steps, he took a deep breath and jumped.

Richard hit the ground hard before rolling down a small embankment and coming to a stop. Hopping to his feet, he brushed himself off and looked back at the train. The conductor was hanging onto a railing on the outside steps of the car and shouting something in Arabic at the top of his lungs. Richard gave a little wave before sprinting toward the town of Asyut.

He had a steamboat to catch—and this time he didn't intend to be late.

CHAPTER 17

RICHARD HID BEHIND A SMALL HUT AND PEERED around the corner as the steamboat docked at Asyut, a bustling city and a significant trading hub within the region. The captain of the ship strode out onto the deck and shouted directions to the dockhands. At the back of the ship, workers hustled on and off with various supplies: food, firewood, mailbags, barrels of beer. Richard noticed his chance to sneak about and seized it.

Snatching up one of the vats and hoisting it onto his shoulders, Richard scurried aboard without drawing a second glance from anyone. With his face shielded, he moved freely through the ship until he reached the galley. When he deposited the ale onto one of the large cutting tables, he dashed down a corridor leading back to the ship's cabins. He shuffled his way along until he reached third class.

He carefully checked several cabin doors to see if he could find one that was unlocked. After his fifth attempt, one of the doors sprang open. Inside, he found no sign of occupancy and decided to stay there for the duration of the trip. Once he had settled in, he took a short nap before launching his expedition to find Jabari Gamal.

Richard went into the dining hall and found a hat hanging from a nearby rack in the entryway. He donned the cap, tugging it down low across his face as he roamed the ship in search of the Reichswehr unit and their coopted guide. Richard flashed by the parlor, scanning the room as he strode past. Inside were several familiar faces, including Wilhelm, who was raking in a pile of poker chips from the center of the table as he smiled big. But there was no sign of Jabari.

Later that evening, Richard finally spotted Jabari. While on a walk along the upper deck in the cool of the evening as the sun was setting over the trees, Richard noticed Wilhelm's right-hand man engaged in an animated conversation with a man who appeared to be Egyptian. At one point, he attempted to walk away, but the Reichswehr soldier grabbed the man by the arm and pulled him back. Jabari sighed and nodded, remaining pat as he listened. Standing in the shadows, Richard watched the scene play out until the soldier escorted Jabari off the deck.

Richard followed the duo down the stairs to the third class cabins before Jabari entered one of the rooms. The Reichswehr soldier delivered a stern warning, shaking his finger vehemently at Jabari before disappearing down the corridor.

Unsure if another opportunity would arise before the steamboat made port in Luxor, Richard boldly approached the door and knocked. After a few seconds, Jabari answered. While he didn't appear to be beaten physically, his posture and demeanor told a different story.

"Who are you? And what do you want?" Jabari asked, his cheeks sagging, his stare cold and penetrating.

"Let me in," Richard said. "I need to talk with you."

"Not before you tell me who you are and what you want."

Richard wedged his foot between the door and the frame. "I just saw Sagira this morning. She's worried sick."

Jabari opened the door and then looked down the hallway in both directions before securing the locks and joining Richard inside.

"They're going to kill you if they find you in here," Jabari said. "You don't know how ruthless these men are."

"On the contrary," Richard said. "I know *exactly* how brutal they can be—and I'm here to stop them. My name is Richard Halliburton, and I was hoping you might be able to answer some questions for me, Jabari."

"Before I tell you anything, I want to know how Sagira is."

Richard nodded. "She's holding it together, as much as any good mother could do under such circumstances."

"And my children?"

"They are coping, though they miss you dearly."

Jabari buried his head in his hands and took a deep breath. "I tried to fight them, but there was no use. They essentially stormed my house and forced me to go with them or else there would've been a bloody confrontation."

"These men are bullies of the highest nature," Richard said. "And we must do everything we can to stop them. Can I count on your help?"

"You told me your name, but I don't know anything else about you," Jabari said. "Forgive me if this seems rude, but I've been working in this business long enough to know that you can't trust anyone."

"I understand as I'm sure being forced into a job so suddenly would make even the most naïve person cautious. Hopefully, I can put your mind at ease by telling you that I'm a writer and I, too, find myself here on a most unexpected adventure in an effort to help the American government stop these German soldiers from obtaining great wealth through illegal means. All I was asked to do was to find out what they were doing and then report back to my superior. But it's turned into so much more."

"It seems as if we're both being used."

"However, I'm participating much more willingly than you are," Richard said. "This is a noble—if not vital—cause. We mustn't let the Germans find ways to get their hands on the resources to rebuild their army. And if they have their way, they're going to steal a part of Egypt."

"It's more than that," Jabari said.

"What do you mean?"

Jabari crossed his arms and leaned against the wall. "They intend to take a part of our Egyptian heritage."

"What exactly are they planning?"

"When they first apprehended me, they showed me a map and asked me if I could read it," Jabari said. "I've seen plenty like it before, a document that speculates where the treasure might be hidden and the exact route one must take to reach it. However, I've assisted on many digs around the Valley of the Kings, and reaching hidden tombs isn't easy. A number of attempts are often required before the entry is identified. However, there is one thing that is always assured."

"And what is that?"

"The treasure will be immense—and these men have every intention of taking it back to their own country and profiting from the treasure that they find."

"Do you know what treasure they're after?"

"I haven't had a chance to study the map, but I saw a name at the top that intrigued me, if anything because of all the stories I've heard about this vast treasure belonging to this particular pharaoh."

"What's his name?" Richard asked.

"King Tutankhamun."

"I've read plenty about ancient Egypt, and I'm not sure I've ever heard of him."

"Information about his rule is scarce, but for those archeologists and other scholars who have studied the tombs of the ancient pharaohs, the legend of King Tutankhamun is a well-known secret. The problem is nobody knows if it's simply a legend or fact."

"So the Germans seem to think they have a map that leads to Tutankhamun's tomb," Richard said.

Jabari nodded. "From what I've gathered so far, that is my assumption. But I still need to inspect the document more closely."

"Then we need to get a better look at it," Richard said.

"How do you expect to do that?" Jabari asked. "This Wilhelm character won't let it out of his sight, keeping it tucked inside his coat pocket at all times."

"Don't despair, my friend. I have a plan."

CHAPTER 18

RICHARD RETREATED TO THE ROOM HE'D CLAIMED and looked at himself in the mirror. The five o'clock shadow he'd had just a few days before had now sprouted into the makings of a beard. With little effort, he managed to snag a pair of reading glasses off one of the small tables in the dining room. Each facial-changing device on its own wasn't enough of a disguise, but Richard was confident the combination would create enough of a different look to help avoid detection while roaming about on the ship. And while he was ready to take action before arriving in Luxor the next day, Richard had learned something from Hank Foster—the art of patience.

While Richard knew it was imperative to follow the Reichswehr unit to the dig site, he had one glaring problem: the means by which to accomplish his goal. Without any resources to pay for transportation by horse or camel, he was stuck. He couldn't reasonably walk out to the site each day, especially if he intended to operate stealthily. And if he was going to sabotage the Germans' efforts, he needed tools, which also required money. Since he was in short supply of everything, he wondered if he was running a fool's errand as opposed to actually making a difference and stopping some grave danger.

Despite being given a hefty amount of money to

complete the mission, Richard knew he was hired for his resourcefulness. Foster had made that point clear. And it was for times like these—times where he couldn't easily access the funds necessary to hire beasts of burden and other workers willing to unearth a treasure—that he needed to lean on his creativity.

He stepped into the corridor and noticed a man wearing a jacket with the Thomas Cook & Son logo embroidered over his left breast pocket. That's when the idea hit Richard like a raging bull.

"Excuse me, sir," Richard said as the man approached.

"Yes."

"Do you happen to work for Thomas Cook & Son?"

The man nodded. "I'm one of the guides for this Egyptian tour."

"Would you be so kind to introduce me to your boss?" Richard asked. "I've studied in the field of archeology and would like to know if the tour company requires any additional help."

The man shrugged. "Why not? I heard my boss say that we're in short supply of guides for this trip—and I just so happen to be on my way to see him now. Would you like to tag along?"

"I'd be honored," Richard said.

He followed the guide down the hallway and then up a couple of flights of stairs until they reached the deck where all the first class cabins were located. After a knock on the door, a man bid them to come in.

"Sir, I brought someone to see you who I thought you might be interested in meeting," the man said. "This is—"

"Jonathan Francois," Richard said as he offered his hand.

"Vincent Vance," the bespectacled man said as he took

Richard's hand. "And why do I need to meet this young fellow?"

"Aren't you looking for some more guides?" the other man said.

"I am," Vincent said. "What kind of experience do you have?"

"Well, as of right this minute, none—but I wager a job on the fact that I know more than enough to handle some of your tours."

Vincent stroked his beard and cocked his head to one side. "Anthropology major?"

"I took classes at Princeton—okay, just one class," Richard said. "But I've been obsessed with Egypt since I was a young child."

"Have you been to Egypt before?"

Richard shook his head. "No, sir. This is my first trip, but I—"

"Look, Mr. Francis—"

"Francois," Richard corrected.

"Mr. Francois, I'm afraid that here at Thomas Cook & Son tours, we pride ourselves on employing the most experienced and knowledgeable guides in the business. And seeing that you have neither the experience or the knowledge necessary to serve in one of these positions, I'm afraid you're not the right fit for us."

"Sir, I kindly ask you to reconsider," Richard said. "I'm very well versed on the geological history of the Giza Plateau as well as the history of Napoleon's exploits around the tombs in the late 18th century, not to mention the history of the Medjay, the secret police that guarded the tombs."

Vincent's eyes widened. "You certainly seem to have a grasp on the facts, but the real secret to being a great guide is spinning a tale that enraptures your clients to the point that they retell your stories, ultimately cultivating a steady stream of future tourists. And that's the secret that I'm not able to discern in a meeting such as this."

"If it helps, sir, my true aspirations are to become a writer," Richard said.

Vincent chuckled. "You and everyone else fresh out of college. It's as if this new generation of kids thinks that people have nothing better to do but sit around and read."

"I've been published," Richard insisted. "Do you subscribe to *Field and Stream* magazine?"

Vincent templed his fingers and looked over the top of his glasses at Richard. "I can see that you're a persistent chap and not going to stop pestering me until I relent. But at the moment, I'm afraid we just don't have such an urgent need for guides that I would hire someone as inexperienced as yourself. Now, if you'll excuse me, I have other business I need to attend to."

Richard turned to go when another man rushed into the room to speak with Vincent.

"Sir, we have a problem," the man said. "Marcus has come down with a fever, and the ship's doctor has recommended quarantining him for a minimum of a week."

Vincent sighed. "Isn't Marcus scheduled to handle Lord and Lady Drummond for tomorrow afternoon's outing once we reach Luxor?"

The man nodded. "I'm afraid so."

"Then we'll shuffle the schedule around," Vincent said.

"But, sir, most of the clients have made specific requests. If you start adjusting the assignments, you may not have just one upset client but a whole boat full of irate customers. Besides, you could probably fill in for Marcus."

"I can't," Vincent said. "I have a meeting with a big investor in Luxor during the scheduled tours. The board has stressed how critical this meeting is to the future of our company. I can't miss it."

"In that case, we could combine a couple of groups."

Vincent shook his head. "That won't work either. All of these couples paid premium prices to get the individualized attention."

Richard took a step toward Vincent and his employees. "Sir, I don't mean to interrupt, but I believe I could help you with your quandary."

"With all due respect, Mr. Franklin—"

"Francois," Richard correct again.

"Mr. Francois, Lady Drummond isn't the kind of woman who wants to be regaled by all your academic knowledge. She's a sophisticate of the highest nature and is more enamored with movie stars and culture than your legends."

Richard smiled. "Then you're in luck, Mr. Vincent. I just so happen to know a few movie stars as well."

"Is that so?" Vincent asked, stroking his chin.

Richard nodded. "I met several when I was at the Battle Creek Sanitarium as a boy, some I even consider to be my friends to this day."

The other man raised his eyebrows and eyed Vincent. "He could be an adequate replacement, especially if he can spin a yarn."

"I'm not so sure he isn't spinning one right now," Vincent said.

"Which should tell you all you need to know about my storytelling ability," Richard said with a wry smile.

Vincent sighed. "Very well then, Mr. Frazier—"

"Francois," Richard said.

"Welcome aboard, Mr. Francois."

The two men shook hands.

"One more thing, sir," Richard said. "I'm a bit cramped in my third class cabin. Would it be possible to upgrade to first class?"

Vincent shrugged. "If I say no, you'll just aggravate me until I change my mind, won't you?"

Richard nodded slowly. "It's only one night, sir. But I promise you'll remember the day you hired Jonathan Francois."

"Let me see what I can do," Vincent said. "Meet me at dinner tonight, and I'll try to make arrangements by then. It's probably the least I can do for someone who just might be the solution to one of my biggest predicaments on this trip—or any trip I've ever led for that matter."

"Thank you, sir," Richard said.

"One more thing before you go," Vincent said.

"Sir?"

"You need to shave," Vincent said. "Thomas Cook & Son has a strict policy barring employees from wearing beards and mustaches."

"You could scarcely consider this much of anything," Richard said. "It's just some stubble."

"I didn't make the policy," Vincent said. "I just enforce it. Alexander here will fetch you a fresh razor if you don't have one."

Richard glanced at a portrait of Thomas Cook on the wall behind Vincent. "Did this rule come about because Mr. Cook was jealous due to his serious deficit of hair?"

"God rest his soul," Vincent said. "Poor Mr. Cook's head wasn't exactly fertile ground for such growth."

"His son, on the other hand, could've woven a nice rug out of his beard," Richard said.

Vincent eyed Richard carefully. "If you want the job, you'll shave. Understood?"

Richard nodded.

"Good. I'll see you at dinner tonight, hopefully with a new room key for you."

* * *

LATER THAT EVENING, VINCENT REMAINED TRUE TO HIS word, seeking out a freshly-shaven Richard at dinner.

"You're in room one-eleven," Vincent said, handing Richard a key as well as a book. "This is our guidebook for how we expect our employees to handle clients. Read up on this tonight because tomorrow you may not have much time between unloading the boat and preparing for the tours the next morning."

"Thank you, sir," Richard said.

Cutting his dinner short, he retrieved his items from the third classroom he'd claimed and placed them in his new home in first class. Even though it was only for one night, he was looking forward to sleeping in a cozy bed, something that had eluded him for more than a week.

Once he settled in, he placed his hat back on and adjusted his reading glasses so they sat low on the bridge of his nose. He needed to return to the parlor and find Wilhelm. Before they made it to port, Richard wanted to see what was on that document that Wilhelm had stolen from Dr. Miller—had killed Dr. Miller for—and then guarded so closely.

After Richard entered the hallway, he was locking his door when a gentleman down the hall called out.

"Don't I know you?" The man cocked his head to one side and shook his index finger at Richard.

He turned to his right and saw one of the Reichswehr unit leaders, Wilhelm's second in command. The man eyed Richard more closely.

Richard tugged his hat a little lower down across his brow and then shook his head before speaking in a husky voice. "I'm afraid you must have me confused with someone else. You don't look familiar to me."

"Are you sure we haven't met?"

Richard shook his head. "Sorry, sir."

"What's your name?" the man asked.

"Jonathan Francois," Richard said. "I'm a guide for Thomas Cook & Son."

"Well, I would swear I've met you before somewhere."

Richard nodded. "Have a nice evening, sir."

The man entered the room next door before Richard turned to lean against the door and exhaled in relief. He was about to walk away when he heard the man's voice carrying through the paper-thin walls.

"Sir, are you ready to go play cards?" the man asked in German.

Another man answered—and Richard instantly recognized the voice and smiled. He had been given the adjacent room to Wilhelm.

In an instant, Richard's plans for the evening changed.

CHAPTER 19

RICHARD SCRAMBLED BACK INSIDE HIS ROOM AND climbed up onto the upper bunk that was attached the wall adjacent to Wilhelm's cabin. After careful examination, Richard determined that the flimsy material used in construction could easily be burrowed through without much trouble. To cut as stealthily as possible, he slithered beneath the bottom bunk in a prone position and began to wedge his pocketknife into the wall, making small, slight movements. The whole process took no more than two minutes before the new hole allowed both light and sound to pour into his room.

With his face flattened against the floor, Richard winked his right eye shut while peering through the opening with his left. Only the feet of two men were visible, but Richard didn't need long to figure out which shoes belong to whom.

"Have you let the guide study the map?" Wilhelm's second in command asked, a man Richard figured out went by the surname of Reinhard.

"Yes," Wilhelm said. "He's confident he can guide us straight to it."

"Are you sure he's not attempting to compromise us?"

"You can never be sure of a man's intentions, but he's acting like a man who believes we will keep our promises with regards to his family."

"What about the issue of the permits?" Reinhard asked.

"He understands that he must accomplish everything we ask him to do or suffer the consequences. And he will never be able to gain the upper hand with us."

"When we arrive, I'll secure the necessary supplies."

"Excellent," Wilhelm said.

"And what of the issue of Seeckt's spy in our midst? Have you resolved that yet?"

"I'm working on it. Someone will regret accepting such an assignment while on my team, that much I am sure of."

Reinhard muttered something before exiting the room and leaving Wilhelm alone.

Richard backed away from the hole before covering it with a dirty sock. After sliding out from beneath the bed, he stood and paced around the room. The brief conversation had shed more light on the team, its hierarchy, its ruthless methods, and a potential weakness that Richard intended to exploit at some point if necessary. But he needed to connect with Jabari, his lone ally in the quest to prevent the Reichswehr unit from looting the tomb.

* * *

THE NEXT MORNING, THE STEAMBOAT EASED INTO THE Luxor port just after breakfast. All across the ship, the passengers were giddy, buzzing with excitement over finally reaching their destination and getting to explore what they'd all come to see. First class exited before everyone else as young boys hustled to earn a few coins by helping wealthy travelers with their luggage. Richard was approached by a small boy with huge brown eyes. He looked up at Richard and gestured to take his pack. While Richard politely declined, he couldn't resist depressing a piece of money into the boy's hands, despite the limited amount remaining for Richard to survive with. He hoped that his pay from Thomas Cook &

Son would ease his financial worries, but he knew better than to rely on a promise of a salary. Until the money was in his hands, he needed to keep a tight rein on his purse.

Richard strolled along the dock and gawked at his surroundings, both natural and man-made. The Egyptians were far ahead of their time when it came to architecture, and Richard couldn't help but marvel at all the buildings and homes crowding around the dock. When he squinted into the distance, he noticed the ruins of the ancient Luxor temple. Though the structure was merely a shell of its former self, Richard didn't find it difficult to imagine the building's splendor with all that remained. Thick columns soared skyward, casting long shadows on the courtyard. The pylon gateway leading into the heart of the temple was every bit as grand as he'd seen in pictures, yet the sight was far more vivid witnessed in person.

Richard was still soaking in the scene when Vincent Vance waddled up to his newest employee.

"What do you think of Luxor, Mr. Franks?" Vincent asked.

"Francois, sir," Richard corrected. "And from what I've seen while standing here, I can't wait to explore all the fascinating history around us."

Vincent took his glasses off and cleaned them with his handkerchief. "You'll have some time to do that when you're not leading a tour. But your primary responsibility is going to be handling Lord and Lady Drummond on a trip to the Valley of the Kings."

"Is there anything specific they want to see?"

Vincent placed his glasses back on his nose and then reached into his coat pocket and produced a map. After opening it, he held it up for Richard to see.

"This is the official Thomas Cook & Son guide for the

Valley of the Kings," Vincent said. "It will require a ten-mile ride by horseback to the valley."

Richard's eyebrows shot upward. "Ten miles on horseback? Have you interacted with Lady Drummond? I met her briefly on the boat. She doesn't seem like the kind of woman who will enjoy such a long excursion."

"She's English nobility. This won't be the first time she's been on a horse."

"But ten miles there and back over rough desert terrain? I'm not sure how many of the people I saw on the boat could handle a trip of that length."

Vincent chuckled. "Your job isn't to assess the physical fitness of our clients, though, given the amount of complaining we usually have to endure, such a requirement might not be such a bad idea. But nevertheless, you're hired to take them there. If it takes three hours, it takes three hours. And then simply explain the consequences. It either means less time exploring the tombs or embarking on a risky return through a place I like to call the Valley of the Thieves."

"That dangerous, huh?"

Vincent put his hands up. "Don't let it scare you. It's not common, but we've had a few incidents in the past."

"Do these robbers carry guns?"

"This isn't the Wild West. They mostly use either a scimitar or a dagger and travel in packs of anywhere from four to six. But they're more apt to rob our wealthier clients using motorized transportation."

"I'm always up for a good horse chase."

Vincent scowled. "The adventure we offer here, Mr. Frampton—"

"Francois."

"The adventure we offer here, Mr. *Francois*, is centered around our sightseeing, not enticing Arabian bandits into a horse race across the desert sands."

"You have to admit that one would be far more entertaining."

Vincent wagged his finger. "Not to the upper crust of British royalty, who is our intended clientele. Now, stop this foolish talk before I rescind my offer of employment."

Richard smiled and nodded. "Lord and Lady Drummond will be in my capable care, sir, and I promise you won't regret hiring me."

"Let's hope not," Vincent said. "They'll meet you outside the Winter Palace Hotel in one hour. I suggest you go get checked in there now and come downstairs dressed in the proper attire and ready to embark on your tour."

"Of course, sir. Thank you again."

Vincent waved dismissively. "Just do a good job." He spun on his heels and then headed in the opposite direction.

Richard hustled inside the hotel and spent the next hour preparing for his first opportunity to lead the Drummonds.

On his way downstairs to meet them, he heard someone trying to get his attention and looked around to see where the noise was coming from. He descended slowly, scowling as searched.

"Pssst. Pssst," came the whisper again.

Richard stopped at the bottom of the steps and then saw a boy hiding behind a nearby statue.

"You trying to talk to me?" Richard asked, pointing to his chest.

The kid nodded.

Richard eased over to the boy and crouched next to him so they were eye to eye. "What do you want?"

"You go to the Valley of the Kings?" he asked.

Richard nodded. "I'm about to leave right now."

"Be careful. The Arabean Lusus plan attack tonight."

"Who is the Arabean Lusus?" Richard asked.

A man started walking toward them, and the boy dashed away. Upon reaching Richard, the man sneered and hustled after the kid.

Richard wasn't sure what to make of the warning or the man chasing the boy, but the Drummonds were waiting. Several tours were preparing to leave, which started with a short ferry ride across the Nile before reaching the stable contracted by Thomas Cook & Son.

Richard strode up to the Drummonds and introduced himself.

"Jonathan Francois," Richard said, offering his hand to the lord.

Lord Drummond shook it vigorously. "It's a pleasure to meet you, Mr. Francois. I can't tell you how much Lady Drummond and I have been looking forward to this adventure."

Richard smiled and took Lady Drummond's hand before kissing it.

"My Lady," Richard said.

She chuckled softly before giving him a coy look. "You're more—how should I say this—muscular looking than other Thomas Cook & Son tour guides we've had in the past."

"I'll take that as a compliment," Richard said, glancing at his left bicep and then his right. "Hopefully, the services of my muscles won't be required. I'm expecting a smooth trip out to the Valley of the Kings this morning."

"We are as well," Lord Drummond said. "This excursion has been the one we have been looking forward to most since we signed up."

"I hope I can help make that so," Richard said. "Now, if you'll follow me. We need to take this ferry across the crocodile-infested waters of the Nile in order to arrive safely on the other side and begin our trek by horseback to the tombs."

"There are crocodiles in the water?" Lady Drummond asked.

"The Nile is rife with them. I know from firsthand experience that it's not impossible to survive an encounter in the water with them. But it takes a fair amount of skill and luck."

"Which apparently you have or else you wouldn't be standing here," Lady Drummond said as she blushed.

"Lady Drummond, I believe you're creating an image of me that I might not be able to live up to."

"Those bulging muscles and tales of adventure suggest otherwise," she said as she stepped onto the ferry. She sat down and Lord Drummond joined her on her left. Patting the empty seat to her right, she look up at Richard.

"Thank you, but I'd rather stand," Richard said. "We're going to be riding for hours, so I want to stretch my legs as much as possible."

"Oh, Mr. Francois, I don't bite."

"Oh, leave the gentleman alone, dear," Lord Drummond said as he waved dismissively at her. "I'm sure he has other things to do."

She stamped her foot. "Well, he's our guide—and our tour starts now as far as I'm concerned. I want to hear more about how he managed to escape a crocodile."

Richard shook his head. "It sounds far more exciting than it really was."

"Any brush with death is exciting. I want to know exactly how it happened."

Richard shrugged and sat down before spinning a tale that only sounded vaguely like the truth. By the time he was finished, the story had evolved to include spear-throwing Egyptians, multiple reptiles encircling him, and a tiger prowling along the riverbank.

"Do you think we'll see any tigers on this trip?" she asked.

"Perhaps," Richard said. "Egypt is a curious place. You never know what you might come across, especially while out in the open desert plains."

Richard was telling the truth, as far as he knew it. Since he'd never *been* to Egypt, he had no experience to draw upon. While he had read that the wildlife was relatively tame in populated areas, the likelihood of seeing ferocious predators prowling about was slim. But it wasn't out of the realm of possibility. Or maybe Lady Drummond was joking with him. Despite his voracious reading habit and his mother's love for exposing him to so many different books that opened the world for him, Richard wasn't sure he knew as much as the Drummonds. He imagined they sat around their grand estate immersing themselves in books, taking breaks only for meals and teatime.

Once the ferry reached the opposite side of the Nile, Richard pointed out several crocodile sunning on the bank about a hundred meters away. Lady Drummond clapped her gray-gloved hands with delight.

"This is going to be so much fun," she said.

As the small groups filed off the boat, they made their way to the stables where horses were already assigned. Richard glanced around at the other guides who were helping their clients up into their saddles. Then he looked at Lady Drummond and swallowed hard.

Lady Drummond wore a flowing dress that couldn't hide her rather large frame. Despite her comments about his muscular appearance, Richard wasn't sure he was strong enough to hoist her onto the animal. He also didn't want to insult Lord Drummond by asking him for help. Richard stared at the horse for a moment and then glanced back at Lady Drummond.

He clenched his jaw and approached her from behind, preparing to boost her up. But something else caught his eye in the distance beyond the stables. Taking a few steps backward to move around a series of posts obstructing his view, Richard gazed at a scene that made him sick: Jabari leading the Reichswehr unit toward the Valley of the Kings.

"Mr. Francois," Lady Drummond called. "Yoo, hoo. Are we ready to begin?"

"Oh, yes," Richard said before rushing back to assist her. He interlocked his fingers and held them next to her left foot. She placed her hand on his shoulder for balance and stepped into his hands.

Richard resisted the urge to grunt as he strained to lift her up and over. Much to his surprise, he succeeded. Lady Drummond applauded for herself before earning plaudits from her husband.

"You look like a real explorer," Lord Drummond said, turning to Richard. "Please keep her safe. She has no idea what she's doing up there."

Richard nodded before assuring Lord Drummond that she was in capable hands. Once they had all mounted their steeds, Richard went over a few basic instructions about riding the horses, tips he'd learned while riding on his family's Tennessee farmland as a young boy.

"Be gentle with these animals," Richard said. "The environment here can be very unforgiving, and we don't want anyone striking off across the desert on a runaway animal. Does everyone understand?"

Lord and Lady Drummond both nodded, giving

Richard the signal he needed to continue. He eased his horse in front and struck off in the direction he'd seen Jabari take the Germans.

"Mr. Franks," called a familiar voice.

Richard almost ignored it, but Lord Drummond shouted too.

"Mr. Francois, I believe Mr. Vance is trying to get your attention," he said.

Richard jerked on the reins and turned back to see Vincent scowling and shaking his head about twenty meters away. He gestured for Richard to come over.

"What is it, sir?" Richard asked after galloping to his supervisor.

"The fastest route to the Valley of the Kings is *that* way," Vincent said, pointing in nearly the opposite direction. "Trust me, you don't want to go the way you're headed. You're likely to run into the Arabean Lusus if you don't change your route."

"You're the second person to mention the Arabean Lusus today," Richard said. "What is that exactly?"

"The fiercest group of Arabian thieves you've ever seen. It means 'Forty Thieves' in English. And if you aren't careful, they'll not only take everything you own, but they'll also kill you."

Richard cocked his head to one side. "I thought you said that there were only a few bands of robbers in the desert, small groups of like four to six who most likely would attack your clients using motor vehicles to reach the site?"

Vincent shrugged. "So, I omitted a few things. You were the one so eager for the opportunity, and I needed someone. Besides, who tells *everything* on the first day on the job?"

Richard pulled out his dagger and flicked the tip of the

blade against his thumb. "Fine, I'll stay away from that route. But I'm not happy with the fact that you hid the real nature of the danger from me."

"Sorry, Mr. Frankle, you and all the sense of adventure you have will get over it, I'm sure, once you lay eyes on the tombs."

Richard had been so engrossed in his conversation that he didn't hear Lord Drummond gallop up. His horse whinnied and then snorted, interrupting the curt discussion.

"Our guide has never been to the Valley of the Kings?" Lord Drummond said, his eyes widening. "I thought you said you were teaming us up with one of your most knowledgeable leaders."

"I'm afraid you've stumbled into the middle of our conversation," Vincent said. "What you heard was—"

"Correct," Richard said. "This is my first time leading a tour to the Valley of the Kings, but I promise you that you will get the adventure you seek or else Mr. Vance here will refund your entire trip."

Vincent set his jaw and narrowed his eyes, locking his gaze on Richard. Before Vincent could say a word, Lord Drummond broke into a gentle smile.

"In that case, let's get going," he said before steering his horse back toward Lady Drummond.

Vincent was still glaring at Richard. "I swear to you if—"

"It's going to be fine," Richard said. "Problem solved. And you didn't have to lie about it."

"Better get moving," Vincent said, relaxing his icy stare.

"Sure thing, chief," Richard said before digging his heels into the side of his horse and joining the Drummonds.

"How long will this take?" Lord Drummond asked.

"Depends on how fast you want to ride," Richard said. Before Lord Drummond could respond, Lady

Drummond kicked her horse, which took off into the desert. She hadn't gone more than fifty meters before she started leaning to the right and was headed for a disastrous fall without a quick intervention.

Richard raced after her in an effort to prevent a potential injury. As he was riding, he shot a quick glance in the direction of Jabari's caravan. It had disappeared over a dune.

CHAPTER 20

RICHARD WAS CERTAIN HIS LIST OF NEW EXPERIENCES was growing by the second, and noon was still an hour away. Serving as a tour guide and striking out for the Valley of the Kings were among the things he had never done—and so was speeding across the desert on a horse at top speed to save a woman.

Storming up to the right side of Lady Drummond's horse, Richard reached beneath her armpit and yanked hard. She didn't budge and slipped farther, creating even more instability. Remaining by her side, Richard sought a different solution. He needed to get her momentum moving in the opposite direction and required an unconventional way to do it.

He reached over with his free hand and grabbed the reins in an effort to guide both horses toward the remains of a dilapidated rock fence. Richard tugged hard, pulling both animals toward a collision course with the boundary. When they reached the obstacle, both horses leaped in unison, and Richard held Lady Drummond steady.

When they hit the ground, Lady Drummond bounced upward. Richard seized the opportunity to get her upright again and shoved her as hard as he could. She shifted in her seat and landed in the correct position. Tugging on the reins again to slow her horse down, Richard eased both animals to a stop.

Lord Drummond kicked up a dust storm as he skidded to a stop next to them.

"Are you all right, Lady Drummond?" Richard asked.

She nodded and smiled. "That was quite an athletic feat, but it doesn't surprise me given how burly you are."

"Lady Drummond," Richard said, shaking his head.

"Thank God you're all right," Lord Drummond said. "That was incredible. I thought she was going to break every bone in her body—or worse. I could hardly stand to watch and have no idea how you managed to return my wife into an upright position. How can I ever repay you?"

"Your enjoyment of the Valley of the Kings will be payment enough for now," Richard said. "Now, let's start moving, but not quite so fast, okay?"

The Drummonds nodded in unison. Instead of a fierce gallop, Richard led them in a steady trot.

Two hours later, they arrived at the Valley of the Kings. Several employees of the Egyptian Antiquities Society roamed the grounds, ushering guests toward more popular tombs and answering any questions that arose. Richard soaked in the experience as well as the information he learned. Touring with a woman as inquisitive as Lady Drummond challenged Richard in many ways, including being able to retain everything he heard about all the pharaohs laid to rest there.

One of the employees warned them about straying beyond the boundaries demarcated by a yellow rope. There were several tombs that were closed off over a nearby ridge. Small campsites were set up close to the dig areas, while the smell of delicious grilled meat wafted down into the valley.

"What is being excavated up there?" Richard asked.

"More tombs, I presume," said the employee. "But please heed our caution."

Richard nodded in agreement, but he had something else in mind.

When they finished investigating the tombs of Amenhotep I and Ramses X, Richard walked outside and looked up at the tents on top of the rim overlooking the valley.

"I wonder whose tomb they're digging up over there?" he said, gesturing toward the encampment.

Lady Drummond's eyes grew wide. "We should go investigate."

"Dear, you heard the man earlier," Lord Drummond said. "We shouldn't stray beyond the ropes. It's for our safety."

She wagged her finger at him. "It's because they don't want us to see what's really going on. Perhaps it's some famous pharaoh that they're unearthing, or maybe they've found gold."

"Nonsense," Lord Drummond said. "We've had more than enough adventure for today, not to mention your episode on the horse."

She narrowed her eyes. "That beast just took off running, and you know it."

"What I know is that you dug your heels into his ribs just before he dashed off into the desert."

"Well, this time, it'll be me dashing off into the desert."

With that, Lady Drummond glanced around before lifting up the rope and slinking beneath it. She scrambled up a narrow path comprised of sand and loose rocks, slipping every few steps.

Lord Drummond buried his head into his hands. "Why me? She does this every time."

"Would you like for me to go after her, sir?" Richard asked.

"Do you mind, Mr. Francois? You've already saved her once today."

"What's one more, right?" Richard said, flashing a grin.

"You're more than earning your keep on your first tour with Thomas Cook & Son."

"No one ever told me that this job would be easy, though I was told it would be different each day."

"Welcome to my life," Lord Drummond said. "Fortunately, the dowry has been worth it—so far."

Richard chuckled before scrambling up the path after Lady Drummond, who was about fifty meters ahead of him. He quickly made up ground, but he slowed for a moment to get a closer look at the camp. If Jabari had led the Reichswehr up here, Richard wanted to know—and if so, he would make plans to come back later tonight.

But upon drawing nearer, Richard noticed that the men appeared to be mostly Egyptian nationals, while the man seemingly in charge was barking out orders in English with a French accent. Then he saw several vehicles parked behind the tents. Jabari had led the Germans across the desert on horses and a few camels.

That can't be them.

Richard ascended along the path and strained his neck to see anything else over the top of the ridge. But nothing appeared to be the makings of a camp, small or otherwise. He was still scanning the area when a shrill scream snapped him back to the main purpose of his venture up the hill: Lady Drummond.

"Where did she go?" Lord Drummond asked from the bottom of the trail as he shielded his eyes.

"I'll find her—don't worry," Richard said.

He raced back down the hill a few meters until he came to a small opening dug into the rock. While many of the tomb entrances were grand and contained numerous hieroglyphics and other artwork signifying the room's inhabitant, this was little more than a dank cave, barely lit by the outside light.

"Lady Drummond," Richard called as he waited for his eyes to adjust to the darkness. "Are you in here?"

"Yes, I'm—" she said, the rest of her sentence suddenly muffled.

"Lady Drummond," Richard called again as he grabbed his dagger and held it outward while moving forward.

Another muffled scream erupted, but she wasn't saying anything intelligible.

Before he could call out again, a small fire ignited against the cave wall in front of him, illuminating Lady Drummond— and a man who had his hand clamped over her mouth.

"Just let her go, and nobody has to get hurt," Richard said.

The man yelled something back to him in Arabic. Richard wasn't sure what the man said, but his tone communicated more than enough. As he was screaming at Richard, Lady Drummond squirmed to get away.

Richard's mind hummed. He needed to come up with a way to assuage the hostage taker before something drastic happened.

Holding his hands up in a gesture of surrender, Richard crouched down.

"I have money," he said. "Do you want my money?"

The man nodded. "All."

He does know some English.

"It's in my boot," Richard said as he pulled up his pants leg and dug into his sock with his left hand. But with his right hand, he palmed the dagger he'd tucked into the side of his belt.

Richard calmly stood, tucking the knife up his sleeve. He held out his hand, showing the man his last bit of money. The robber scowled as he peered down to look at it. As he went to snatch it, Richard quickly released the knife, sliding it into position with the blade out. He then slashed the man's wrist, resulting in him instinctively reaching for the wound to stop the bleeding. With Lady Drummond released, Richard yanked her toward him. Seeing that the hostage was getting away, the man fumbled for his knife, but it was too late. Richard slammed the man's head into the cave wall and knocked him out.

"Let's go," Richard said, pulling Lady Drummond toward the exit.

She ran so fast that she passed him, bursting outside and falling into Lord Drummond's arms as he reached the mouth of the cave.

"Are you all right?" he asked.

Lady Drummond sobbed and muttered that she was, keeping her head buried in her husband's chest.

"What happened?"

"I was attacked by one of those crazy Arabs. He threatened to kill me. But Mr. Francois saved me."

Richard stayed a few feet away, allowing the Drummonds to have a moment without intruding. But a moment was all Richard was willing to give them.

"We need to get going," Richard said. "Who knows if there are others nearby. We can't afford to risk it."

Lord Drummond nodded and assisted his wife down the hillside to their horses. They all mounted their steeds and proceeded to tear out across the desert back to Luxor.

Richard let the Drummonds go before he stopped and stared back at the dig sites scattered around the ridge. None of them appeared to be occupied by the Reichswehr unit, but he needed to get closer to make sure. However, with the Drummonds racing ahead, he couldn't let them get much more of a head start before he wouldn't be able to catch them.

I'll be back tomorrow.

CHAPTER 21

THE WINTER PALACE HOTEL RESTAURANT WAS teeming with who's who in the archeological world—and Richard couldn't wait to find out more about the treasure the Reichswehr were pursuing. With a substantial tip from the Drummonds for his services as well as his bravery, he approached the bar and ordered a drink. After some friendly banter with the server, Richard inquired if there were any archeologists present.

The bartender scanned the room. "There in the corner," he said, pointing toward the back. "That's Dr. Howard Carter. If you want to speak with anyone, he's the man you want to see."

"I'm familiar with him," Richard said before thanking the man and sauntering off toward Dr. Carter's table.

Clad in a dark three-piece suit and wearing a tan top hat, the mustachioed archeologist sat with his legs stretched out while sipping a cup of tea. He scanned the room as if he was expecting someone to join him.

"Dr. Carter," Richard said as he offered his hand, "I'm Jonathan Francois here as a guide for Thomas Cook & Son on the Valley of the Kings tour. Would you mind if I joined you?"

Dr. Carter rolled his eyes before half-heartedly gesturing for Richard to sit across the table.

"Thomas Cook & Son, huh?" Dr. Carter said. "Can't you find more meaningful employment?"

"I was desperate," Richard said as he sat down. "I was robbed of almost all my money and needed work. However, I'd gladly switch to working for you if you need any help on one of your digs."

Dr. Carter took a big swig of his tea and then sighed. "I wish I had a dig for you to join me on."

"Funding troubles?"

"That's never a problem with Lord Carnarvon, my patron. However, the Egyptian Antiquities Services is another matter. I don't believe I could imagine a more corrupt organization—and that's saying something since I've had dealings with more than my fair share of companies that seem to specialize in improprieties."

"Is this a new development?" Richard asked.

Dr. Carter nodded. "As of this morning, my entire project was placed on hold. The Egyptian Antiquities Services limits the number of digs occurring at once to three, and someone must have offered a large bribe to Pierre Lacau, the official who oversees the permit department, because he personally visited me on my way out this morning to inform me that my work must cease immediately."

"Is someone digging on your site now?"

"I hope not, though I didn't bother making the trek to the valley today. Honestly, I don't mind a little break, despite Lord Carnarvorn's constant pleading with me to uncover more tombs or risk having the funding pulled. This business isn't for the faint of heart."

Richard took a long pull on his drink. "Whose tomb are you expecting to find? I've heard that they've all been uncovered."

"That's merely conjecture," Dr. Carter said, waving his

hand dismissively. "You can't definitively know that without continuing to dig since there's no written record of all the kings buried there."

"So there *is* one you're targeting," Richard said.

"Ever heard of King Tutankhamun?"

"As a matter of fact, I have."

Dr. Carter's eyes shot upward. "Maybe I should hire you when our digging resumes. Outside of the academic community, I've never met anyone who's even heard of him. Very little is known about his reign. And some archeologists and historians think King Tutankhamun is merely an ancient legend. But I'm going to do my best to prove that he existed—if he indeed did."

"You don't sound so sure yourself."

Dr. Carter shrugged. "It's never a good idea to be sure in our line of work. Between scam artists who fake artifacts and the tenuous nature of bringing buried items to the surface, most of what we do is educated conjecture. However, if the Egyptian legends about King Tutankhamun are true, Lord Carnarvorn will be delighted that he saw this excavation process out."

"I've heard that the treasure was substantial," Richard said.

"Perhaps the most significant of all the kings in the valley," Dr. Carter said as he nodded. "But again, that's pure speculation."

Dr. Carter glanced at his watch and abruptly stood. He offered his hand to Richard.

"Pardon me, Mr.—"

"Francois. Jonathan Francois."

"Mr. Francois, I have a prior engagement that I'm going to be late for if I don't hurry. It was a pleasure speaking with you."

"I can assure you that the pleasure was all mine," Richard said.

"And if things don't work out for you with Thomas Cook & Son, please come see me. I think I was wrong about you earlier. You'd actually make a great addition to our dig team."

Richard smiled as he watched Dr. Carter saunter off. Spending hours sifting through sand wasn't the most appealing career to Richard, but he imagined he could do it for a few weeks if he had to. However, the lure of uncovering a king's tomb was irresistible.

He went outside and stared at the large moon hovering above the ruins of the Luxor temple.

Oh, Grandpa, if you could've seen this . . .

Richard soaked in the scene for the next ten minutes before retiring to his room for the evening, where he found a note from Vincent about his next assignment as well as a thank you based on the gushing praise about his bravery in rescuing Lady Drummond from their tour.

After washing up, Richard climbed into bed, anxious to get a good night of sleep after a long day. He drifted away while reliving all the adventure he'd experienced. It made him feel like the earlier portion of his trip across Europe had been relatively uneventful.

Richard was deep in dream state when he was rudely awakened. He opened his eyes when he felt a large hand clamp down across his mouth.

"Don't make a sound," the man said.

CHAPTER 22

RICHARD ATTEMPTED TO PROCESS HIS STARTLING awakening, which was challenging due to how disoriented he was. The pale moonlight streaming through the curtains turned the figure over him into nothing more than a hulking silhouette. Despite the order to remain silent, Richard tried to scream. Only a muffled noise escaped, which wasn't loud enough to alert any potential passerby in the hallway.

Next, he lunged for his dagger stashed inside the bedside table. Unable to reach the drawer, he struggled to get away, only to be pinned to the bed by the man's knee.

"It's me," the man said. "Jabari."

Richard studied the man's profile before sitting upright in bed.

"Are you insane, waking me up in this manner?" Richard asked. "I could've killed you if I'd kept my knife within arm's reach."

"That's actually a wise thing to do in this area of the world," Jabari said as he eased off Richard and moved to sit at the foot of the bed. "There's a thief lurking in every shadow. In fact, I heard you ran into one today."

"Who told you that?"

"I overheard it in the dining hall, and I assumed it was you based on the story that was related to me," Jabari said.

"Two members of English nobility out with a guide on his first tour and the woman wanders into the cave only to be rescued by the man?"

"And you just assumed that was me?"

"Only a foolish person would enter a cave like that without a small group," Jabari said. "It's a well-known fact that members of the Arabean Losus spend their days there before pillaging unsuspecting foreigners and vulnerable Egyptians at night. A more seasoned guide would've known better."

"A more seasoned guide would've let a woman die today?"

Jabari nodded. "But you're different, aren't you?"

"If you say so. I just try to do what I think any decent human being would do."

"A decent human being without any shred of fear in his body."

Richard chuckled. "You're starting to sound like my mother. But I'm sure that you didn't come here just to tell me that you heard people talking about my exploits at dinner."

Jabari shook his head. "I came here to warn you that Wilhelm has posted lookouts all around their dig site and has ordered anyone who sees anything suspicious to report it to him. And one of the hired guards reported that he saw a tour guide trying to snoop around some of the sites. And the guide was escorting a pair of middle-aged English clients, including a portly woman who entered a cave. Sound like anyone you know?"

"I wasn't anywhere near the dig sites," Richard said. "I was just trying to see if I could see you, though I thought it was foolish since you led them in a different direction."

"Wilhelm wanted me to take a long route to throw off

any marauders who might be following us. He wanted us to appear as if we were simply heading off into the desert, not traveling to the Valley of the Kings to dig."

Richard nodded. "Wilhelm is no fool. And he did such a good job at disguising the site I couldn't tell which one was yours."

"We're on the fringe of most of the other sites," Jabari said.

"And what have you found so far?"

"We're never going to find anything where we're digging—at least, not what Wilhelm is searching for."

"You've seen the map then?"

Jabari nodded. "And I'm leading them to dig in a different place to ensure that they find nothing."

"How long do you think you can keep up this charade before he figures out what you're doing?"

"Long enough for you to find the real treasure," Jabari said as he placed a rolled up map into Richard's hand. "I deciphered Dr. Miller's original map and have extrapolated it here for you."

"So, what am I supposed to do with this? I've never done this before. Besides, when am I going to have time to do this? I'm still working for Thomas Cook & Son, leading tours to the valley. I even have one in the morning."

"I've taken care of most of the arrangements for you, including paying off the Egyptian Antiquities Services so you can begin work as soon as possible."

"How did you—"

"Wilhelm gave me money to pay them off to secure a dig permit," Jabari said with a smile. "It was far more than necessary, so I doubled it to get you access as well."

"Now I'm supposed to go find some random people and start digging around?"

"I hear Dr. Carter isn't doing anything these days," Jabari said with a chuckle.

"I'm sure you didn't just wake me up to tease me with this," Richard said. "I need more specific instructions than that."

"There is a mercantile two blocks south of the hotel. You can't miss it. Go there and ask for Sherif Nazari. Go there and tell him Jabari Gamal sent you."

"He's not going to pull a dagger on me, is he?"

Jabari laughed. "He's my cousin and one of the most knowledgeable men in Luxor when it comes to the Valley of the Kings. He knows where all the tombs are and whom they belong to. He's also worked for Dr. Carter on several digs over the years."

"And he'll be able to interpret this map?"

Jabari nodded. "Don't let anyone else see this but him."

"How will I know it's him?"

"Just ask him to show you his tattoo of a pyramid on his left ankle."

"Then what will we do exactly?" Richard asked.

"Find the tomb, of course—and make sure the Germans never see it. Good luck, and stay clear of those caves."

Richard ushered Jabari into the hallway, locking the door after he left. Collapsing into a chair in the corner of the room, Richard turned on the light and unfurled the map. He studied it closely for several minutes before rolling it back up and stuffing it into his sack. His tour in the morning wasn't scheduled to start until 10:00 a.m., which gave him enough time to pay Sherif Nazari a visit and get the process started.

Richard crawled back into bed. He struggled to go back to sleep as visions of ancient tombs—and their treasures—flitted through his mind. Eventually, he drifted off, excited to start a new day.

CHAPTER 23

RICHARD AWOKE A HALF HOUR BEFORE HE WAS supposed to meet everyone at the ferry to begin his morning tour. He threw on some clothes, combed his hair, grabbed a pastry from the dining hall, and hustled down to the docks. A visit to see Sherif Nazari would have to wait.

Vincent Vance was pacing back and forth while studying his pocket watch every few seconds when Richard arrived.

"Where have you been, Mr. Franks?" Vincent said, shaking his index finger at Richard. "I was beginning to wonder if you'd abandoned me."

"It's Francois—and I would never abandon you without good reason," Richard said with a wink. "Now, is everyone here and ready to go?"

Vincent sighed. "All the clients are here and restless. Good luck today—and don't go running into any caves."

"Yes, sir," Richard said before turning toward the anxious crowd surrounding him.

Richard clapped his hands together before addressing them.

"Who's ready for a little adventure?" he said with a smile. "I know I am."

All their hands shot into the air as everyone began

talking nervously with each other. Richard caught a few words of several conversations as the patrons studied him closely.

". . . and then he broke the thief's neck."

"He threw the woman over his shoulder—and she was not exactly a light load—and raced down the hill, saving her."

"We need more strong Americans like him working for Thomas Cook & Son . . ."

Richard shook his head in disbelief. Through the gossip mill of England's high society, it only took one night for him to achieve near legendary status. While he didn't mind the fame, experiencing adventure was his main objective—and he was more than happy to drag along a dozen or so interested tourists.

* * *

THE RIDE TO THE VALLEY OF THE KINGS WAS UNEVENTFUL in comparison to that with the Drummonds. Most of the people stayed in line and held their horses at a steady trot.

While they explored the tombs, Richard decided to hike up to the top of the ridge to see if he could identify which dig site Jabari had led the Germans to. With another permit pulled to open up a spot for Richard's impending team, there were only two areas being excavated. His cursory glance of the personnel assisting with the closer of the two locations gave him a strong reason to believe the Reichswehr were digging at the spot farther away.

When he strained to see how the Germans were operating, a man walked outside and glared at Richard. He turned his horse aside and returned to the valley to rejoin with the tourists.

"Which cave did Lady Drummond go into?" one of the men in the group asked Richard.

"Now, now," Richard said, holding up his hands in a gesture of surrender. "We're here to look at the tombs of ancient kings, not make trouble for ourselves. Besides, I was warned against letting any of you wander into anything other than the designated attractions."

Richard looked up and noticed two men from his party venturing near the mouth of one of the caves. He scrambled up the hill and stood in front of them before escorting them back down to the rest of the crowd.

"I have my gun," one of the men bellowed. "It's not like I was in any danger."

"I'm sorry, sir, but you must abide by our regulations on a Thomas Cook & Son expedition," Richard said. "It's for your own safety."

After rounding everyone up, Richard led all of the clients back toward the ferry. He was in a slow trot when the gun-toting gentleman rode up next to Richard.

"Did you really sock it to that Arab?" the Englishman asked.

Richard furrowed his brow. "I only acted instinctively to save a tourist. Despite the stories that seem to be buzzing about, I never sought out a confrontation."

"Why not?" the man said as he grabbed Richard's bicep and gave it a firm squeeze. "You look like you might be able to handle just about anybody."

"I haven't been to Japan yet, but I hear their sumo wrestlers would be difficult for anyone to defeat."

The man chuckled. "I'm sure you could handle them."

"Look, Mr.—"

"Nathaniel Thomas, Earl of Locksley," the man said as he offered his hand. "But you can just call me Earl Thomas."

"Earl Thomas, I appreciate your sense of adventure, I really do. In fact, you have no idea how much I admire your willingness to charge into the unknown and experience it with complete abandonment. But I have to draw a line somewhere. It's one thing to venture into a new environment with your eyes wide open for the first time to see something new, but it's another to tempt your fate by rushing headlong into an established danger."

"Come on," the earl said. "You can't tell me that you didn't know marauders were using those caves near the tombs as hiding places. I'm sure you heard the warnings, just like we all did. It was one of the first things they told us at the orientation meeting when we boarded the steamer."

"Unfortunately, I wasn't at that meeting," Richard said. "This is my first time leading groups to the Valley of the Kings, and at no time did I ever perceive we were in such danger until I saw that thief's dagger at Lady Drummond's throat."

They plodded along for a few moments in silence before Earl Thomas spoke again.

"What kind of wages do you earn out here?" he asked. "I can't imagine it would be much."

"It's sufficient for my current needs," Richard said.

"What if I offered your five hundred pounds to take me back out to the caves tonight?"

Richard scowled. "Are you mad? We will be robbed for sure if we return at night. It will be as if we're inviting the thieves to attack us."

"Not if we're prepared."

"Sir, that is not the kind of adventure I seek. I have no intention of dying at the hands of the Arabean Losus for the change in my pockets."

"I'll pay you up front," Earl Thomas said.

"I'm sorry, but I'll have to decline."

"You don't have to give me an answer now. Just think about it. Five hundred pounds."

"I have thought about it, and I will again decline,"

Richard said. "Now, please fall back into line. We need to pick up the pace if we're going to get back to the hotel so you can all have your four o'clock tea."

* * *

FOLLOWING JABARI'S DIRECTIONS, RICHARD WENT TWO blocks south and found the mercantile. Richard strolled around the store once, inspecting many of the items for sale. Pickaxes, scarves, ropes, gloves, cargo nets, fuel cans, burlap sacks, mesh sifters, chests, and other sundries related to excavation lined one wall of the shop. The other side was filled with various souvenir items such as porcelain pyramids, glass bottles of Egyptian sand, "magic" carpets, and oil lamps.

Richard fingered a few of the items as he browsed.

"Is there anything I can help you with, sir?" the man behind the counter asked.

Richard pointed at one of the rugs hanging from the wall and winked. "Does that one fly?"

The man broke into a sly grin. "The ones that actually work are in the storage room."

Richard chuckled. "Actually, I'm looking for someone. Sherif Nazari—do you know him?"

The man shrugged. "That depends."

"On what?"

"Who's asking?"

"Jabari Gamal sent me here."

The man stroked his chin for a moment before nodding. "I will go ask if he's available."

"Thank you," Richard said.

While waiting for the man to return, Richard strolled around the store again and made mental notes on all the items he would need if he were to indeed begin digging. His cursory calculations left him dismayed that he wouldn't have enough money to afford all the necessary supplies, even if he could talk Vincent Vance into a small advance. Richard's final tally was just north of thirty pounds, which was around one hundred U.S. dollars.

The clerk returned about a minute later and leaned on the counter, eyeing Richard. "I heard you were looking for me."

Richard closed his eyes while pinching the bridge of his nose.

"Is something the matter, sir?" the man asked.

"Didn't I just see you?"

"That was my twin, Abu. We often get confused."

Richard gave the man a wary glance. "And you still wear the same clothes?"

"This is the attire the owner of this mercantile demands that we wear. It can be puzzling at times."

"Look, I'm not here to play games. Jabari Gamal sent me to ask for Sherif Nazari, and if you want to make a fool out of me, that's fine, but I'm leaving now."

"Wait, Mr.—"

"Francois," Richard said.

"Mr. Francois, I'm sorry if I offended you. You can't be too careful in our line of business. There are all kinds of questionable characters who simply want to presume upon our helpful nature in this part of the world. Ever since we escaped the oppressive British regime, we have endured wave after wave of treasure hunters simply wanting to come and pillage our country's great riches. So pardon my healthy suspicion."

"Oddly enough, that's why I'm here," Richard said. "To protect one of your country's great artifacts from being stolen right out from underneath your noses by a less than reputable country these days."

"The Germans?" Sherif asked.

Richard nodded. "It's up to me—*us*—to prevent that from happening now."

"I saw a few of them milling around the last couple of days and couldn't imagine it was anything but trouble."

"You're right about that—though it might be more trouble than you could ever imagine. So, here I am. Jabari said you were the best and would know what to do with this."

Richard reached for the map but stopped for a moment. "Before I show you this, I need you to show me something."

"What do you want to see?"

"Your left ankle."

Sherif scowled and raised his left ankle, which was devoid of any markings.

"Sorry to have troubled you," Richard said before hastily heading toward the door.

However, the man slid over the counter and grabbed Richard by the back of his shirt collar.

"Hand me the map," the man said with a growl.

CHAPTER 24

RICHARD STEADED HIS BREATHING BEFORE HE reached inside his coat pocket for his dagger. But before he could make another move, he heard a loud thump on the floor. He spun around to see the impostor collapsed in a heap with a knife in his back.

Richard looked up and threw his hands in the air in surrender once he noticed he was eye to eye with another man.

"Who was that?" he asked.

"I was hoping you might be able to tell me, especially since you just killed him."

The man chuckled. "For the past couple of minutes, I was hiding in the back, watching everything that was happening through a crack in the door. I knew he was a dangerous man when he started pretending to be me."

"I'm Sherif Nazari," the man said before lifting up his left ankle to reveal the pyramid tattoo Jabari had mentioned.

Richard offered his hand. "Jonathan Francois—and it truly is a pleasure to meet you."

Sherif knelt next to the man and checked for a pulse. "He's dead now, and we need to get him out of here. We might get some more customers in here any minute. Would you mind helping me remove this impostor from the shop?"

Richard nodded. Sherif hustled over to the front door

and locked it before lugging the dead body into the back of the store with Richard.

"Do you own this business?" Richard asked between grunts as shuffled toward a stack of pallets.

Sherif nodded. "I opened it a few years ago to help fill the time between digs. However, I don't do much of that anymore. This mercantile is far more prosperous with an income I can depend upon."

"You seem like a wise businessman."

Sherif chuckled. "You might be ascribing too much to my idea. However, I read about the gold rushes in your country and Australia, too. And what I learned was that the people who really got rich were the ones selling supplies to the prospectors. As long as there were foolish people driving their axes into the ground, they needed food and other items to survive. I just took the same principle and applied it here, where the prospectors are world-renowned archeologists with wealthy benefactors. And fortunately at the moment, I have no competitors."

"So did you hear everything I told our friend here?" Richard asked, gesturing toward the dead man.

Sherif nodded. "My brother, Jabari, sent you."

"Your brother?" Richard asked.

"In spirit only, but I would do almost anything he asks me to do. Follow me."

Sherif led Richard back to the front of the store and proceeded to wash the floor.

"How are you going to handle what just happened here?" Richard asked.

"I'll tell my real brother, who is the chief of police in Luxor. The man was robbing one of my customers. What else was I supposed to do?"

Once Sherif finished, he stood and admired his work.

"It's like it never happened," Richard said as he stared at the area devoid of even a trace of blood.

Sherif patted Richard on the shoulder. "And it's not the first time either."

Heading toward the back, Sherif strode quickly. "So what exactly does Jabari want me to help you do?"

Richard glanced around the room once more to make sure they were alone. Once satisfied that no one else could possibly hear or see them, Richard reached into his pocket and produced Jabari's hand-drawn map.

"What's this?" Sherif asked. "This doesn't seem like any archeological map I've ever seen."

Richard shrugged. "It's what Jabari gave me. The original was written in code by Dr. Miller."

"Dr. Thurston Miller?" asked Sherif.

"That's the one. The Germans murdered him in order to get the coded map."

"But let me guess: There was no cipher?"

Richard chuckled. "How long have you been doing this?"

"I was a teenager when Dr. Howard Carter first started excavating in the Valley of the Kings. He was looking for volunteers, and I jumped at the opportunity. Once you uncover an ancient artifact, it's almost like a fever that overtakes you. I couldn't get enough of the work."

"But it's lost some of its luster since you don't dig anymore?"

Sherif shrugged. "I suppose. I got married, had a few kids, and then the Egyptian Antiquities Society got involved in the digs and regulated everything so heavily. I guess you could say it stole my joy for searching for these relics."

"But you'll still help me with this venture?"

"If Jabari believes this is that important, I will do whatever you need me to do."

"He said you're the best."

Sherif shrugged. "Maybe the most experienced, at least of anyone around here that you'd be able to hire on such short notice. But if Jabari wants to say that about me, I won't dispute him. He's been coming to the valley many years."

"I don't care if you're second best or the worst dig expert," Richard said. "What I do care about is stopping the Germans from sneaking out of Egypt with a bounty of treasures. And if you can help me prevent that from happening, I'll be most grateful."

"If by stopping the Germans you mean uncovering a tomb before they do, then I'll be able to assist you. I'm not exactly handy with many modern weapons."

"Then it's a deal?" Richard said, thrusting out his hand.

With his arms still crossed, Sherif didn't move. "There's still the matter of my fee to negotiate."

"What kind of fee are we talking about?"

"One hundred British pounds per week."

Richard's eyes bulged. "One hundred pounds?"

"Plus twenty pounds for all of my men."

"How many men do you need?"

"My usual crew size is ten men."

"Are you mad?" Richard asked. "Three hundred pounds. I don't even have twenty dollars to my name. Where am I going to get that kind of money?"

"You'll also need to pay for supplies, which will cost approximately fifty pounds."

Richard rubbed his temples and considered an alternative solution. "What if I let you take a percentage of the profits from the treasure we find."

Sherif chuckled. "That'd be beyond foolish. Do you know how many times people have sold me the promise of getting a portion of the profits from a dig? Honestly, I've lost count. And I'd be far poorer than I am today if I'd agreed to chase dreams of wealth instead of building it by demanding a fair wage for my help."

Richard sighed. "I'm afraid this has been a mistake. I can't afford this venture—and unfortunately the world can't afford for these soldiers to return home having looted one of the ancient Egyptian king's tombs."

"It wouldn't be the first time some European country raided Egypt's sacred burial chambers."

"You don't seem bothered by this."

"Mr. Francois, I am a businessman, not a philanthropist. It's unfortunate that Jabari didn't warn you about my fee, but I'm afraid I can't help you if you can't pay me and my men a fair wage. We have the expertise to find the tomb if it truly exists, not to mention that I know how to read that map, something you can't do."

"This feels awfully underhanded, if you ask me."

"Perhaps Jabari simply neglected to tell you. I'm sure the oversight wasn't intentional."

Richard furrowed his brow. "Intentional or not, that doesn't change the fact that I can't just wave my hand and conjure up that kind of money. I barely have enough to live off of myself, nor would I be able to get anyone to wire me that amount of money before it's too late—and Jabari is exposed."

"Jabari can take care of himself."

"If he could, he wouldn't be here right now."

"Perhaps he thought it best to steer the Germans in the wrong direction until he could get someone to help him."

"It makes no difference now," Richard said. "Obviously, I wasn't the person who could help him since I can't afford to pay you. I won't take up anymore of your time."

Sherif nodded. "If your financial situation changes, you know where to find me."

Richard remained silent as he strode through the door. He couldn't shake the feeling that he was being taken advantage of by Jabari—at least almost was. Richard thought he might be able to cobble together enough to cover a modest fee. But at least three hundred pounds per week, plus fifty for expenses? He calculated the exchange rate in his head. The costs were equivalent to one thousand U.S. dollars. If he could reach Hank Foster quickly, which was highly unlikely, Richard wasn't sure he'd be able to get approval for that kind of expense, not to mention how long it would take to reach him. One day? Two days? A week? Much longer than a day or two, and it might be too late as the Germans excelled at putting pressure on even the most stubborn of hostages and squeezing until the desired result was achieved.

As Richard walked back to the hotel, he kicked at a few stray rocks along the street. If he had the money, he wouldn't have hesitated to pay Sherif the requested salary. But Richard wondered if there was anything he could possibly do other than ditch the assignment and go see Egypt on his own terms, a tempting option given his situation.

Upon reaching the Winter Palace Hotel, he wandered into the restaurant to have a drink. Most of the tourists were finishing up their tea, except for a few more hardy clients who were saddled up to the bar. Richard eyed an empty seat next to Earl Thomas but opted to sit at the other end of the bar.

However, before Richard could sit down, Vincent Vance grabbed him by the arm.

"Great work again today," Vincent said. "I heard nothing but rave reviews."

"It wasn't as eventful as yesterday."

Vincent waved dismissively. "As long as the clients enjoyed their excursion, that's all that matters. Besides, I think we'd both prefer to avoid that type of detour in the future."

"Agreed," Richard said.

"The next couple of days are kind of light," Vincent said. "Why don't you take them off?"

"And my compensation?"

"I'll leave it in an envelope at the front desk for you to pick up later this evening."

"Thank you, sir," Richard said.

"No, thank you, Mr. Francois," Vincent said. "You've upheld your promise."

Richard watched Vincent weave through the tables in the crowded restaurant before vanishing into the lobby. After taking a deep breath, Richard made his way to the empty seat at the end of the bar next to Earl Thomas.

"Was your trip to the Valley of the Kings all you hoped it would be?" Richard asked.

The earl shrugged. "It was interesting, though it certainly lacked the excitement that the Drummonds' trip had."

"Trust me," Richard said. "You don't want that kind of adventure."

"And you don't know me well enough to presume what constitutes adventure in my book. I would've given anything to be twenty years younger when the war started just so I could be a part of it."

"I find adventure in racing into the unknown, not running into danger. There is a stark difference."

"On that point, we disagree. Perhaps I'll find someone willing to take me back to the valley and allow me to explore the tombs and surrounding caverns how I choose."

Richard ordered a drink and sat in silence as he weighed the consequences of the next few words out of his mouth. Confident that he had no other choice, he looked at the earl.

"About that return trip to the Valley of the Kings," Richard said. "Does your offer still stand?"

"Five hundred pounds, not a shilling more."

"All up front?"

"I'll give it to you right now if you like."

Richard nodded. "It'll be dark in two hours. Can you meet me at the dock in an hour and a half? That is unless you have any prior engagements."

Earl Thomas dug into his pocket and counted out five hundred pounds before pushing the money to Richard. "Whatever I have, I'll cancel it. See you at the docks in ninety minutes."

Richard collected the money and stuffed it into his pocket. The bartender slid a drink in front of Richard, which he promptly drained. He got up and hustled back down the street to Sherif's mercantile.

Sherif was standing outside talking with a policeman as several other law enforcement members carried out the dead man's body. Patting the officer on the shoulder, Sherif excused himself and strode over to Richard.

"Is everything all right?" Richard asked.

"It's being handled," Sherif said. "What brings you back here so soon?"

"You told me to let you know if my financial situation changed—and it has."

"Do you have the money?"

"In my pocket, though we probably shouldn't exchange it right now given the circumstances. That officer is watching us."

"Agreed," Sherif said.

"Just have your men ready to head to the valley at sunrise," Richard said. "I'll give you the money when we meet."

After shaking hands with Sherif, Richard rushed to the docks to meet Earl Thomas. The evening was only just getting started.

CHAPTER 25

RICHARD DUG OUT HIS POCKET WATCH AND GLANCED at the time. Earl Thomas was already ten minutes late, not that Richard cared too much. He enjoyed the brief respite, though he would've preferred to use the extra time to stash the money in a good hiding place in his room. Another ten minutes passed and Richard was on the verge of leaving when Earl Thomas sauntered into view. He weaved back and forth along the dock before coming to a stop a few feet away from Richard.

"Did you make a return trip to the bar?" Richard asked.

The moment the earl opened his mouth, Richard realized a reply wasn't necessary. With the earl smelling as if he'd fallen into a vat of ale, Richard took another step back.

"Are you sure you're up for this tonight?" Richard asked.

"Of coursh, I a-am," the earl said, slurring his words as he spoke. "This is what I've been waiting for since I arrived. Danger's lurking."

"In most cases, I'd say I hoped you were armed, but given the circumstances, I'm not sure that's the greatest idea."

"Don't worry, Mr. Francois. I—I won't shoot you, if that's what you're worried about."

"I'm concerned that you're more of a danger to yourself than to me. And I doubt you'll be quick or agile enough to evade any potential thieves."

The earl chuckled. "Drunk or sober, makes no difference there. I can barely outrun a crippled snail. But don't underestimate my marksmanship. It's saved me plenty of times."

"You've been attacked before?"

The earl nodded. "Many times—it's how I got this slight limp. I fell down the stairs chasing after some ruffian. Fortunately, I still got a shot off. Hit the bloke in the back of his head."

Richard shrugged. "It's your expedition."

"It sure is. Now, let's get moving."

They hustled down the dock and boarded the final ferry of the evening. After arriving on the opposite side of the Nile, they went to the stables where Earl Thomas forked over the hefty overnight rental fee for two horses.

They rode to the Valley of the Kings at a steady pace. Richard was curious about the life of an English earl and asked plenty of questions. However, when he noticed a small tool belt around the earl's waist, Richard grew curious.

"What kind of tools are those?" Richard asked.

"They're used for excavation purposes."

"That looks like a chisel."

The earl nodded. "I should be able to remove a substantial portion of one of the walls for my collection. I'd love to secure some portion containing hieroglyphics."

Richard scowled. "Do you know how much trouble you're going to be in for doing that?"

"If you haven't figured this out by now, I'll let you in on a little secret. Earls don't get in trouble. And in the off chance that we do, it's relatively easy to make such problems disappear. Money will fix everything. But you already knew that, otherwise, you wouldn't be here right now."

"I'm not like that. I—"

"Oh, save me your trip to the moral high ground. You needed money for some reason, and I offered more than enough to motivate you to take me up on the offer, even if it did take you some time to decide."

"I don't care how much money you have, word about your collection will eventually leak out," Richard said. "You're not immune from consequences."

"Only the kind that can't be handled with a payoff. Now, let's get going. I've got a piece of a tomb to steal."

Richard sighed as he goaded his horse to move faster.

A half hour later, they reached the Valley of the Kings in time to watch the moon rise over the ridge. Richard stared with his mouth agape as more beams of light trickled over the valley floor with each passing second until it was fully lit.

"Do you see this?" Richard exclaimed. "The Valley of the Kings under the light of the moon—I'm not sure it gets more beautiful than this."

Richard waited for a response but didn't receive any.

"Earl Thomas?" he asked as he glanced around him.

After dismounting, he hustled around the area in search of his impulsive client, but he wasn't readily visible.

"Earl Thomas?" Richard called again. "Where did you go?"

"Over here," the earl said, already shuffling up a path leading to one of the tombs.

"Perhaps you should wait for me," Richard said.

"You got me here. That's all I really wanted."

Richard rushed up the path after the earl, who had turned his attention to navigating his way up the hillside toward one of the caves.

"Earl Thomas!" Richard called again. "Wait for me."

The earl ignored the plea as he limped ahead. A few seconds later, he wandered off the path and entered one of the tombs. Moments later, the chink of his chisel reverberated throughout the valley.

Richard noticed faint traces of smoke rising from the mouth of a nearby cavern. He concluded that either Earl Thomas was a lunatic or had a death wish, though given the man's eagerness to visit an area teeming with thieves under the shadow of night, Richard realized the brazen move shouldn't have surprised him.

By the time Richard entered the tomb, the earl was steadily chipping away at the wall.

"Do you *want* to die?" Richard asked.

"Eventually, but not tonight," Earl Thomas said. "Now, be a good helper and stand at the entrance for me. This shouldn't take long."

"The Medjay will hear you and—"

"Who?"

"The secret police that roams this area to protect Egyptian heritage."

"Oh, that's just a myth. Those people died off long ago."

Richard shook his head. "With the ruckus you're making, you may need to be more concerned with them than any member of the Arabean Losus."

"Right now, I'm only worried about getting this piece chiseled off the side of the wall here."

Richard sighed and shuffled toward the tomb entrance. Straining to read what Egyptian king was once buried in the chamber, he pulled out a lighter and flicked it. He read the sign aloud.

"Here's lies the—"

Before he could finish, someone swatted the lighter out of his hand. Richard glanced up to see a man standing in front of him, wielding a scimitar. He shook his head as he glared at Richard.

"Earl Thomas, we need to go now," Richard said.

"Give me a moment," the earl said. "I'm almost there."

"I'd recommend you stop what you're doing right now and heed my advice."

The earl ignored Richard, continuing to chip away. With narrowed eyes, the Medjay soldier took a swing at Richard, who dove to the ground and rolled to safety.

"We need to leave right now," Richard yelled.

"Almost there."

"No, now."

Gripping his dagger, Richard ventured back into the tomb. He squinted as he peered into the darkness. When he rounded the corner, he saw the silhouettes of Earl Thomas and the Medjay agent.

"No need for that," the earl said while raising his hands in surrender. "What do you want? Money?"

The man growled and muttered something in Arabic.

"Here, let me pay you handsomely," Earl Thomas said as he reached for his bag. The soldier placed his blade at the earl's neck and coaxed him to his feet.

"So you don't want money," he said. "I understand. It's not for everyone."

Once the earl reached his feet, he made a quick gesture with his hand and suddenly the area filled with a thick smoke. Richard heard what sounded like a brief physical struggle before a thud echoed in the chamber.

A few seconds later, Earl Thomas emerged from the haze. "He should've taken the money."

With eyes bulging, Richard's stared at the English nobleman. "How did you—did you kill him?"

"Good gracious, man. I'm not a murder, but a little smoke and a rock never fail to disappoint. We better get going before he wakes up."

Earl Thomas hustled outside, clutching his new prized possession and wearing a wide smile.

Richard outpaced his client down the embankment and hurriedly prepared the horses.

"Come on," Richard said, coaxing the earl to move faster. "He's going to wake up soon."

"I doubt that," Earl Thomas said. "Just have everything ready when I get there."

He took no more than a minute to reach the valley floor where Richard was waiting with their transportation. The earl took his time securing the tomb wall piece into his horse's saddle pouch.

"You're going to regret not moving more hastily," Richard said. "I'm sure that man wasn't the only Medjay guard patrolling the area."

"Don't get your knickers in a knot."

Richard sighed and waited for the earl to finish. When he did, Richard interlocked his fingers and held them at knee-level to boost Earl Thomas into his saddle. Once situated, the earl dug his heels into his horse's ribs and took off. Richard sprang up onto his horse and followed suit.

They raced across the desert with Richard taking the lead not long thereafter. However, the jaunt across the desert beneath the moonlight was short lived when several bandits pursued Richard and the earl before eventually running them down.

Richard jerked hard on his reins, bringing his horse to a halt next to the earl, whose bravado had disappeared.

"Whatever you do, don't hurt us," the earl said, dropping his head and raising his hands. "We'll give you whatever you want. Just please let us go."

Richard shook his head, surprised at how little pressure was applied before the earl folded. The entire attitude stood in stark contrast to his brazen getaway attempt at the tomb, which made Richard consider that perhaps the earl had another trick.

"Are you all right?" Richard whispered.

The earl placed his palm out flat toward Richard, gesturing for him to calm down. He read the signal but remained confused about the glaring lack of the earl's chutzpah.

Before he could do anything else, one of the other robbers leapt off his horse, yanked the earl to the ground, and held a blade to his throat.

Richard contemplated for a moment if his horse was fast enough to outrun the bandits.

CHAPTER 26

RICHARD WATCHED THE SCENE UNFOLDING BEFORE him and swallowed hard. Death at the hands of Arab marauders certainly wasn't the kind of outcome he'd expected when he agreed to work for Hank Foster in the name of the U.S. government. *Surely, this isn't worth it.* Despite any misgivings Richard had, it was too late to consider what would've happened had he taken a different path. Instead of wasting any more time mulling over hypotheticals, he realized the importance of tackling the problem in front of him that wasn't going to vanish no matter how hard he wished it away.

"If it's money you want, I have it—and I'll gladly give it all to you," the earl said. "I have five hundred pounds in my pocket here. If you'll allow me, I'll reach inside and hand it to you."

One of the thieves jerked his horse back and forth in front of them before holding out his hand.

"Do you think this is a fair deal?" the earl asked.

"Let me see your money," the man said.

Earl Thomas reached inside his coat and produced a stack of bills. He held it out in front of the man and waved it back and forth.

"Is that all you have?"

"I swear, that's it," the earl said. "Please, just let us go."

"What were you doing out here?" the thief asked as he thumbed through the stack of cash.

"Just on a little nighttime ride across the desert."

The thief muttered something, which led to several of his cohorts dismounting and rushing over to the earl's horse. Just as they were about to dig into his pouch, Earl Thomas threw his hands in the air.

"I'm sorry," he said as he reached into his pocket. "Did I say five hundred pounds? I meant a thousand."

He nodded at Richard.

"What?" he asked.

"Give them your money," the earl said. "Or else it's going to get worse."

Richard reached into his pocket and produced the tightly-stacked notes totaling five hundred pounds he had received from the earl and tossed them on the ground.

"Feel free to search me," the earl said. "That's all I have."

The man in charge nodded at his minions, who worked feverishly to pat down both the earl and Richard. After a lengthy process, one of the thieves looked at the man in charge and shook his head.

"Tonight is your lucky night," the thief said. "Don't ever come back here again with anything less than two thousand pounds."

As Richard watched the earl hustle back onto his horse, the situation seemed to be defused as the thieves began to mount up.

Then the man in charge uttered something in Arabic and pointed at Richard.

In an instant, the robbers snatched him back off his horse and dumped him on the sand again.

"I don't have any more money, I swear," Richard said, squirming away from the men.

One of the thieves put a boot on Richard's chest and

motioned for him to stand up. He eased to his feet, raising his hands in the air. The men patted him down and after a few seconds seemed content that Richard was penniless.

"Worthless," the head thief said.

One of the men shoved Richard, sending him sprawling face down into the dirt. He skidded to a stop a few feet away from his steed. He looked up and noticed the creases in the earl's forehead.

"What?" Richard whispered.

"Get on your horse before they try anything else," the earl said.

Richard slipped into his saddle and turned his horse in the direction of the Nile. Earl Thomas jammed his heels into his steed and began galloping away with Richard close behind. They rode hard for several minutes before Richard finally turned around and noticed the thieves weren't visible any longer. After the earl peeked over his shoulder, he slowed his horse to a trot.

"That was close," Richard said. "I suggest you don't ever tempt fate again like this."

"I got what I came for," Earl Thomas said.

"But I've got nothing," Richard said.

"Don't worry, lad. I'll take care of you."

When they reached the river, the man paid by the earl to keep a ferry there for them to return to Luxor on was nowhere to be seen—and neither was his vessel.

"Looks like we're going to be spending the night here," Earl Thomas said.

"Not if I can help it," Richard said. "I can pilot a boat across this river."

"There's just one problem," the earl said. "We don't have a boat."

"After all that we've encountered tonight, I would rank

not having a boat somewhere around four or five among the top ten challenges we've faced."

"It's that high?" asked the earl with a snicker.

"You know what your problem is?" Richard asked. "You don't take situations like these seriously enough."

The earl shrugged. "You're not the first person to tell me that, though I could say you take things too seriously."

"And you would be the first person on earth to utter those words to me," Richard countered. "I'm usually doing what you do, much to the chagrin of those who would prefer I travel a more traditional path, though I hardly find those routes interesting."

"Yet, here you are, acting as if you're my mother."

"I'm never going to regret going on an adventure that results in death," Richard said. "I made a vow a few years ago to spend the rest of my days living without regrets. If there's some challenge I want to face head-on, I will—and I'll enjoy the process along with all the sacrifice required to conquer it. But you're playing Russian roulette with your life—and mine. It's not a gamble I appreciate."

"But when you spin the wheel and survive, you'll never feel more alive. Isn't that right?"

Richard shrugged. "Over the past hour, I experienced far more feelings of fear as a result of our circumstances than I have life-giving exhilaration."

The earl chuckled. "One day you'll look back at this situation with fondness."

"That day is many years from now, a day I hope I live to see. But for now, I'm regretting every minute of this."

"You'll have many adventures in front of you if you seek them," the earl said.

"As I mentioned before, there's a chasm between our definition of the word *adventure*."

Before the earl could respond, a man approached the dock on a ferry. He cast a long shadow over the water, while his cigarette was little more than a fiery blip hovering in the air.

"Did you think I forgot about you?" the man piloting the ferry asked.

"I was beginning to wonder," the earl said.

"Well, the price has gone up. I'm going to need double what you gave me in order to return to Luxor."

"I guess we'll take the long way," Richard said.

"That's not a good idea," the man said, wagging his finger. "The Arabean Lusos are out in full force tonight and waiting on unprotected travelers such as yourselves."

"We've already run into them," the earl said. "It's why I can't offer you a dime more than our already agreed upon price."

"Perhaps I can accompany you back to your hotel for the balance," the ferry operator said.

"You take us back across or I'll see to it that you're flogged in the center of the city," Earl Thomas said.

The man laughed heartily. "That day will never come. Now, are you going to pay me or the thieves prowling in the shadows?"

"Neither," the earl said. "You're going to take us."

"Perhaps you're not listening, old man. I've already told you—"

The man abruptly stopped when he noticed the earl's gun.

"I'm not going to tell you again. Instead, I'll just shoot you, feed your dead body to the crocodiles, and take your boat back across the river myself."

Richard watched the man closely as he eyed the earl. It was clear the ferryman remained suspicious about the earl's bluff.

"Good luck on your way home."

The earl didn't flinch, other than to pull the trigger on his revolver. With the shot piercing the still air, the bullet flew straight and true before embedding itself deep into the ferryman's skull.

Earl Thomas shrugged. "Maybe listening wasn't his strong suit."

With the danger subsided, Richard needed an answer to the question that was nagging him.

"Why didn't you use that gun earlier?" he asked.

"It's a single shot pistol. I wouldn't have been able to ward all those thieves off."

"You could've at least scared them away," Richard said, his eyes growing wide with disbelief.

"It all worked out," the earl said with a wry grin before patting Richard on the back. "Now, let's shove off."

While disapproving of the earl's methods, it was just past 1:00 a.m. and all Richard really wanted to do was climb into bed and get a few hours of sleep before leaving at daybreak on the real mission that had an unbreakable spell on him: finding the mysterious tomb before the Reichswehr unit did.

Richard guided the ferry through the water, stopping halfway across to dispose of the previous owner's body. Dumping the carcass into the water led to a feeding frenzy among the half-dozen crocodiles that were barely hovering above the surface of the Nile. The reptiles devoured the body in a matter of minutes, ripping the man limb from limb. Mouth agape, Richard watched the raw force of nature having its way with the cadaver.

"Don't look like that," the earl said. "He got what he deserved. That was extortion, not to mention a possible death sentence. We could've very easily died had we pursued a different route home—and you know it."

"That doesn't make this any less difficult to watch."

"Everyone lives with the consequences of their decisions. Sometimes the results are more painful. But either way, life doesn't give us the option to peer into the future and choose the best way. We either know it intrinsically or we don't. It's an intellectual form of Darwinism. Consider this ferryman at the bottom of the food chain."

"He's at the bottom of the Nile now," Richard said.

"And it's where he belongs for what he tried to do to us. Now, let's get this thing across the water. After all we did today, I'm absolutely exhausted."

"Killing and thieving will wear a man out—or so I'm told," Richard said.

When they arrived back at the hotel, Richard walked the earl to his room.

"Are you afraid I'm going to run into some more trouble?" the earl asked with a chuckle.

"No, I want to make sure I get my money."

The earl unlocked his door and gestured for Richard to join him inside. After shutting the door, Earl Thomas shuffled over to a chair in the corner of the room and collapsed into it. He buried his head in his hands.

"Where's my money?" Richard asked. "I'm tired and want to get to bed."

The earl leaned back and sighed without saying a word.

"Why do I have the feeling that you don't have any money for me?" Richard finally asked.

"Because I don't."

"What? You told me not to worry and said you would take care of me."

The earl sighed. "I only have about fifty pounds left, which should be sufficient for the rest of my trip until I return home to England. When I get there, I'll make sure to wire you the money immediately."

"But I need the money in the morning."

"I'm sorry, but I won't be able to get you any until I return. I know this might be disappointing for you, but—"

"Disappointing? I risked my life for you tonight and all you can do is give me a glib shrug and a promise."

The earl shook his head. "I thought you claimed to be an adventurer. The first maxim of journeying into lands unknown is this: Nothing ever goes as planned. I'm sorry you're having to learn this the hard way."

"I'm well aware of that fact," Richard said as he narrowed his eyes. "But you don't understand how desperate I am to get that money. Now you're going to figure out a way to get it to me before sunrise."

"Settle down," the earl said. "There's no getting blood out of a turnip."

"Maybe one of your fellow noblemen here owes you a favor."

"Not a favor worth five hundred pounds."

"I'll settle for three hundred."

The earl shook his head. "I'm sorry to disappoint you—I really am. But I won't be able to get you what you're owed until I get back. It might not seem like much of a consolation right now, and perhaps you don't trust me, but I am an honorable man and will make sure you get every shilling that's due."

Richard sighed and was lost in thought as they returned to the banks of the Nile. His plan had suffered another setback—and he was struggling to come up with an idea that could change his fortunes. Sherif Nazari wasn't going to take the news well.

CHAPTER 27

THE CLANGING OF THE ALAR CLOCK CONTINUED FOR nearly a minute past 6:00 a.m. before Richard woke up enough to recognize where he was. With a swift slap, he ended the irritating sound. Not even eight hours earlier, he would've sprung out of bed. But the dread of having to tell Sherif Nazari that there wasn't any money for the dig put a damper on Richard's outlook.

Richard considered sleeping in and waiting until later to inform Sherif about the previous night's misfortune. However, Richard decided he couldn't shirk that responsibility for several reasons, among them being the fact that an opportunity might still arise to acquire the funds necessary to move forward with the dig. While getting in touch with Hank Foster via telegram was one option, Richard wasn't sure how viable it was. He didn't know how long it would take before he would receive another response from Foster, never mind if the U.S. government would be willing to send that amount of money to a brand new agent. But in Richard's foggy state of mind, he couldn't conceive of any other way.

Soaking in the tub woke up Richard's sense, but his mind remained lethargic.

I need a cup of coffee.

He slid down in the water to rinse his hair one final

time. When he resurfaced, he gasped and flailed for the sides as he saw a man standing over him.

"Jabari!" Richard exclaimed. "Do you lie awake at night imagining new ways to startle me?"

Jabari subtly shook his head. "I'm not fond of knocking."

"I'm well aware of that by now," Richard said, using the back of his hand to shoo Jabari away. "If you don't mind, I need to get out and would appreciate some privacy."

Jabari turned his back to Richard. "I had to sneak out early so I can slip back in before anyone notices me missing. I'm taking a big risk just by being here. The Germans aren't very trusting of me."

"They aren't fools, that's for sure. So, I suppose you want an update?"

Jabari nodded. "Have you made contact with Sherif?"

"I have," Richard said as he toweled off. "We're *scheduled* to begin work this morning."

"Excellent. The sooner you get to work—"

"Don't get excited just yet," Richard said. "I emphasized the word *scheduled* for a reason."

"What's wrong?"

"Sherif isn't exactly what I would consider affordable for a man in my position. In fact, he demands quite a handsome sum for both himself and his workers."

"But you did come up with the money, didn't you?"

"Again, the emphasis is on the past tense here. I *had* the money."

"What happened to it?"

Richard sighed as he pulled on his underwear and pants. "I took a crazy British nobleman to the valley last night, and we were robbed by some thieves."

"What were you thinking?" Jabari asked.

"I was thinking I had to come up with a way to raise the money for Sherif to prevent you from getting tortured— or worse—once the Germans eventually figured out that you led them to the wrong site. And the only opportunity I had to raise the amount Sherif required was to do something risky. *High risk, high reward.*"

"That must be an American saying," Jabari said. "And it's an absolutely dreadful one. Look where that risk got you now. *Nowhere.*"

"I can assure you that the last thing I need is someone else beating me up over this," Richard said. "I feel foolish enough as it is without having someone else heaping more shame upon me. And no matter how awful I feel, nothing is going to change the fact that I have no money—and Sherif assured me he won't as much as pick up a tool if I don't hand him the money up front."

"That is his standard operation procedure," Jabari said. "Don't take it personally."

"I'm not taking anything personally," Richard said while buttoning his shirt. "I'm just upset at myself for letting all that money slip away because of my recklessness."

"Then find another way. Perhaps a member of your government could wire you the money."

Richard shrugged. "Maybe, but it would take several days for that to happen. By then it could be too late for you and me both."

Jabari nodded as he paced around the room, his fingers steepled and pressed against his lips.

"What are you thinking?" Richard asked.

"There's a safe in one of the rooms where we're staying that contains all the Germans' money."

"How much is inside?"

"Enough to meet Sherif's usual asking price, I'm sure."

Richard furrowed his brow. "I'm sure they don't leave it unguarded."

"Not very often," Jabari said. "I've noticed that one soldier always remains behind to stay with the safe. They also take turns sleeping in that one room. When we get back from our day's expedition, most of the men are tired and go right to bed following dinner. Now, I'm not sure if the soldier must stay awake or not, but I imagine they are at least told they should."

"Even if we get inside, how do you expect us to break into the safe? That's not exactly my area of expertise."

"When you have the combination, it doesn't matter."

"You have the combination?"

Jabari nodded. "I have a cousin who works at our hotel. He'll think nothing of giving it to me for a small fee."

"And what happens when he's accused of stealing? I've heard the punishment here isn't too pleasant."

"Just leave that to me," Jabari said before the two men finished going over the rest of the details.

* * *

RICHARD WAS SCHEDULED TO HAVE THE DAY OFF, BUT A NOTE slipped beneath his door stated otherwise. Instead of spending the first part of his day waiting to steal the Reichswehr unit's money, Vincent assigned Richard a half-day tour to the Valley of the Kings with a pair of brothers. He didn't mind as sitting around all morning would've made him antsy. But before Richard could do anything else, he needed to deliver the bad news to Sherif.

An hour before Richard was scheduled to meet the brothers at the banks of the Nile, he rapped on the door of Sherif's mercantile, which had yet to open. After several knocks, a man appeared on the other side. He pointed to the sign that showed the store was closed.

"I'm here to meet with Sherif," Richard said.

The man shrugged and walked away. Richard tapped on the door again but didn't receive a response. After several more attempts to get the man's attention were ignored, Richard turned and started walking back toward the Winter Palace Hotel. He was more than half a block away before a strong hand grabbed his shoulder.

"You were supposed to meet us at the water," a man said.

Richard spun around to see Sherif standing there eye-to-eye, wearing a scowl.

"I thought I would try to catch you at your shop before you went down there," Richard said.

"Why would you do that?"

"The money—it's gone."

Sherif cocked his head to one side and glared at Richard. "What do you mean it's gone?"

"Last night, I took a client to the Valley of the Kings, and on our way home, we were robbed. All the money he promised me was taken by a bunch of bandits."

"The Arabean Losus control the area of the desert between the river and the tombs. That was foolish."

"It was the only way I could get the kind of money that you demanded."

Sherif sighed and shook his head subtly. "I've already promised these men their money. This is going to damage my reputation."

Richard held up his hands. "Think of it as a delay, not a permanent setback. We have another plan to acquire the money this afternoon and should be able to begin work as soon as you can begin."

"You better not disappoint me—or else you better hope I never see you again," Sherif said with a growl. "I've worked a long time to get the kind of reputation that I have. If others find out that I'm not trustworthy, my entire business could crumble. Egyptians have little grace for dishonest men, as do I."

"I promise you'll get your money," Richard said. "Just give me until this afternoon."

* * *

UPON RETURNING FROM THE EXPEDITION WITH THE BROTHERS, Richard retreated to his room to find Jabari already inside.

Richard wore a furrowed brow as he looked at Jabari. "How did you—"

"We're about to steal some German soldiers' money from a vault and you're concerned about how I got into your room?"

"It's unsettling," Richard said. "If you can get in here, what's stopping others from doing the same?"

"Nothing, which is why you must always be on guard."

"That's not making me feel any safer."

Jabari chuckled. "The feeling of safety will betray you in an instant. We're all just a heartbeat away from death."

"Aren't you a ray of sunshine today?"

Jabari stood and paced around the room. "Are you ready? Because this will get you killed if we fail."

"And what about you?"

Jabari shrugged. "If the guard sees me, I'm going to claim that I was following you because you looked suspicious. I'll be a hero to the Germans."

"Then I guess we better not fail."

The two men strode downstairs, exiting several minutes apart before reconvening at Jabari's hotel down the street. Instructing Richard to remain in the stairwell for a few minutes, Jabari hustled up to the floor where all the Germans were staying and peeked around the corner to see if a guard was on duty. A man was seated in a chair at the far end of the hallway, his head resting against the wall. With his mouth gaping open, he was clearly asleep.

Jabari motioned for Richard to join him. They crept down the hallway to the room with the safe inside. After inserting the key into the lock, Jabari opened the door and eased in with Richard. Jabari worked on the safe's combination, while Richard locked the door then stood next to it, listening for any movement down the corridor. In a matter of seconds, Jabari cracked open the vault and grabbed several stacks of cash before closing the door.

"Think that's enough?" Richard asked.

"Enough for Sherif but not enough to be so obvious," Jabari answered.

As soon as he finished re-securing the safe, Richard held his hand up.

"What is it?" Jabari asked.

"Someone's coming," Richard said.

"Are you sure?"

Before Richard could answer, the sound of a key sliding into the lock sent both men scrambling.

CHAPTER 28

WITH THE GERMAN SOLDIER PACING AROUND THE room, Richard was certain his heartbeat had reached an audible level from underneath the bed where he was hiding. His hands dampened with sweat, he wondered how long the man needed to inspect the room. Richard glanced toward the closet, which was packed full of clothes and Jabari. After stomping around for a few more minutes, the soldier's cursory examination seemed to satisfy him. He exited, locking the door behind him.

Richard exhaled slowly and waited for a minute before deciding to move. After easing out from beneath the bed, he crept over toward the closet.

"It's clear," he whispered.

Jabari crawled out and jumped to his feet. "Now how are we going to get out of here?"

Richard nodded toward the window. "You should be able to escape without any trouble. We're only on the second floor, which means it's not that far of a jump."

Jabari shook his head. "Have you seen what's outside these rooms?"

"How bad can it be?" Richard asked as he sauntered over toward window. He peeled back the curtains a few inches and peered down. On the sidewalk below were two members of the Reichswehr unit casually patrolling the area.

"Any chance they won't notice us scaling out of this room?" Richard asked.

"They're far more alert than the guard who was sleeping at the end of the hall—and he even thought he heard something."

"What about up?" Richard asked.

"Up?"

"Yeah, the roof. We can climb up to the top of the roof and then exit through the stairwell."

"There are five stories. One of those soldiers will see us."

Richard nodded. "Perhaps, but by that time they must just think we're strange people, not suspects in a heist."

"I can't do it," Jabari said. "I'm scared of heights. Besides, I have work to do in here to avoid getting accused of stealing some of their money."

"What do you have planned?"

Jabari smiled. "I'm going to cause a little chaos among our German friends."

"I like that," Richard said.

"Well, it won't matter if you don't find that tomb before they do. And I'm not sure how much more time they're going to give me."

"If Sherif is as good as you say he is—and this map is accurate—we'll make sure they never get their hands on it."

"Good luck," Jabari said, patting Richard on the back and then slipping him the stacks of German money. "You're going to need it."

Richard nodded knowingly and then eased open the curtains before slipping onto the balcony. He glanced down at the patrolmen, who seemed to be more interested in their cigarettes than anything happening above them.

Richard picked his way up the side of the hotel wall,

grabbing ledges and balconies to reach the top. Just as he was about to disappear onto the roof, his foot slipped and he grunted as he tried to maintain his grip. As he looked down to see where his feet were, he noticed the guards below staring up at him. They pointed at him and started yelling in German.

Without any place to put his feet and push off for leverage, Richard strained to pull himself up by his fingertips. After struggling for a few seconds, he managed to wriggle his way onto the roof, flinging his legs over and rolling out of view of the guards. Richard made his way down the stairwell and exited through an alleyway. He thought he was in the clear before he heard someone shouting behind him. As he turned to see where the voice was coming from, he noticed one of the German guards in pursuit.

Richard darted across the street, weaving his way through irked street vendors as they tried to maneuver their carts safely away from him. As he hurdled a man shining shoes outside of a restaurant, Richard winced as he realized he was about to topple over an old lady. Instead of continuing forward, he spun his body to the side, narrowly missing her. However, he wasn't able to maintain his footing and stumbled to the ground. With a quick glance over his shoulder, Richard scrambled to his feet and continued on his path.

While his hotel was only half a block ahead, Richard didn't want to lead the guard straight to where he was staying. Instead, he dashed across the street and hustled up next to a moving car going in the opposite direction. Richard used the vehicle as a shield while doubling back to lose the soldier.

After dashing into a nearby open market, Richard browsed through a store packed with artisan rugs and blankets. He kept an eye out on the street and didn't relax until he saw the German soldier hustling in the opposite direction. Richard stepped out and waited until the man disappeared before returning to the Winter Palace Hotel.

Once he was safely in the confines of his room, Richard pulled out the money and inspected it. While he flipped through the money to count it, he chuckled at his good fortune. Not only had the Germans been vulnerable with their safe, they were using the British pound on their trip, exactly the currency Richard needed. It saved him a time-consuming trip to an Egyptian bank.

Richard changed clothes and returned to Sherif's mercantile just after 5:00 p.m. He was about to lock the front door when Richard appeared wearing a wide grin.

"I take it you got the money," Sherif said as he opened the door and locked it behind Richard.

"It's all right here," Richard said. "Feel free to count it if you don't trust me."

"Do I want to ask where it came from?"

"It's better that you didn't know."

Sherif nodded. "I hope you won't take it as a sign of mistrust if I do count it. But given the rough start to our partnership, I'm going to make sure it's all here."

"Be my guest. I won't be offended."

After Sherif finished tallying the cash, he turned to Richard. "Everything appears to be in order."

"Excellent. When can we get started?"

"Tonight," Sherif said. "I'll meet you at the docks after dark. We'll have to secure some more horses and camels for the journey to the Valley of the Kings, but I don't think that'll be a problem."

"I'll leave those details up to you," Richard said as he turned to leave. "I'll see you at dark by the river."

Sherif nodded as he strode past Richard to unlock the door for him.

* * *

AFTER A QUICK MEAL, RICHARD GATHERED ALL THE SUPPLIES he figured he needed for the excavation. He headed toward the docks. Along the way, he kept his head down while passing several German soldiers returning from their day shift. Jabari had told Richard that since the process was taking longer than expected, Wilhelm hired a few more workers and split the Reichswehr members into two teams to make sure that the digging never stopped. While they had received a permit to stay there, it was a temporary one, limiting them to two weeks. The deadline created extra stress for Wilhelm and his men, resulting in high tension.

Richard knew how desperation made a person more dangerous than ever. He'd seen it in Gibraltar firsthand, an experience he preferred never to relive. And he could only imagine Wilhelm would be even more unhinged than anything Richard ever experienced if the Reichswehr unit leader witnessed the treasure yanked right out from underneath his nose. That only amplified the importance of finding the secret tomb Dr. Miller believed existed before anyone else did, particularly Wilhelm.

At the docks, Richard found Sherif and his band of nearly a dozen workers, all enthusiastic and eager to begin.

"This is quite a crew," Richard said as he walked up and shook Sherif's hand.

Sherif took Richard by his shoulders and kissed both his cheeks. "This is Egypt, my friend. We are partners. We don't just shake hands any more as you do in the west. Now, it's time for you to start learning how we do things here."

Richard nodded. "I'm just a boy from Memphis— Memphis, Tennessee, that is. But you show me what I need to do and I'll do it. I'm completely capable of adapting to my environment."

Sherif nodded as he ushered Richard aboard the ferry. A half hour later, they were on the other side of the Nile and packing their animals to begin the expedition in the Valley of the Kings.

"Look over there," Sherif said. "That German crew is heading the same place we are."

"We'll never be able to get out of their shadow," Richard said.

"Shadows don't appear at night."

"Good point," Richard said. "It also reminds me of a question I have for you: Shouldn't we do this during the day?"

Sherif chuckled and shook his head. "Sweltering heat, scorching sand, underground digging. Only one of these things happens in the dark. There's absolutely no reason to do it during the day unless you're about to make a major discovery or you're on a tight schedule."

"The quicker we can unearth this tomb, the better."

"Faster is always better except when it isn't," Sherif said with a wry grin.

"You sound like a fortune cookie."

"A what?"

Richard sighed. "Never mind. It's not important. I know that we're working in a different part of the valley than the Germans, but we must make sure they don't intercept our findings and claim them as their own."

"It wouldn't be the first time that's happened here," Sherif said. "Discovery theft happened all the time a few years ago. So many of the people who allegedly discovered certain tombs were simple thieves who were able to muscle the actual archeologist out of the way. But the Egyptian Antiquities Society has done a good job of preventing that from happening recently."

"So the society *is* good for something."

"That might be the only thing," Sherif said. "But for some people, that's an important task."

They saddled up and began their trek across the desert, which was cooling rapidly since the sun had dipped below the horizon. Richard held a lantern out in front of his horse while riding at the head of their caravan with Sherif. Both men plodded along on their beasts of burden for several minutes in silence until Richard asked a question that broke the stillness.

"Are you certain that you'll be able to read this map?" Richard asked.

"The only thing I'm unsure of is if your beloved Dr. Miller knew what he was talking about," Sherif said.

"Do you have reason to question him?"

"The entire story of Tutankhamun is one that divides many scholars. I've met men on both sides of the debate— men who think that Tutankhamun is real and those who think he was just a legend. We don't know much about him, but it seems difficult to believe that a young king could be buried with so much treasure as many archeologists believe."

"So you believe we might be wasting our time?"

"Perhaps, but the Germans are paying for it, right?"

Richard shot Sherif a look. "I never said that."

"I know you didn't, but I saw Jabari after you left. He told me everything. You are quite daring. Your willingness to risk everything to get to this treasure first let me know just how important it is to you. And if it's important to my client, it's important to me."

"Just don't expect a bonus if we find it," Richard said. "All I can do is recommend you to Dr. Howard Carter if you want more work like this."

"It depends on how this dig goes. If we find the tomb, I might be more inclined to return to my roots and explore more of the tombs around here with an expert like Dr. Carter."

"Let's hope it goes perfectly."

Sherif chuckled.

"What's so funny?" Richard asked.

"This is definitely new territory for you," Sherif said. "If you'd been doing this for a while, you'd know how nothing ever goes as planned."

"Maybe this will be a first."

"Maybe the tomb itself will rise out of the sand for us the moment we put a spade into the desert sand."

"A man can dream, can't he?"

Sherif just smiled. "I like you, Mr. Francois. You always keep me smiling."

"If you can find this tomb, you'll keep me smiling for a very long time."

An hour later, they arrived at the dig site, already staked off by the Egyptian Antiquities Society. Someone for the society used a few pegs and some twine to cordon off an area that would be inspected regularly to ensure that the excavation wasn't extending beyond the boundaries. Sherif's lackeys quickly erected a tent over a large portion of the area and lit it. Each day, two of the men would take a turn remaining at the site to ward off any marauders. It was relatively safe during daylight hours between the roaming Medjay members and the Egyptian Antiquities Service patrolmen. But Sherif suggested that at least two men needed to stand guard around their tent each night to avoid an attack from the Arabean Losus or some other group of bandits.

Sherif's workers weren't more than an hour into their dig when a ruckus outside the tent arrested Richard's attention. He rushed into the open air and found a handful of men clutching torches and swords while intently glaring at them.

"Where is your leader?" one of the men demanded in Arabic.

The man next to Richard pointed at him.

"What are you doing?" Richard asked.

"He wanted to know who our leader was," the man said.

Richard sighed and shook his head. "What do you want?"

Before he could utter another word, two guards seized Richard and then thrust him to the ground. One of the men yanked Richard to his feet and quickly tied his hands behind his back.

Richard looked at the sharp blade placed up next to his throat before scanning the area for Sherif, who was nowhere to be found.

CHAPTER 29

S HERIF," RICHARD SHOUTED BEFORE SWALLOWING HARD, "where are you?" The man standing in front of Richard pressed the knife a little harder against his throat. He felt something warm begin to trickle down his neck—and he wasn't sure if it was sweat or blood. With bulging eyes, he glanced around the dig site again.

Still no sign of Sherif.

"If there's any way I can help you—" Richard said before the man gestured for his hostage to be quiet.

"When I want your help, I'll tell you what to do," the man said. "Until then, keep your mouth closed."

Perspiring more than ever, Richard nodded. As sweat seeped inside his eyes, they started to burn, so much so that he stopped looking around for Sherif. Richard squeezed his eyes shut and hoped that the confrontation would come to a sudden end, preferably one where he escaped with his life.

With the fiery sensation subsiding for a moment, Richard took a deep breath and shouted again. "Sherif! Where are you?"

Just when Richard had given up hope that he'd ever see the man who was supposed to be the genius crew leader again, Sherif glided through the tent doors.

"Unhand him right now," Sherif said.

The man glared back, narrowing his eyes while

tightening his grip on Richard. Shouting something back in Arabic, the man made a slashing motion with his knife across the front of Richard's shirt, slicing off the top button. Then the man motioned for all his cohorts to leave.

The moment everyone vanished outside, Sherif charged at the man before stopping short and embracing like long lost friends.

"Yousef, do you have to always make such an entrance?" Sherif asked.

Yousef chuckled as he stroked the bottom of his beard. He paused for a moment, glancing upward while he thought.

"A friendly hello hardly instills fear in the heart of someone," Yousef said, "especially if I expect to get paid."

"I hope you're not counting on getting any money from me," Sherif said. "Because if you are, I'm afraid you'll be disappointed."

"You? No," Yousef said as he pointed his dagger toward Sherif. Then Yousef redirected his blade at Richard. "But I think he might have something for me."

"Mr. Francois doesn't have much. Go easy on him. He's financing this entire project with the help of the Germans."

Richard glared at Sherif. "I thought I told you—"

"What?" Yousef said, sliding directly in front of Richard and raising his chin with the knife. "You're working with the Germans?"

"That's not what I said," Richard explained. "I was merely trying to remind him that—"

"Never mind that," Yousef said. "I don't care who you're working for, Mr. Francois, as long as you have money for me. Consider it a protection fee. We'll make sure that no one robs your site."

"But I hardly have a dollar to my name," Richard said.

Yousef shrugged. "Makes no difference to me. I deal in

many different currencies. I'll take whatever you can give me."

Richard eased back a few steps, away from the sharp edge. "I've got ten pounds I can give you."

"That'll suffice for the next couple of nights. But you're going to need to bring more the next time you come back out here. Otherwise, I might have to help the bandits who attack you."

"We'll be ready for anyone next time, even you," Richard said.

Sherif closed his eyes and subtly shook his head. "What he meant to say is that we'll have to make more payments when we return."

"In that case, I'll look forward to working with you, Mr. Francois," Yousef said, slapping Richard on the shoulder.

Richard nodded slowly, resigning himself to the fact that a fee would be required to keep Sherif's friend from raiding the dig site. And without another word, Yousef exited the tent.

"I'm sorry," Sherif said. "I should have warned you about the possibility of people like Yousef who take advantage of people who are new to digging in the Valley of the Kings. It's somewhat of an initiation."

Richard narrowed his eyes. "I'm more upset with the fact that you mentioned the Germans, particularly that the money came from them. Do you know what could happen to me—and Jabari, too—if they found out what we did?"

"I'm sure Jabari was careful."

"He was and so was I. But that doesn't make us immune to loose lips. And you're the only person who knew before tonight. Now Yousef knows too. Who knows how many people he'll tell."

"Don't worry about it," Sherif said. "I'll handle any issues that might arise from that."

"Unless you're going to personally guard me every minute of the day until I leave this area, your promise means nothing. Let's just get back to work."

Sherif nodded and gathered all the men back inside the tent to continue working.

* * *

RICHARD RETURNED BEFORE SUNRISE WITH MOST OF SHERIF'S team after a long night of work. They hadn't found anything significant, but Sherif insisted excavations—even if they have the specific location identified—can take days, if not weeks to unearth. Richard just wanted to get a few hours of sleep before taking his next group of tourists back to the Valley of the Kings later that morning.

Richard slept for two hours before a knock at his door startled him awake. He scrambled to put on his robe before shuffling across the room to see who his visitor was. Vincent Vance stood outside, hat in hand as he shifted his weight back and forth from one foot to the other.

"Mr. Vance, is something the matter?" Richard said after opening the door.

"I just wanted to let you know that I don't have any clients for you this morning," Vincent said. "And I'm not sure how many more I can steer your way after the incident with Earl Thomas."

"There was an incident with the earl?"

"Don't play dumb with me, lad. I know you took the earl back to the valley a couple of nights ago and you were robbed. He's been telling everyone about it, and now there seems to be a rumor circulating among many of our clients that you're somehow coordinating with the thieves that roam the area around the tombs."

"That's preposterous," Richard said. "I would never do anything like that."

"I would hope not, but how people perceive you unfortunately becomes the truth. If I can't manage to get you anymore work in the next two days, I'm afraid I'm going to have to dismiss you. And that means your room will no longer be paid for."

"But I hardly have any money."

"I'll pay you what you're owed, but I don't think you're a good fit for Thomas Cook & Son. You're too reckless."

Hard lines creased Richard's brow. "People come here for good stories and adventure—and that's what I've given them. The only ones reckless here were the tourists themselves. Who knows what would've happened with another guide."

Vincent shrugged. "We'll never know because oddly enough no other employee had a similar situation arise. Now, if you'll excuse me, I need to get back downstairs so I can coordinate with some of the employees who have booked trips this morning."

Before leaving, Vincent stooped down and picked up a letter that someone slid beneath the door.

"Good day, Mr. Franklin."

"It's—" Richard stopped and sighed as he watched Vincent leave. It didn't matter anymore. Vincent had obviously made up his mind.

Richard shut the door and then shuffled across the floor. Picking up his change purse, he peered inside, concluding that it was far lighter than it needed it to be. Between the few dollars he had and what remained from the heist on the Reichswehr unit's safe, Richard realized his time was limited. He couldn't afford to hire Sherif's men for another week, much less stay at the Winter Palace Hotel after Thomas Cook & Son stopped paying for his room. The feeling he had was similar to the one he had in Monaco when he dove off the cliffs—terrified of the unknown but excited to see how everything would unfold. Even if everything didn't fall his way, he concluded he'd have a good story to write about the time he tried to dig up an Egyptian king's tomb.

Got to find the silver lining.

Richard glanced down at the envelope in his hand. Mr. Francois was scrawled across the front.

"Meet me at the bazaar across the street at 9 o'clock ~ Jabari"

Richard placed the note on his bed stand and then set his alarm. He crawled back underneath the covers to catch another half hour of sleep before paying Jabari a visit.

* * *

RICHARD HUSTLED ACROSS THE STREET IN FRONT OF THE hotel, dodging a car and a horse-drawn carriage as they passed each other. He picked up a copy of the Cairo newspaper and tucked it beneath his arm before ducking into the market. The smell of freshly baked bread wafted through the air, and vendors waved warm breakfast food in front of his nose as he walked by them. After casually strolling through the bazaar for a few minutes, Richard stopped when a firm hand was placed on his shoulder. He turned to see Jabari, who nudged Richard into a nearby jewelry store.

Colorful beads shimmered on the wall and hung from the roof. Richard and Jabari navigated through the tight shop and found a place to chat behind a tall display in the center of the store.

"What's so important?" Richard asked.

"Wilhelm is officially upset at the amount of time it's taking for us to find the tomb," Jabari said.

"This isn't about the money?"

"No, that took care of itself."

Richard cocked his head to one side. "No one's found out yet?"

"I framed the guard," Jabari said. "I took some of the money and stashed it in his room and later went back and unlocked the safe. Wilhelm demanded every man's quarters be searched—and the soldier who reported that someone was rummaging around in the room with the vault was found with the money in his possession. Of course, some of it was missing, which was what Wilhelm needed to hear to let his imagination run wild."

"Where's that soldier now?"

"The bottom of the Nile, according to one conversation I overheard between two soldiers."

"Wilhelm will do that to us if he catches us, won't he?"

Jabari nodded. "And that's why you need to get Sherif to work more quickly. Hire more men if you have to. Because if you don't, we're both going to be in trouble. And my entire family is at risk."

"I don't have any more money," Richard said.

"What about from your job?"

"As of the end of this week, I'll no longer be employed by Thomas Cook & Son. Apparently, no one wants me to lead them back to the valley after the rumors that were spread about me."

"Rumors?"

"The earl who promised to pay me but was robbed is telling everyone I'm working with the thieves. And I can only take that to mean that he has no intention of paying me later."

"Then see if you can convince some men to work off the prospect of uncovering the treasure. Because if you don't,

Wilhelm will visit your site and take it over once he sees you."

"That can't happen."

"I know," Jabari said, nodding knowingly, "for both our sake's."

"And for the sake of peace."

CHAPTER 30

RICHARD ATE BREAKFAST AT THE HOTEL BEFORE stealing down the street to Sherif's mercantile. They debriefed about the previous night's dig along with the encounter with Yousef. Sherif promised to handle the scoundrel if he returned to the site. Satisfied that Sherif would keep his word, Richard moved on to the most pressing matter.

"I know that everyone worked hard last night, but we need help," Richard said. "If we can't find access to the tomb quickly, we are in grave danger."

"The Germans?" Sherif asked.

Richard nodded. "They're growing restless with Jabari's interpretation of the map. He seems to think they'll attempt to take over our site if they don't find what they're looking for soon. We need to make the discovery quickly to halt any rumors before they start about what we've been looking for."

"The truth will eventually come out."

"Of course it will. But if we're the ones who make the discovery, the Germans won't be able to raid the tomb. It will be under the protection of the Egyptian Antiquities Society, not to mention the Medjay. The Reichswehr will be forced to leave the area for fear of further sanctions if they make a brazen attempt to steal the king's treasure. It would be an obvious breach of the Treaty of Versailles."

"While I agree with you, convincing men to work with only the hope of getting paid won't be easy."

"Can you help me?" Richard asked. "I want to go back this morning, and I was hoping to take some men with me."

Sherif grunted and paced around the room. "If I do this for you, I'm going to need more compensation."

"What if I let you help someone else discover the tomb with the promise of a percentage of the profits?"

"I'm listening."

"While I wouldn't mind taking credit for this discovery, I can't," Richard said. "This was Dr. Thurston Miller's life work, and I would prefer that he get some of the credit along with a real archeologist who continued on Dr. Miller's quest."

"And what do I get out of this deal?"

"I'll make sure that you're on the team that excavates this tomb, consistent work for several years—and you'll be placed in charge of managing all the workers with a hefty salary that you'll name."

Sherif smiled. "I like the sound of this."

"And it will forever solidify you as the preeminent authority here in Egypt among the excavators. You'll never have to open this store again."

"But I love my store," Sherif said.

"Then keep it knowing that you don't have to."

Sherif thought for a moment and then nodded his head. "Okay, I'll help you. I know about a dozen men who are also skilled but out of work."

"How long you think you can get them to dig simply with the promise of getting paid for their services?" Richard asked.

"A week, maybe two at the most."

"We don't have that much time anyway, so see if you can convince them to join our venture."

"I'll go see them right now."

* * *

TWO HOURS LATER, RICHARD WAS GLIDING ACROSS THE NILE on a ferry with the dozen men Sherif lassoed into digging in the valley. Aside from one of the men named Omar, they were all relatively quiet. However, Omar made up for everyone with his incessant chatter. Richard deduced that Omar had just grasped enough of the English language to carry on a conversation and seemed determined to hold one with anyone who would listen.

"What is it we search for, Mr. Francois?" Omar asked.

"A king's treasure, hidden in a tomb," Richard said. "Did Sherif not tell you?"

"He told us to work for him or he would hurt our families."

Richard furrowed his brow. "Are you sure that's what he said?"

Omar nodded. "I think that's how you say it."

"Did he say that if you worked for him it would *help* your families?"

Omar looked up, scanning the blue skies with his eyes. "Maybe I am not saying the right word. Is *hurt* when you do something nice for someone?"

"No, that's *help*."

"Okay, he said he would help us if we helped you."

Richard winced. "Are you sure he said he would help you if you *helped* me or *hurt* me?"

"My head hurts," Omar said. "Let's talk about something else."

Richard felt uneasy about his conversation with Omar.

Perhaps there's a reason why everyone is being quiet. They're going to attack me and leave me for dead in the desert.

The thought wasn't a pleasant one, but Richard couldn't shake it. While Jabari sang Sherif's praises, Richard was never certain he could fully trust Sherif. All Richard could think about was the possibility that Omar's translation was twisted. And all of it made Richard wonder if he was about to get blindsided by the man supposedly helping him.

Money makes people do crazy things.

At least, that's what his father always told him. Despite Richard's appetite for luxury, he adapted that same perspective for himself, seeing money as a means to accomplish goals. He never wanted money for the sake of simply having it. There always had to be a purpose for it. And he only wanted more at the moment to afford a team willing to work around the clock to excavate the site. But Sherif? Richard wouldn't have been surprised to learn that Sherif absconded with every last shilling.

Richard couldn't waste time wringing his hands over something that might or might not happen. Any fallout from that was minor compared to the Germans finding the tomb first, keeping Richard focused on his priorities.

Find the tomb. Find the tomb. Find the tomb.

Richard's team scratched at the sand and dug deep in surprisingly quick fashion. According to Dr. Miller's estimations, the entrance to the tomb was buried about six feet beneath the surface. He believed there would be steps leading to a secret entrance. Dr. Miller proffered forth a theory that Tutankhamun actually faked his own death, escaping out of his sarcophagus and fleeing Egypt where he could live a normal life. Richard hadn't learned enough about the life of Tutankhamun to accept or reject Dr. Miller's notion. Such a ploy seemed unlikely for a young boy, but he could've had help from some advisors or even a power-hungry relative who was in line to ascend to the throne. The idea was fascinating to think about, though Richard wondered if Dr. Miller was simply conjuring up a fanciful idea that fit more firmly in the world of fiction than fact.

Three hours into the shift, one man started yelling excitedly in Arabic and gesturing for Richard. He dropped his spade and crawled down into the hole the man had dug that had already reached a depth of more than six feet.

"What is it?" Richard asked.

Omar hustled over to translate, while the man continued speaking.

"He said it looks like a step," Omar said.

Richard's eyes widened as his mind wandered with the possibilities. He didn't move from his spot perched on the surface above where several men were digging away. No more than another minute went by before the men started shouting again.

"It's another step," Omar said.

Over the next hour and a half, the crew worked furiously to remove the sand covering the steps. When they were finished, what remained was a door no taller than five feet.

"It's the perfect size for a young boy," Richard said.

"That's what I think," Omar said. "This is unlike anything I ever saw working in the Valley of the Kings."

"What do you mean by that?" Richard asked.

"Entrances are grand and ornate, but this one is simple."

Richard nodded. While giving tours among the tombs, he had seen enough of them to know that Omar was right. Highly skilled artists' renderings decorated the corridors leading into the tombs. Carvings and treasures adorned the walls and ceilings. But this entryway was almost natural looking, crafted from the rock wall, perhaps in an effort to be hidden in plain sight.

Richard motioned for the men to move out of the way

as he descended the steps. He placed the palms of his hands flush against the door and pushed. It didn't budge. Turning sideways and crouching low, he rammed his shoulder against the rock. Still nothing.

On the side of the map was a short riddle. Richard read it aloud: "To enter life, you must place one foot in the grave."

He studied the area over the top of the door and tried to brush away some of the sand. Gesturing for a handheld broom, one of the men threw one to Richard. He swept away the dirt, revealing a series of hieroglyphic pictures. Unsure of their meaning, Richard cleaned off the final step. An embossed symbol of some sort was etched out of the stone. After raising his foot, Richard stomped on the step. The door started to rumble before it slid to one side to expose a small chamber.

Behind him, the men started to shout. Omar said something to them, and they then poured down the stairs and joined Richard.

"What did you tell them?" Richard asked.

Omar shrugged and smiled. "I told them what Sherif said."

"And what was that exactly?"

"He said you have no money so we take what we find."

Richard glared at Omar. "I told him I would give you a share of the profits, not that you could loot the tomb. Tell them to stop."

Omar relayed the message, which drew long steely stares from the workers.

"Tell them they will get paid, but we still have work to do."

Omar said something in Arabic, and most of the men began to trudge out of the chamber and up the steps. However, one man narrowed his eyes and looked directly at

Richard before breaking into a dead sprint. Richard noticed the knife in the man's hand and sidestepped him before slashing his wrist.

Richard twirled his dagger on his fingers and eyed the man cautiously. "I haven't been in Egypt long, but I've been here long enough. Now if you don't like the payment arrangements, feel free to leave at any time."

The man tilted his head to the side and scowled.

"Omar, please translate for me," Richard said.

Upon hearing Omar's words, the man nodded slowly before leaving the chamber, sneering at Richard.

Meanwhile, Richard hustled over to a corner and peered through a small slot. He couldn't see anything, but he could feel a draft coming from the portal. Glancing down, he noticed a small stone with the same markings as the one positioned just outside the chamber door.

That must be the actual tomb.

The real treasure was inside the kings' tombs. This small chamber was just a passageway of sorts, perhaps designed to appear like a tomb for one reason or another. Richard quickly formed a working hypothesis that this was where the supplies were stored for the boy king. However, the fact that valuable items remained here after all these years puzzled Richard.

Richard found a pouch full of gold, more than enough to give each man on both crews one piece—and it would be worth hundreds of pounds. But he was smart enough to know that the real gold lay on the other side of the wall. That was what the Germans would be after, but a trap would scare them away.

Richard resurfaced and explained to all the men what they were going to do. He informed them that all the treasure had been accounted for and it was much. However, they were each to receive a gold coin, which would be worth hundreds of pounds each. The men all cheered as Richard passed out the coins.

He then directed two of the faster workers to dig a hole just inside the entrance of the chamber. No sooner had they begun then several men stormed into their tent.

"Who is the leader of this expedition?" a man bellowed as he flashed a badge indicating his affiliation with the Egyptian Antiquities Society.

Richard stepped forward. "What do you want?"

"I certainly didn't come here for your autograph," the man said with a snarl. "I want part of your riches."

Richard shrugged. "Sorry, but that reward is reserved for the men who do the work. But if you're handy with tools—"

Richard tossed a shovel toward the man, who swatted it to the side and drew his sword from its sheath.

"I would suggest you put that way before you kill yourself," Richard said.

"I said *I want a portion of your riches.*"

CHAPTER 31

RICHARD FELT THE TEMPERATURE IN THE ROOM rising as the man and his fellow bandits didn't appear to be interested in vacating the dig site. Thinking of a way to avoid a bloody brawl, Richard flipped the thief a coin.

"Split it amongst your men and leave if you know what is good for you," Richard said.

The man tossed the money into the sand and laughed. As he was howling with laughter, Omar flung his dagger into the man's throat. Staggering to his left and then right, the man toppled to the ground.

Richard looked at the man to the guard's right. "It's time for you to leave."

The man's eyes widened as he turned to his fellow officers and gestured for them to leave. They all exited without making a sound while their leader writhed around in the sand, gasping for air. Richard sighed as he watched the man die.

"He can't say he wasn't warned," Richard said.

Omar shook his head. "He won't say anything ever again. Over the years, he's robbed far too many people while working in the valley."

"He won't anymore," Richard said.

Omar smiled a wry grin. "How do you say in America? *Dead as a doornail?*"

"Thank you, Omar. I think I owe this to you," Richard said as he pressed a couple more coins into the palm of Omar's hand.

All the men stood around staring at the lifeless body, the blood still oozing out and staining the sand.

"Let's get this cleaned up," Richard said. "I'm sure we'll have to answer for this."

"I'll be honored to confess," Omar said. "We defended ourselves against his threats. And Egypt looks more favorably upon murderers than thieves. Besides, my brother-in-law is on the board of the society. They are aware of this man's—how do you say it—extension?"

"Extortion," Richard corrected.

"Ah," Omar said with a smile. "I learned a new word today. That makes me happy."

"Happier than getting paid with gold coins?"

"I have many reasons to be happy today," Omar said with a wink.

Richard hustled back down the steps to check on the progress of the two men digging. Once the hole went down deep enough, Richard climbed inside and buried several spears in the ground, their sharp ends pointing upward. If anyone fell into the hole, they would not crawl out without serious injury—if they could even get out. The men had dug the opening in a triangular shape, narrowing from the bottom up. Climbing up the side would be difficult as well as dangerous.

Richard shimmied up with a rope and then covered the hole with a parchment paper before shoveling some sand on top. He then directed several of the men to bring him large rocks and a net. Using some of his Princeton ingenuity, Richard constructed a trip line that would trigger the net to dump the rocks in front of the door, preventing anyone else from getting access into the chamber.

When they were finished, Richard left a note for Sherif and the day crew with instructions on what needed to be done to secure the site. Richard also issued a stern warning not to go into the chamber or risk death.

* * *

UPON RETURNING TO THE WINTER PALACE HOTEL JUST before dawn, Richard stumbled into his room and found a letter someone had shoved beneath his door. He immediately recognized the handwriting—it was Jabari again.

Richard tore open the letter and shuffled across the room to the window, which had just enough light to illuminate Jabari's message.

After tonight, Wilhelm is going to search elsewhere for the tomb. He plans to send a team of men to investigate your site tomorrow night. Beware. ~ Jabari

Richard could only hope that Sherif tied up all the dangling ends left behind from the night before.

The moment of truth had drawn nigh.

CHAPTER 32

REFRESHED FROM SIX HOURS OF SLEEP, RICHARD ATE A quick lunch before hustling down to the Nile. He paid for a ferry ride across the river on a boat that was packed with Thomas Cook & Son tourists. A few of the people noticed Richard and pointed at him, while speaking to each other in hushed tones. Richard tried not to let the ordeal bother him, especially since it was Earl Thomas's face-saving lie that ignited the rumor mill. But the negative attention was hard to ignore.

Richard eventually walked to the stern of the ship and stared out at the water, his back to the other passengers. Although the trip was short, he was lost in thought and didn't see the man approaching him from behind.

"Mr. Francois?" a familiar voice said.

Richard turned around to see the earl holding his hat in his hand. "Come over here to start some more rumors?"

"Actually, I wanted to apologize to you for starting them in the first place," the earl said. "I should've never made up those awful things about you, and I feel dreadful for doing it."

"If you want to truly apologize, you should admit that you fibbed in the first place," Richard said.

"I never meant for word to get around like that. It's just that my wife was upset that I acted foolishly, so I had to tell her something or suffer her wrath."

"Sounds like a wonderful marriage you have there."

Earl Thomas sighed. "When families of nobility are merged through marriage, the end result isn't always happiness."

"I'm sorry about your disagreeable wife, but that's never a reason to sully a man's reputation. In this world, my name is all I've got. And I can assure you that mine has suffered immensely as I've had to endure a burdensome weight beneath your fanciful tales."

"I'm going to double what I owe you when I return to England."

"Give it to charity," Richard said. "In fact, give all of it to charity. I don't need it anymore."

"But, Mr. Francois, you must let me make it up to you in some way."

"I accept your apology, but if you want to be a bigger man, tell the truth—and exaggerate only for the purposes of telling a better story," Richard said with a wink.

"You're a better man than I am, that's for sure," Earl Thomas said as he patted Richard on the back.

"It's not a contest. Just be the best you can be each day and keep growing."

The boat slowed down before hitting the dock and knocking both men off balance for a moment. Richard regained his footing and grabbed Earl Thomas's arm to keep him upright.

"Do me a favor," Richard said as they turned to depart. "At least tell Vincent Vance the truth. I still need the work."

"I will," Earl Thomas said resolutely. "And I'll do it first thing when I return this afternoon. Thank you for being so gracious."

"I'm just glad neither of us got seriously injured—or worse—during our excursion."

Richard bid the earl farewell amidst a sea of snoopy tourists. Everyone cast shameful glimpses at Richard. He decided to smile and nod, defusing the gloom that hung over the short trip.

After hustling ahead of the tour group, Richard saddled up his horse and blazed out across the desert toward his dig site. When he arrived, Sherif and his shortened crew were putting the finishing touches on the last item on the list.

"Where are all the men?" Richard asked.

"A few of them fell ill, so we had to double our efforts."

"Well, it looks like you've done a fine job," Richard said before embracing Sherif with a hug and kiss on each side of his cheek.

Sherif nodded. "We've worked hard to complete everything you asked."

"If you hadn't, we could be in serious trouble."

"Why's that?"

"Apparently the Germans are growing troubled by Jabari's supposed inability to read a map," Richard said. "They think he's toying with them."

Sherif chuckled. "Well, he is."

"Yes, but once they figure that out, they're going to kill him and his family."

"And what are we going to do about it?"

Richard motioned for Sherif to follow him. "Come with me. I want to show you our trap."

Richard led Sherif down the steps and near the front of the chamber door. Turning to face Sherif, Richard explained the purpose of the trap.

"If we can ambush the German soldiers, we should be able to stop their ambitious attempt to steal one of the king's treasures. There are a few more traps I want to install now before this final one, but once they recognize that they're not going to get this fortune, they'll leave."

"And how are you going to ensure that happens?"

"With this specially designed trap," Richard said. "All they have to do is jump on this stone here—"

The door began to slide open slowly.

"And then they can gain access to the chamber," Richard said.

Sherif grabbed Richard's arm and stepped into the chamber, mouth agape.

"This is amazing," he said over Richard's pleas to return. "I've never seen anything like—"

Sherif's foot gave way and he started to fall into the hole Richard's team had dug. Thinking quick on his feet, Richard got down onto his stomach and reached into the hole, grabbing Sherif's forearm and gripping it tightly. Sherif shrieked as he looked down, realizing that death by impalement was a very real possibility if he slipped out of Richard's hand.

"Please don't drop me," Sherif said. "I didn't know. I swear it."

Richard grunted as he strained to keep Sherif from plunging downward to his death.

CHAPTER 33

RICHARD TIGHTENED HIS GRIP ON SHERIF AND URGED him to quit wriggling so much. With forearms afire, Richard wasn't sure how much longer he'd be able to keep Sherif from sliding down into the impalement pit.

"You haven't even set off the trip wire yet," Richard said in an attempt to assuage Sherif's fears. "If you do that, I'm not sure I'll be able to hold onto you. So stop moving if you want to live."

Sherif went limp, hanging there in an almost lifeless state as he let Richard navigate him back to the surface without triggering an avalanche of stones and boulders. Once Sherif was safely back in the stairway, he collapsed.

"I almost . . ." he said, either unwilling or unable to finish the obvious truth.

"But you're not dead," Richard said. "You're very much alive, so stop dwelling on what almost was, and think about how fortunate you are."

Sherif's eyes watered as he looked up at Richard. "You saved my life."

"Now we're even," Richard said. "Let's get back to work. "

Richard reset the trap, this time positioning a small treasure chest just beyond the impalement pit. He placed one gold coin on the ground in front of it, guaranteeing the

Germans would charge in after it. Richard was counting on the first person through to fall into the hole and the second to break the trip wire and all but seal the door. And with such a small unit, Wilhelm wouldn't risk sending more men after that into the chamber to retrieve the treasure for fear of being descended upon by thieves after exiting the Valley of the Kings.

Once Richard was finished, he announced that it was time to pack up and leave.

"I don't understand," Sherif said. "I thought you came here for the treasure."

"The real treasure is preserving whatever is inside there for future generations to enjoy," Richard said. "I only took what was necessary to compensate all the men for their hard work."

"But aren't you curious about King Tutankhamun's sarcophagus?"

"I am, but I'll save that for another trip after someone far more skilled has excavated the tomb and maintained its integrity."

"You're a strange man, Mr. Francois."

Richard smiled. "I'll take that as a compliment."

The team finished packing up its gear and began the short trek across the desert. All the men kept scanning the area in anticipation of an attack. With only six men total, Richard feared they would look like a prime target for the Arabean Losus.

"What does *Arabean Losus* mean?" Richard asked as they plodded along.

"It means *Forty Thieves*," Sherif said. "The leader of the group is named Ali Baba. He has quite the sense of humor."

"I certainly don't find marauders funny, especially when they're killing innocent people."

"You've experienced what they do," Sherif said. "They are harmless."

"Except for the fact that they are plundering the riches of every good man and woman who crosses the desert. Besides, I thought Egyptians took a harsh view toward stealing."

"Only when we're stealing from our own. But taking from the wealthy tourists who visit the Valley of the Kings? No one cares about that as much. The guards for the Egyptian Antiquities Society claim to care, but as soon as they're handed some money, they happily look the other way."

Richard glanced back toward the dunes and saw flames flickering near the top of a ridge.

"Look up there," he said as he pointed toward the lights. "What is that?"

"The better question is *who* is that," Sherif said. "That's the Arabean Losus—and they're headed straight toward us."

Sherif turned toward the men and shouted something in Arabic. In an instant, the horses went from plodding along at a steady pace to tearing across the desert. Richard could scarcely figure out what was going on before he found himself enveloped in a cloud of dust. Digging his heels into his horse, he darted ahead to keep up with the rest of the pack.

After making the trek across the desert for the past few days, Richard felt like he had a solid grasp on how much farther they had to go before reaching the Nile. He estimated at least three more miles. And with the thieves thundering toward Richard and his crew, he sounded the alarm. Based on the thrum of galloping hooves against the desert, he wasn't sure if it even mattered. Every man in the crew appeared to be driving his horse as fast as possible.

Richard edged his way back toward the front next to Sherif.

"We're going to be cutting it close," Richard said.

"It won't matter if the ferryman isn't ready for us," Sherif said.

Richard nodded, remembering the operator Earl Thomas put at the bottom of the Nile.

The herd stormed over a hill and raced toward the water's edge about a quarter of a mile away. As they drew nearer, Sherif shouted in Arabic at the man casually leaning against one of the dock's pylons. He scrambled into action, loosening the ropes tethered to the boat's cleats.

By the time they reached the water, the men worked furiously to collect their tools and remove them from the horses. Richard was safely onboard, but some of the crew was still working when the Arabean Losus stormed over the top of the ridge.

"Tell them to forget about it," Richard said to Sherif. "We need to go."

Sherif said something, and all the men broke into a sprint for the boat. The ferryman didn't even wait for them to get on before he shoved away from the dock. A primal scream erupted from the thieves as they drew closer. With one man still fiddling with his pack on his horse, Sherif shouted a final warning. The man darted down the dock and leaped, hitting the water with a big splash. Other workers fed him a rope and dragged him aboard.

They were nearly fifty meters away from shore by the time the Arabean Losus reached the banks. But that didn't stop several flaming spears from being launched toward the ferry. Fortunately, they all fell short, disappearing into the Nile.

The leader then sat upright on his horse and yelled at Richard's crew.

"What was that all about?" Richard asked Sherif.

"It was a warning," Sherif said. "He said next time we will pay a hefty tax to pass through his desert or suffer the consequences."

"If it's just the same, I'd prefer never to go back—except to make sure that my trap worked on the Germans."

"The Arabean Losus are wicked, but the currency they operate with is fear. You showed them just how courageous you are."

"Courageous? For running away?"

Sherif nodded. "Do you realize how angry they would've been had they caught you after fleeing?"

Richard shook his head. "I wasn't interested in finding out."

"It would have been a bloodbath," Sherif said. "They would've likely killed every one of us."

"In that case, I'll consider us fortunate."

Sherif nodded. "Most fortunate indeed."

* * *

RICHARD SHOT STRAIGHT UP IN HIS BED WHEN HE HEARD loud knocking on his hotel room door. He rubbed his eyes and then looked at the clock.

"What does a man need to do to get some sleep around here?" he mumbled to himself.

The clock displayed 8 o'clock, which meant he managed to get just five hours of sleep. He sighed, wishing for three times that amount.

Just once I'd like a full night of sleep.

He flung his legs over the side of the bed and threw on his bathrobe before shuffling to the door.

"Who is it?" Richard asked.

"It's Vincent Vance," the man said. "Please open the door. I have an urgent message for you."

Richard opened the door slowly, checking through the

crack to make sure the man was actually who he said he was. Upon recognizing his face, Richard gestured for Vincent to enter and welcomed him.

"I didn't expect to see you again so soon," Richard said. "Did you come by to personally fire me?"

"Actually, quite the contrary."

Richard cocked his head to one side. "What did you say?"

"Quite the contrary. I came here to offer you another assignment and pay you."

"You want me back?"

Vincent nodded vigorously. "Most definitely. It's come to my attention that the rumors that were spread about you were in fact fabricated. And I'd be foolish to fire my new star guide over some absurd lies."

"The same lies you were so quick to believe?"

"Please accept my apology," Vincent said. "I made a mistake that I sincerely regret."

Richard eyed Vincent closely. "Something feels amiss here. Why the sudden change of heart?"

"I told you that I learned that the stories about you were lies."

"The truth," Richard said glaring at Vincent.

Vincent chewed on his lip before answering. "Fine, I'll tell you what you want to know, but you need to do some answering yourself, Mr. *Halliburton.*"

Richard gasped.

CHAPTER 34

RICHARD WAS CERTAIN HE COULD OUTRUN VINCENT Vance even with a pair of broken legs. But the greater danger wasn't in the immediate moment—it was in the long term. The fact that he knew Richard's identity was beyond troubling. He'd been careful to perpetuate the Jonathan Francois name on everything he signed and with everyone he met. But he'd slipped up somewhere. He just couldn't recall when it was or with whom.

"How do you—" Richard said.

"Know your real name?" Vincent interrupted. "Or is it just another alias you created as you run from some past crime you committed?"

"I'm not a criminal nor am I running from anything," Richard said, wagging his finger at Vincent. "In fact, I'm running headlong into adventure."

"With a fake name? Now, who's the one who needs to tell the truth?"

Richard sighed. "My real name is Richard Halliburton, but I go by Jonathan Francois for various reasons, the most important of which is to protect my identity from some ruffians who are after me. How on earth did you find out my true identity?"

Vincent smiled. "A Miss Elizabeth Corbett can be thanked for that. And she's also your next client for a half-day tour that starts in the hotel lobby at noon."

"Oh, Miss Corbett," Richard said, shaking his head. "She caught me in a moment of weakness in Cairo."

"That's not exactly how she described it," Vincent said with a chuckle.

"I certainly wasn't thinking straight since I was in—" Richard stopped himself for fear of undoing the story he'd just sold Vincent as being a man of virtue.

"Handcuffs is the word you're looking for," Vincent said with a grin.

"What did she tell you?"

"Everything. She saw you at the dining hall and pointed you out to me while we were sharing drinks. I told her you were a guide, and she suddenly wanted to book a tour with you as her guide. She insisted that your name was Richard Halliburton, not Jonathan Francois."

"If I take her on a tour, please swear to me that you won't divulge my true identity to anyone."

Vincent nodded. "Your secret is safe with me. Now, wash up and get ready to show her a good time this afternoon. She's a very influential woman, and a good review from her could translate into more business from London's elites."

"She'll be singing the praises of Thomas Cook & Son by the time we return," Richard said.

"That's what I like to hear," Vincent said, patting Richard on the shoulder. "Now get cleaned up. She'll be expecting more than a disheveled fugitive for a tour she's paying a hefty sum for."

Richard nodded and ushered Vincent toward the door. He turned and slapped an envelope full of money into Richard's chest.

"For what it's worth, I wish I had a dozen men like

you," Vincent said. "Be safe."

Richard locked the door behind Vincent and exhaled slowly. While Richard's secret was safe, he needed to keep Vincent happy—and quiet—or else Wilhelm would be able to find his chief competition for the tomb with a simple inquiry at the front desk. And even though Richard had apparently defeated the Reichswehr on that front, he wasn't about to announce his presence. Jabari had made it abundantly clear that Wilhelm's patience had worn thin and he was ready to pursue a more violent course of action to attain his goal.

Richard needed to be extra careful, especially with Elizabeth Corbett. Her request was puzzling, making him unsure if it was made out of genuine affection for him or if there was some other sinister ploy in the works.

* * *

RICHARD DESCENDED THE STAIRS SPILLING INTO THE WINTER Palace Hotel's central lobby, dressed in neatly pressed khaki pants, a white shirt, with a sports coat flung over his shoulder. He glanced at his watch before scanning the lobby for Elizabeth Corbett. After one sweep around the room, he made a second, this time spotting her at the bar, drinking a beer while wearing pale-green pants and a tan loose-fitting, long-sleeve shirt. She appeared more ready for war than a simple tour to the Valley of the Kings.

Sauntering across the floor toward her, he eased into the empty chair on her left.

"Is this seat taken?" he asked.

She turned and noticed him before a warm smile spread across her face. "I'd only sit there if you want to miss out on all the fun."

"And where are you off to today, Miss Corbett?" he asked.

"Where do you think I should go?"

"I was thinking the Valley of the Kings, but only because I'm paid to suggest such things."

Her eyebrows shot upward. "Is visiting the tombs of a slew of dead Egyptian kings really worth all the trouble?"

"Would you prefer to swim with the crocodiles in the Nile? Or outrun the infamous Forty Thieves across the valley desert? Or evade the ever-dangerous Medjay while digging for your own tomb?"

She shook her finger at him and smirked. "Am I to assume that's what you've been up to since you arrived in Luxor?"

"How do you Brits say it? It's a *wee bit* more fun than listening to some tour guide drone on about the historical significance of each king and his impact on the world thousands of years ago."

"But I love history," she said. "And I'm dreadful when it comes to defending myself with a dagger or gun."

"What if I told you that I can't guarantee those other things won't happen," Richard said. "This is Egypt, after all."

"Well, I accept whatever adventure you decide for us— as long as you promise no Germans will kidnap us."

Richard sighed and looked down. "That's one thing I can't promise. But we'll steer clear of their dig site."

"They're looking for a tomb?"

Richard waved her off. "It's a long story, but it's not worth retelling at the moment."

"Whatever you say, Mr. Halliburton," she said with a grin.

Richard leaned in close. "Please call me Jonathan Francois. If my real name slips out, it could cause serious problems for me."

"Fair enough," she said as she rose to her feet. "Shall we?"

Richard offered her his arm, which she gladly took, and ushered her outside and down to the ferry. They waited a half hour before the boat returned, allowing Elizabeth to recount everything that had happened since she arrived in Luxor. For the most part, she had been subjected to little more than museum browsing and souvenir shopping.

"I prefer to collect adventures, not artifacts," Richard said when she asked him what he had done.

"And you wouldn't the least bit interested in unearthing some piece of pottery or jewel from one of the early Egyptian dynasties?" she asked.

"That would be a wonderful experience, but I'm quite certain it wouldn't finish very high on my list of personal favorites since arriving in Egypt."

"Your life is that exciting, is it?"

"Perhaps a tad too exciting for some and downright frightening for others. Escaping the Arabean Losus in the nick of time across crocodile-infested waters while the bandits fling flaming spears at you—it can be a bit much for some people."

"Oh, stop it," Elizabeth said, playfully punching Richard in the arm. "You best be careful, or your fanciful imagination is going to carry you off one day, like a runaway dirigible."

"I only wish I was making this up. If I recorded in a book just half of the things that have happened to me since I was in France, I'd be accused of writing fiction."

She shot him a sideways glance. "Don't get any ideas about this trip. The last thing I want is a brush with death."

"Better a brush than the alternative."

"I want an uneventful trip to the Valley of the Kings," she said. "Is that too much to ask?"

"It's not—for most guides," Richard said with a wry

grin. "But you requested me, so it's not unreasonable for me to believe that you actually do want something more."

"If I wanted to play roulette with my life, I would've stormed across the desert on my own."

"The only promise I'll make to you right now is that you won't die."

She chuckled. "I guess I'll have to settle for that then."

Judging by her reaction, Richard could tell she didn't believe that danger was so imminent.

* * *

Two hours later, they arrived at the Valley of the Kings. Richard dismounted from his horse first and rushed over to help Elizabeth, which was a futile gesture since she was already on the ground and securing her horse to one of the nearby posts.

As he led her around to the tombs, she had plenty of questions. Richard knew the answers to some, while he created entertaining stories for the others. Elizabeth laughed so hard at some of his explanations for the hieroglyphics that he figured she knew he was spinning a tale—and she didn't care one wit.

By the time the sun started to dip low on the horizon, Richard glanced at his watch.

"It's getting late," he said. "Are you ready to return to Luxor for the evening?"

She shook her head slowly. "There's still so much I want to see."

"We can come back tomorrow, if you like," Richard said. "I don't have any plans."

"I'd rather spend more time here and see this place beneath the stars."

Richard cocked his head to one side. "You were the one who said you wanted an uneventful tour. If we stay, everything could change quickly."

"But I'm with the great Richard Halli—Jonathan Francois. What do I have to be afraid of?"

While Richard wanted to play along with her whimsical attitude, he couldn't help but notice the movement from the shadows of the surrounding caves. Most of the tourists left a half hour ago. Aside from a few stragglers making their way back to their horses and camels, Richard and Elizabeth were nearly all alone.

"If only I had half your confidence," he said. "However, I've witnessed firsthand what these thieves will do to you if you aren't willing to acquiesce to their demands. And it's not pretty. However, I can't imagine what they would do if they found a woman roaming across their desert. I strongly suggest we go back now."

Elizabeth sighed. "Fine. I don't know how you transformed into being such a stick in the mud in a matter of hours."

"And I'm still trying to figure out how you evolved into some woman willing to tempt fate just hours after pleading with me for a boring visit to the tombs of dead kings."

"You've rubbed off on me," she said with a wink.

"While I appreciate adventure, my experiences the past few days are hardly the kind I want to relive."

"But now I want to see the tombs under a blanket of twinkling stars and behold these ancient sands."

Richard reached into his satchel and pulled out a sandwich.

"Since I know attempting to convince you otherwise would be futile, may I offer you something to eat?" he asked.

She chuckled and snatched the half of the sandwich he held out to her.

"I'm going to tell Mr. Vance that you truly are the best

tour guide I've ever had on a Thomas Cook & Son excursion."

Richard shrugged. "That's an awfully kind gesture, but I'm not sure this job is something I want for much longer. There's still so much of the world I haven't seen."

The pair sat down on a rock and munched on their sandwiches as the sun vanished behind the hills. A half hour later, the first star appeared overhead.

"Perhaps you would like to dig for gold," Elizabeth said. "That might be a job more suited for your thirst for adventure."

"Gold?"

"Or treasure," she said. "Maybe you could even look for one of the buried tombs out here."

Richard shook his head. "Believe it or not, I've tried that already. And it's not exactly my preferred profession either. Too much of a rote task, scratching at the dirt while hoping to find something incredible."

"Did you ever find anything?"

Richard nodded. "What I found was amazing, but it didn't stir some dormant passion within me to become an archeologist. However, discovering the treasure was exhilarating."

"You found treasure out here?" she asked as her eyes widened.

"It wasn't life-changing, but I found a small amount."

"I knew it," said as she leapt to her feet. "You do love searching for treasure."

She continued on for at least another minute, blathering about how she was right regarding Richard's future. But he was focused on something else near the top of the ridge, near his dig site. Slowly rising to his feet, he walked past Elizabeth as she talked and peered into the distance.

"What is it?" she finally asked once she realized he was engrossed by something else.

"It's our site," he said. "They found it."

"Who?"

"The Reichswehr unit searching for the tomb."

"Is this the same tomb you discovered?"

Richard waved her off. "We need to get closer and see what they're doing."

"Why? I thought we were going to enjoy this scenery beneath a star-lit sky."

"The stars are barely out, but the Germans are on the prowl."

Without any explanation, he hustled up the hill and took up a position on a large boulder. Elizabeth scrambled after him.

"What are you doing?" she called after him. "I thought you were a gentleman, but apparently you aren't after leaving me in the dust."

He turned around and froze before putting his index finger to his lips. Once she caught up with him, he crouched and spoke in a whisper.

"I'm truly sorry, but I must see this."

She smirked. "I knew you wanted to be an archeologist."

He shook his head. "It's not like that, though I wish it was."

"So, you wish to spy on the Germans?"

Richard peered through his binoculars, ignoring her question.

"What is Jabari doing?" Richard said to himself as he lowered his binoculars and widened his eyes.

CHAPTER 35

WILHELM MARCHED THE REICHSWEHR NIGHT SHIFT crew right by the site they had been digging in for the past few days and led them elsewhere. Jabari protested that they were abandoning the place Dr. Miller had specified on his map, but Wilhelm ignored the Egyptian guide. If it weren't for his connections in securing a few knowledgeable workers, Wilhelm would've killed Jabari already. But his time would eventually come, that much Wilhelm was sure of after getting hoodwinked.

Following several days of unsuccessful digging, Wilhelm sought out another local expert and showed him the map. His conclusion varied greatly with Jabari's. Wilhelm could only conclude he was being toyed with, especially after the man seemed genuinely surprised that Jabari would have directed them to such an area.

"Everybody knows there is nothing in this portion of the valley," the man had said.

Wilhelm decided he wouldn't waste another minute searching in the wrong location. However, when he arrived at the new site, Wilhelm was incensed when he realized someone had been working there recently.

"What is this?" Wilhelm bellowed as he investigated the spot. "Someone was just here."

"But they're gone now," Hans Reinhard said. "I checked

this morning with the Egyptian Antiquities Society, and they said the location had been vacated as of last night."

Wilhelm cursed as he paced around. "What do you think that means, Hans? It means that they found what they came for?"

Reinhard shrugged. "Or maybe they didn't find anything or ran out of funding. Not everyone is after the same thing we are out here."

Wilhelm sighed. "Everyone must get to work now."

After setting up their site, one of the crew members noticed large rocks piled up against a boulder.

"What is this?" Wilhelm asked.

"It looks like an entryway of some sort," Jabari said.

"Have your men remove these rocks immediately."

For the next hour, they scuttled everything away from what appeared to be a door. Once it was all clear, Jabari called Wilhelm over to inspect it.

"Is this what I think it is?" Wilhelm asked.

Jabari shrugged. "There's only one way to find out."

"That's right," said a man from behind the crowd of onlookers. "Open it up, and let's see what's inside."

Wilhelm spun around and noticed one of the guards from the Egyptian Antiquities Society pushing his way to the front.

"I'm afraid I must ask you to leave," Wilhelm said. "You'll be able to investigate after we've finished exploring the tomb. Only authorized personnel are allowed to be on our excavation site."

"I'm an inspector," the man countered, flashing his credentials. "We have permission to investigate any site at any time."

Wilhelm glared at the man before whipping out a knife and slashing the man's throat. He staggered to the ground in a futile attempt to stop the bleeding.

"Drag his body outside," Wilhelm said in German, pointing his blade at a couple of his men. "Make it look like he was murdered by thieves."

The men hustled into action, hoisting the body off the ground and carrying it outside the tent. Wilhelm returned his attention to the door while carefully positioning his feet to avoid the blood. To his left, Jabari looked on as he shifted his weight from one foot to the other.

"Nervous?" Wilhelm asked as he looked at Jabari.

"I'm anxious to see what's inside."

"Perhaps if you knew how to read a map, we could've seen the inside of this tomb several days ago."

"I apologize for the mistake. It was my best guess based on everything I know about the valley as well as Dr. Miller."

Wilhelm scraped dirt away from a divot in the door that ran five feet up from the ground. He stopped for a moment and turned to Jabari again.

"Based on what I was told, I'm not sure I believe you," Wilhelm said.

"I swear that site was where I thought Dr. Miller's map pointed to," Jabari said.

"We'll discuss this more later."

After another minute of intense work clearing the sand away from the door, Wilhelm dropped to his knees and swept the sand away from the stone in front of the entrance. He studied the inscription on the stone, stroking his chin while he thought. Still unsure what to make of the markings, he stood upright.

"What do you think this means?" Wilhelm asked Jabari.

"I'm not sure," he said before kneeling to get a better look.

However, when he did, the weight of his knees

activated the door, opening it and revealing the chamber inside. Wilhelm stared, his eyes wild with wonder at the mystery that rested in the darkness. Upon pulling out his flashlight, he illuminated the room and gasped.

"What do we have here?" he said.

CHAPTER 36

RICHARD COULDN'T PULL THE BINOCULARS FROM HIS eyes as he watched Jabari lead the Germans inside a tent erected over the site Dr. Miller demarcated on the map. While the trap had been sprung, Richard wasn't sure if it was going to work. With a penchant for ruthless action, Wilhelm was certainly a worthy adversary. But Richard couldn't help but wonder if such a trait would be a hindrance or a help for Wilhelm when faced with a daunting obstacle.

"What is it?" Elizabeth asked. "What do you see?"

He reluctantly handed her the binoculars. She peered through them for a moment.

"I don't see what the excitement is," she said, offering the eyeglasses back to him. "It's just a tent in the middle of nowhere."

Richard gazed through them at the scene. Everyone was gone.

"They're all gone," he said.

"Who?" she asked.

"The Germans, the Reichswehr unit, my friend Jabari. They were all outside just a moment ago."

"I'm sure they just went inside the tent. Is it that important to find out what they're doing that you're going to spoil this incredible moment?"

Richard looked heavenward and sighed. "The sky is

amazing, and it's only going to get better. But while more stars populate the sky, I'm going to watch what's happening over there. In fact, I believe we need to get a little bit closer."

"I'm starting to wonder if you have an appetite for death. Or have you already forgotten what the Germans did to you last time they caught you?"

"But they're not going to catch us because I'm not going in there," he said. "Besides, my job is not to apprehend a unit of elite German soldiers."

"Then just what *is* your job?"

"I'm a curious explorer," he said.

"Quite precisely," she said. "Your job, as you call it, is to stir up adventure so you will have fanciful tales to share with all your American friends living in drudgery oceans away from here."

"I'll investigate from afar. I promise," he said, offering her his hand. "We need to get a little closer."

She looked pensively at his hand, reached to grab it, and then withdrew suddenly.

"What's the matter?" Richard asked. "You said you agreed to my adventure as long as I assured that you wouldn't get captured by the Germans."

"I'm just playing a hunch here, but if the only goal we have is to not get kidnapped by these monsters, it makes sense to avoid detection. And the simplest way to keep from being seen is to stay far, far away."

Richard nodded. "It does cause problems when two objectives clash in this manner. However, adventure and danger often work in tandem. It's the danger that causes the adventure."

"Quite frankly, I've had enough of it for today, and I'd like to go back to our hotel."

"Give me ten minutes," Richard said. "Let's watch the

site for a spell, and then we'll go back to staring at the stars at a safe distance from the encampment. Fair enough?"

Elizabeth sighed and closed her eyes. "I guess I can go along with that. But I'm counting down the minutes on the watch right now."

Richard reached out and took her hand before steadying her as they climbed a steep embankment. Upon coming to rest near a large boulder, they both eased into a prone position.

Pulling out his binoculars again, Richard peered through them at the site. Figures dashed back and forth before a man's body was hurled into the sand. Without hesitating, Elizabeth shrieked.

"Elizabeth!" Richard said in a whisper as he continued to study the scene. "The last thing we want is to get caught here."

She didn't make a sound or even move. After a moment, he turned to look at her and noticed she was wide-eyed and tight-lipped.

Then he felt a cold piece of steel jammed into the back of his neck.

CHAPTER 37

RICHARD DUG HIS HEELS INTO THE SAND AND REFUSED to move despite the violent nudge from his Reichswehr captor. Tears streamed down Elizabeth's face as she pleaded with him to do something. One of the soldiers promptly slapped her, sending her sprawling to the ground.

"Just leave her alone," Richard said. "She's done nothing."

"If you don't start walking, I'll hit her again," the soldier said with a sneer.

Richard trudged forward, careful not to incur the German's wrath again for Elizabeth's sake. She sniffled as she stumbled along, begging Richard to help her.

"There's nothing he can do," snarled the man prodding her forward. "You better pray for mercy."

After a short walk, Richard and Elizabeth were ushered down the stairs to the chamber entrance.

"We found these two snooping around outside," one of the guards said in German.

Wilhelm, who was studying the inside of the chamber with a flashlight, stood and turned around. He glared at Richard.

"You found this man outside?" Wilhelm asked, poking Richard's chest.

The soldiers both nodded.

"Your timing couldn't be any more perfect," Wilhelm said, his gaze still locked on Richard. "I need to send in another person to check for more booby traps. Unfortunately, I lost one of my men."

Wilhelm shined his flashlight down into the chamber, illuminating the impaled body of a member of the Reichswehr crew. Grabbing Richard's head, Wilhelm forced his captive to stare at the dead man.

"Not a pretty sight, is it?" Wilhelm asked. "But that over there is."

He then directed the beam onto the treasure chest situated in the corner of the room.

Richard shrugged. "There's nothing stopping you from taking it."

"Maybe, but I'm going to let you fetch it for me. I have a feeling you've been here before."

"If I'd been here before, I wouldn't have left the treasure."

Wilhelm put his left hand around Richard's neck and squeezed. "You better get in there and find me the treasure— or else your girlfriend here will pay a steep price."

Richard shot a glance at Elizabeth. Tears streamed down her face as she looked at him with pleading eyes.

"I need a light," Richard said.

One of the soldiers handed a flashlight to Richard. Shining it on the ground, he gingerly stepped inside the chamber, careful to avoid the trip wire. He crept over to the treasure box and held it open. There were a few artifacts and a couple of gold pieces inside. When he first found the chest, the valuable items inside were scarce, though he'd managed to take most of them. However, the real prize was behind the hidden door.

"That's not what we came for," Wilhelm said. "This is an entry chamber. The real tomb is behind that wall. Find it."

Richard watched as Wilhelm snatched Elizabeth by her hair and jerked her head backward, all illuminated by his flashlight. She screwed up her face, convulsing as she sobbed.

"Please, help," she said.

The image of Elizabeth writhing in fear at the hands of Wilhelm pained Richard. He couldn't let her suffer simply for being in the wrong place at the wrong time, thanks to his obsessive curiosity. If he could do everything all over, he would've taken her back and then returned to see what the Reichswehr unit was doing. This wasn't the adventure either of them wanted.

"Everything's going to be all right," he said. "Trust me."

"I did trust you—and look where it got me," she said, her words biting.

Wilhelm stamped his foot. "Enough. Find me that treasure now."

Richard turned his focus back toward the far wall. The night before, he'd peeped through a hole and into the actual tomb of King Tutankhamun, but he wasn't sure how to get inside.

Maybe the hole can help open it up.

He stuck his finger inside and tried to move the wall. Nothing happened.

"Quit stalling," Wilhelm said. "Open that door."

Richard stepped back and studied the area once more, scanning it with his light.

This has to be it. But where's the key?

Richard carefully moved around the room, searching each wall for something that could be placed into the hole. But there was nothing but ancient writing in a language he couldn't understand. He studied the chest again to see if any part could fit inside. When he failed to find a match, he searched the area. Digging through all the items, he could only find rounded artifacts that were flat edged. A crown, rings, golden cups, coins, belts—none of them could fit into the hole.

"If I have to send someone else in there, the first thing they're going to do is drag your dead body out," Wilhelm shouted.

Richard glanced toward the open door, blinded by Wilhelm's light.

"I'm working as fast as I can," Richard said.

"Work faster," Wilhelm growled.

Richard turned his focus back to the chest. Studying it for a few more seconds, he tipped it up and looked underneath.

This looks promising.

Fastened to the bottom was a small stick that had several nodules jutting out around the center. The tip was narrow, the width widening toward the bottom. Richard dug the device out of its nesting spot and looked at it for a few more seconds before walking over to the wall. He knelt in front of the hole and placed the narrower end inside first. The sounds of gears clicking echoed in the room before a section of the wall slid aside and revealed the tomb.

Richard gasped at the sight. Golden objects around the room glittered beneath the shine of his flashlight. In the center was a small sarcophagus.

"It's the boy king," Wilhelm exclaimed. "Dr. Miller was right."

Richard turned and glared at Wilhelm. "And it's a shame he'll never be here to see this moment."

"Get me that treasure unless you'd like to join him," Wilhelm said.

Richard approached the sarcophagus, intrigued by the work of art that encased the body. Ornate carvings along with vivid paint decorated the box that rose about four feet off the floor. The walls were adorned in a similar fashion, a combination of chiseled out tributes to Egyptian gods and hieroglyphics.

As Richard leaned over the coffin, he placed his hands on the side and it began to rumble. A few seconds later, it split open, revealing the mummified body. However, it was the golden death mask over the face that captured his attention—and Wilhelm's too.

While Richard had yet to inspect it fully, his initial assessment of the object was that it was the real treasure. Inlaid with colored glass and precious gems, it stood out in a room teeming with coins and other ancient artifacts that would fetch a hefty sum on the collector's market.

"Bring that mask to me," Wilhelm said.

Richard shook his head. "It's wrong to disturb the dead."

"You can bury your own dead if you don't," Wilhelm said with a growl.

Richard turned back to see Wilhelm jamming his gun into Elizabeth's head as she groaned.

With a sigh, Richard returned his attention to the mask. He studied it for a moment before wrapping his hands around the top and bottom and then tugging upward. He was surprised at how easily it lifted from its position despite its heavy weight.

"That's it," Wilhelm said. "Bring it to me."

With Wilhelm creating a pathway with his flashlight, Richard moved steadily across the room toward the outer chamber. However, when he attempted to cross the threshold, the ground started to shake. He froze as a statue in the corner toppled and smashed onto the floor. Pieces of the ceiling crashed downward, stirring up dust. Quickly dropping to his knees, Richard covered his head.

"I need that mask now," Wilhelm said.

Richard looked up and shook his head. "I can't get this to you."

"Figure out a way," Wilhelm said as he glanced at his gun.

Before Richard could move, the tripwire he'd set snapped and the rocks tumbled down from above and partially blocked the doorway. There was little chance that he could fit through a small opening, though Richard assumed the odds that he would survive if he got through were lower with an armed Wilhelm just waiting for his prized treasure.

As much as Richard wanted to keep the golden death mask out of Wilhelm's hands, Elizabeth's life was still at stake. Richard couldn't just let her die.

Scrambling over the rocks, Richard fed the heavy piece through the opening to Wilhelm. Once it was through, he picked up his gun and started firing at Richard. With the ground still moving, Richard darted away from the clearing in search of a place more difficult for Wilhelm to reach with his gun.

Once Richard ran out of room, he crossed back into the tomb and the shaking stopped. So had the gunfire. For a moment, Richard wondered if the Reichswehr unit had vanished since they got what they came for. Poking his head around the corner, he peered into the chamber and toward the doorway. Two more bullets whistled past Richard's head.

"Come on out, Richard," Wilhelm said. "I hear a bullet to the head is far better than being buried alive."

Two more Reichswehr members followed Wilhelm's orders to pursue Richard. Unsure of what do to next, he eased inside the chamber, which began to shake again. The pair of soldiers lost their balance and fell as a couple of columns toppled onto the men and flattened them.

Wilhelm fired several shots into the chamber again, desperately trying to hit Richard as he bunkered behind some debris on the floor.

"Have fun being buried next to a king," Wilhelm said before dashing away from the entrance.

Richard eyed the soldiers again to make sure they were dead. Neither of them moved. As the ground finally stopped shaking for good, all Richard could hear in the distance was Elizabeth screaming.

Two more gunshots ripped through the air, followed by silence.

Richard leapt over the soldiers' bodies and tried to yank the rocks away from his only way out. But the stones wouldn't budge.

CHAPTER 38

DUST FLITTED FROM THE CEILING OF THE CHAMBER as Richard darted around in search of an exit. His initial scan revealed that the only way out was the way he came in, but he took a second look. Standing inches away from the wall, Richard placed his hands flush against it and crept his way along. Checking the full breadth of three sides including the one that connected the two rooms, he didn't find the slightest crack or ridge that would indicate the presence of an opening. But there was still one wall left.

As Richard eased his way down, his index finger caught a small trough running near the bottom. He knelt and brushed away the surrounding debris. Stepping back, he illuminated the area with his flashlight and noticed the distinct outline of a space about three feet wide and two feet tall.

While reading up on the tombs, Richard remembered about how young boys were trained to finalize the burial chambers after the walls had been sealed. Once they finished, a boy would slither out through a small passageway. Due to its size, potential thieves would have a difficult time smuggling out the bulk of a king's treasures, discouraging such attempts. Between the presence of the Medjay lurking around the Valley of the Kings and the numerous other failsafes built into the sites, raiding a tomb would likely result in certain death.

Richard figured he would be able to shimmy his way through the tunnel, though it would be a tight fit. He just didn't know where it led—or how to open it. Pulling out his dagger, he scraped more dirt out of the edge of the stone door until it loosened. The next painstaking process included inching the piece from side to side while pulling on it to displace it from the front of the shaft. After several minutes, he managed to free the block.

After a brief inspection of the area with his flashlight, Richard scooted inside, his stomach against the ground while propping himself up on his elbows. He guessed he had a clearance of maybe two inches for his head and half that on either side. With his knife in one hand and light in the other, he wormed his way along. The dust stirred up as he moved, drying out his mouth. When enough particles filled his lungs, he broke out into an unpleasant coughing fit, which kicked up more dirt. The whole journey took about ten minutes until he came to a dead end.

Richard reached forward and cut around the edge of the block. Satisfied that he sufficiently cleared the edges, he nudged it forward. After another couple minutes, the small doorway slid forward into a larger space until it wouldn't move any farther. In order to get out, he slid the rock to the left. Inhaling the blast of fresh air, Richard worked quickly to get out. Once freed, he stood and shined his light around and realized the place looked familiar. It was the antechamber of King Ramses VI's tomb, which had been excavated twenty-four years earlier and was a popular site for tourists. Richard could only assume that the pillar positioned in front of the tunnel was glossed over by archeologists searching for Ramses's burial chamber, unaware of what was underneath their noses.

After catching his breath, Richard returned the stone

to its position, re-sealing King Tutankhamun's tomb. Convinced no one would notice the disturbance near the base of the wall, he raced outside in search of Elizabeth. Richard hustled down the side of the hill and over to the dig site that was virtually abandoned. The tent, the tools, the workers—everything was gone. He shined his light against the area where he had dug with Sherif. Nothing but a pile of rocks.

Richard hustled to the top of the ridge and peered out across the sea of darkness in an attempt to spot Wilhelm. For a few seconds, he surveyed the valley below and didn't see anything. Then he stopped when a glint of fire moving quickly in the distance caught his eye.

Wilhelm.

Richard raced down the hill and found his and Elizabeth's horses where they'd been left. As he was untying his steed, Richard noticed two men lying on the ground, surrounded by a pool of blood. He rushed over to check on them. One man was dead with a bullet hole in his forehead, while the other one was clutching his chest.

When Richard knelt next to the man to help him, he shook his head.

"It's too late," he said in a whisper. "The Germans—you must stop them."

Then he exhaled his final breath.

Richard shut the man's eyes before standing back up and scanning the area once more. There was no doubt that the small caravan racing across the valley floor was the Reichswehr unit. Richard mounted his horse and tore off across the desert. He wasn't sure he'd be able to catch the Reichswehr entourage before they reached the ferry, but he had to try, if not for the sake of the treasure, for Elizabeth.

When Richard reached the dock at the Nile, the ferry was gone, already halfway across the river. Richard's only chance of catching them was to ride a couple kilometers up the river, cross the bridge, and chase them down in Luxor. He dug his heels into the side of his horse and raced to the bridge.

As he rode, he pondered the best approach to fighting off the entire Reichswehr unit, despite the reduction in number of troops. He needed to reach them before they arrived at their hotel and regrouped.

The breeze created by the swift jaunt along the sandy path sent a chill over Richard. With the moon beaming brightly above, he would've preferred to stop and admire the scenery. Galloping across the Egyptian desert beneath a starry sky is the kind of moment he knew his grandfather would have wanted to experience, though likely in a different scenario. The winding road that led Richard to Egypt and ultimately the Valley of the Kings was unexpected in many ways, but he chose to embrace his assignment and count it a unique adventure. Such a perspective was the only way he kept from wondering if he'd actually gone mad.

Hoofs thundering across the bridge echoed in the still of the night, interrupted only briefly by the shrill train whistle in the distance. Richard guided his horse back toward the hotel where the Reichswehr had been lodging. When he arrived, he dismounted and then sprinted toward the entrance, stopping short on the veranda when he heard a familiar voice.

"They're gone," the man said.

Richard swung around to see Jabari slumped against the wall, applying pressure to his right bicep with his left hand. Trickling blood glistened in the faint light.

"I tried to stop them," Jabari said. "But one of the men I was fighting surprised me and slashed my arm."

"Are you going to survive?" Richard asked.

"I'll live, but your lady friend is in grave danger. They plan on using her as a pawn until they get out of the country."

"Do you know where they were going?"

Jabari shook his head. "I'm guessing the train depot. Once they leave, they'll be nearly impossible to catch."

Another whistle broke the otherwise serene evening.

"Better hurry," Jabari said again.

Richard leaped up to jump onto his horse. He rode hard and arrived at the station several blocks away in a matter of minutes only to see the train pulling away from the platform.

"Do you speak English?" Richard asked one of the nearby attendants.

The man nodded.

"Did you see any Germans board that train?"

"There were quite a few. And they looked like they were in a hurry to leave."

The lights on the caboose dimmed as it rolled away. Richard darted back toward his horse before saddling up and charging down the tracks after the train. He managed to catch the train before it reached full speed and grabbed on to the handrail. Pulling himself aboard, he steadied his feet and took a deep breath. Then he eased inside the cabin, which was little more than a rolling supply closet, littered with train parts, dry goods, and luggage. He also found several attendant uniforms hanging from a rack. Without hesitating, he suited up in one, figuring it would give him the best chance to maneuver throughout the train without drawing suspicion.

Upon exiting the caboose, he leapt across the coupler links and entered the last passenger car. He smiled and nodded at some of the passengers who made eye contact with him as he flitted down the aisle. Richard went through both second and third classes on the train without the slightest hint of the Reichswehr presence. For a moment, he wondered if the man on the platform had been intentionally misleading. Then Richard reached first class.

The first thing he saw when he stepped inside the dining car were two familiar German soldiers sitting at the bar, drinking. Richard pulled his hat down low across his brow and eased past them without earning even a glance. He hopped across another set of couplers and into the first class sleeper cabins. Moving steadily down the corridor, he tried to determine which ones belonged to the Reichswehr. As he sauntered past each one, he strained to hear any conversation inside. Based on previous observations, Richard knew that Wilhelm would likely have a compartment all to himself. And with only seven other soldiers and Elizabeth, the group required a total of three rooms.

When Richard neared the end of the car, there were only three rooms left.

This has to be where they're staying.

He leaned in to hear a snippet of the conversation. The combination of German along with Elizabeth's voice confirmed his suspicions. Richard spun and headed along the corridor. When he reached the bar, he grabbed a napkin and scribbled a note on it. Then he ordered a drink and billed it to what he presumed to be Wilhelm's room.

Upon gathering the cocktail, Richard strode back down the hallway and knocked on the door. He kept his head down when one of the soldiers answered.

"For the lady," Richard said in his best thick English accent.

The man rolled his eyes and took the glass along with the napkin positioned underneath before sliding the door shut. Richard headed toward the dining car to lie in wait.

The instructions were simple: Go to the restroom in the dining car right now.

Richard clung to the rails on the outside of the car as he waited. Less than a minute passed before the door from the dining car slid open and the two soldiers jumped between the pair of cars. One of the men glanced at Richard with a furrowed brow, but he quelled any suspicion by wishing the men a good night with a thick English accent.

Almost immediately, the train headed across a large ravine that had a sizeable tributary branching off from the Nile. Moments later, the sleeper cabin door opened and Elizabeth stepped through, leaping to the other side. She gasped as she looked down. Then her eyes widened upon noticing Richard.

"Go to the caboose, and wait for me there," he said.

She nodded and didn't hesitate. Then a Reichswehr soldier followed after Elizabeth. But as he was in midstride between the two cars, Richard rocked back and drove both his feet into the man's midsection, knocking him off balance. He grasped for the railing and came up empty before he plummeting into the ravine.

Richard sighed then poked his head back into the sleeper cabin. With the hallway clear, he moved to the next part of his plan. He stole down the corridor and exited through the front of the car before climbing on top of the roof. Lying prone, he looked down and lined up his target: Wilhelm's window.

With a thunderous crack, Richard kicked through the glass and tumbled into Wilhelm's room. The sudden interruption caught the German unit chief off guard as he scrambled to his feet. Richard kept Wilhelm on the defensive, landing a flurry of punches before spotting the golden mask.

Richard snatched it and headed back toward the window. With Wilhelm staggering to his feet, the other Reichswehr members rapped on the door, which was locked.

After not getting a response, they tried to kick the door down.

Richard worked quickly to knock the stray fragments of glass out of the frame before climbing back through and onto the roof. And Wilhelm followed.

* * *

WILHELM GRABBED THE GUN AND TUCKED IT INTO THE BACK of his pants before scrambling after the thief. Still woozy from the pounding, Wilhelm closed his eyes and shook his head to rid himself of the dull ache. The move didn't work, but there wasn't time to worry. The treasure was no longer in his possession.

"I'll handle this," Wilhelm shouted to his men, who were still trying to kick down the door to his room. His *wolfsrudel* were certainly capable of handling the job, but this was personal. He underestimated the American and had failed to eliminate him not once but twice, a mistake Wilhelm wanted to correct on his own.

When he reached the roof, he saw a silhouetted man sprinting across the tops of the cars. Wilhelm pursued without hesitation. His training had prepared him for a moment such as this. With the opportunity to make a sizeable deposit into Germany's future war chest, he couldn't let this expensive gift vanish into the Egyptian night along with the pesky American, Richard Halliburton. Wilhelm had invested too much into this expedition, both from his own personal finances and the skimpy Reichswehr treasury.

Using his long, lanky steps, Wilhelm almost overtook Richard before tackling him from behind. The mask slid toward the back of the car, farther away from the grasp of both men. Richard swung first, but Wilhelm had wised up from the earlier beating. The order of punches seemed rehearsed and predictable as he dodged every one. Then he went on the counterattack, slamming his fist into Richard's face repeatedly until the American was left bloodied and sluggish.

Wilhelm staggered to his feet before spitting onto Richard and then stepping over him. With the treasure just a few feet away, Wilhelm staggered toward it before looking up to see a fast approaching tunnel. Diving back down, he remained prone on the roof and hoped the clearance was high enough to keep him from suffering a life-ending head injury.

The darkness seemed to last an eternity as he lay still. At last, the moon illuminated the rooftop again as they emerged from the tunnel. But when he looked toward the spot where the treasure had come to a rest, it was gone.

And so was Richard Halliburton.

CHAPTER 39

RICHARD STASHED THE GOLDEN MASK IN A CHEST tucked away in the corner of the caboose. He glanced up at Elizabeth, who was shaking. Taking her hand, he gave it a reassuring squeeze.

"Stick with the plan," he said. "It's all going to work out."

"Are you sure?"

Richard shrugged. "It's like roulette. Red or black? Someone has to win."

"You're not exactly instilling me with much confidence."

Before he could respond, a thud hit the platform just outside the door.

"Get ready," he whispered.

Seconds later, the door flew open as Wilhelm stormed inside with his gun trained straight ahead on Richard.

"You're a sly fox," Wilhelm said. "But you won't be able to get away from me again. Now, hand it over."

Elizabeth swung an iron skillet at Wilhelm, connecting with his arm and knocking the gun out of his hand. Richard dove for the gun as did Wilhelm. In the scuffle, it skidded across the floor and slipped out of the door.

Wilhelm put his knee into Richard's chest and pinned him to the ground. "I guess we'll have to do this the old-fashioned way."

The German got off two more punches before Elizabeth wielded her skillet again in a fit of fury. However, Wilhelm ducked as the iron collided with the wooden door, splintering it and sending shards flying in all directions. Wilhelm grabbed the pan and ripped it from Elizabeth's arms.

Seizing his opportunity to regain the upper hand, Richard wriggled free from Wilhelm amidst the bustle and scrambled to his feet. After backing up a few feet, Richard took a run at Wilhelm and drove him against the wall. Wilhelm groaned as his back slammed hard into the wooden siding. Richard proceeded to punch Wilhelm several more times, bloodying his face.

"It's time for you to leave," Richard said as he backed up and surveyed the damage to Wilhelm's face.

"Not without my gold," Wilhelm said.

The Reichswehr leader spun to his right and dug a gun out of his shoe before attempting to get a shot off on Richard. However, Wilhelm had become so engrossed with Richard that he didn't see what was happening to the side. Elizabeth drew back and smashed Wilhelm in the face with the skillet, knocking him out.

Richard sighed in relief before springing into action. He grabbed Wilhelm beneath his armpits and dragged him toward the door.

"Can you get his ankles?" Richard asked.

Elizabeth nodded and then hoisted his feet off the ground.

Richard shuffled back and outside to toss the body onto the third class train's platform.

"Why don't we just kill him?" Elizabeth asked. "You know he's a bad man."

"I'd prefer not to have the full weight of the Reichswehr chasing me down the rest of my life," Richard said, pausing before he hoisted up Wilhelm and flung him to the third class train. "It'd be a short one if that was the case."

Richard dashed back inside the caboose and located a large pair of bolt cutters. He returned outside and hacked away at the coupler that attached the caboose to the rest of the train.

"You sure this is a good idea?" Elizabeth asked as the train crossed another deep ravine.

"I'm certainly not interested in fighting all those German soldiers who will hunt us down if we stay on the train."

"It's too late for that," said an unfamiliar voice.

Richard looked up to see a pair of Reichswehr unit members standing on the platform in front of him. As the train started to move uphill, Richard returned his focus to the coupler and made one final snip, freeing the caboose from the rest of the train.

Although disconnected, the caboose's momentum carried it upward and hadn't yet separated much from the car in front it when one of the soldiers acted as if he was going to jump to the caboose.

"I wouldn't do that if I were you," Elizabeth said.

Richard looked over and saw her with Wilhelm's gun in her hand, trained on the soldiers. Then he saluted the soldiers and winked.

The other soldier went for his weapon. Richard noticed what he was doing and instinctively pulled Elizabeth inside the caboose, which had drifted farther away from the other cars. Several shots ripped through the wall.

"Stay down," Richard said as he attempted to cover Elizabeth with his body.

He heard a couple more shots, but they didn't hit anything. That's when Richard realized they were drifting backward.

"What's going on?" Elizabeth asked.

"We're on our own."

Richard kept his arm over Elizabeth until they were barely moving. He then stood and looked out toward where they had been coupled with the train. It was nowhere to be seen. Elizabeth hopped up and smiled.

"We're finally rid of them," she said.

"I wouldn't celebrate yet," Richard said as he surveyed the area. They were stuck over the center of the ravine.

Elizabeth's eyes widened. "How are we going to get off here?"

"Walk?"

She shook her head. "I'll sprout wings and fly before I do that."

"Perhaps the possibility of death will inspire you to reconsider."

"Absolutely not. I think I'd rather die than walk across the tracks."

Richard sank to the floor and leaned against the wall. He couldn't just leave her, but he knew that they only had a small amount of time before a train came roaring from the other direction.

"There's a train that arrives in Luxor just after 1:00 a.m.," he said as he glanced at his watch. "It won't be long before it gets here."

"What kind of bloody comment is that?" she asked. "Is that supposed to motivate me?"

"I was hoping it might."

She shook her head. "You obviously don't understand my fear of heights. Death is preferable."

Richard found his satchel that he'd stashed in the caboose and threw it around his neck. He opened the chest, pulled out King Tutankhamun's mask, and studied it closely.

"Amazing, isn't it?" he asked.

"Quite decadent, especially for something that ancient,"

she said. "I wouldn't expect such a lavish golden mask from that era, but what do I know?"

"This is quite incredible," Richard said, unable to take his eyes off it. "It's no wonder the Reichswehr chose this artifact to escape with. I have no idea just how valuable it is, but I'm sure it'd fetch a pretty penny."

He turned the object over in his hand, studying each detail closely. After a couple minutes, he stuffed it into his bag and cinched it shut.

"Now what are you going to do?" she asked.

"I'm going to walk across the tracks," he said. "Are you going to come with me?"

"I already told you that I'm not going anywhere."

Richard froze as the tracks started to shake and rumble. He dashed outside and looked back up the hill and saw the light of another locomotive chugging straight toward them.

"Well, you need to make up your mind fast because we're going to die if we stay here," Richard said.

He didn't wait for her to respond, instead searching all over the caboose for a rope. Once he found one, he scurried outside and secured it around one of the railroad ties.

"You coming?" he asked.

She sighed and shook her head. "I'll be fine here."

"You're going to die," Richard said before he snatched her around her waist and carried her outside while she screamed.

He ignored her pleas to be released as he shimmied down the rope suspended over the ravine. Digging his heels into the twine, he braced for the shaking overhead. The rickety bridge clattered as the train rumbled toward them.

Seconds later, the oncoming train plowed into the caboose and sent it careening over the edge. When their car hit the water, there was a big splash in the water below.

Richard clung to the rope as Elizabeth held on tight.

"Did you see that?" he asked.

"I'm not opening my eyes," she said. "Tell me when it's all over."

Richard felt his hands burning along with every other muscle in his body that he used to keep from slipping downward. When the train finally passed over them, he took a deep breath and started to climb.

"Hold on tight," he said.

Elizabeth's fingernails dug into Richard's shoulders, piercing his skin. He was sure that he was bleeding as he muscled his way up and onto the track.

"Can I look now?" she asked.

"I'm not sure that's a good idea for someone afraid of heights."

He watched her open her eyes before closing them tight again almost immediately.

"You should've warned me," she said.

"I did," Richard said as he wriggled up onto the bridge.

Lying on their backs for a moment, they both stared upward at the starlit sky, dulled only by the moonlight.

Richard rolled over and stood upright. He offered his hand to Elizabeth.

"I don't want to do this," she said.

"You don't have a choice," he said. "Let's go."

Richard held her arm and repeatedly reminded her to look anywhere but down. After about five minutes, they cleared the ravine and were on solid ground. He led her over to the surrounding sand and they both fell to the earth, exhausted and grateful that they'd survived the ordeal.

"Now what?" she asked.

"We go back to Luxor," he said. "I still have some unfinished business to attend to."

CHAPTER 40

RICHARD AND ELIZABETH MANAGED TO HITCH THE short ten-mile ride back to Luxor with a produce delivery truck making its nightly run to some of the surrounding villages. Holding his satchel close against his chest, Richard did his best to cover the artifact poking out of the top. The driver glanced over at Richard and eyed the object.

"What's that?" he asked.

"Just a souvenir," Richard said.

The driver nodded but didn't say another word the rest of the trip.

He was kind enough to deliver them to the front steps of the Winter Palace Hotel. Elizabeth asked him to wait so she could go inside and get some money to pay him for his generosity, but he declined the gesture.

After he drove away, Richard turned to Elizabeth. "Think he suspected anything?"

"I'm sure he did," she said. "It'd be presumptuous to think this evening would end so calmly. I'm sure he only offered to drop us off at the hotel so he can return with five other lads to steal your *souvenir*."

Richard chuckled and nodded. "This does feel too easy, doesn't it?"

She shook her head. "Let me assure you that there was nothing easy about tonight."

"Well, I hope you had fun on your tour."

She smiled. "Is that what you think this was? Just an average tour venture?"

Richard shrugged. "Since I've only given out a handful of them, I'd have to seriously ponder where this one ranked. I can assure you that they've all contained their share of excitement."

"The kind that includes suspension from a rope over a ravine? Or getting held hostage by an elite group of German soldiers?"

"Perhaps you're right," Richard said. "This may have been slightly more exhilarating. It's not every day that you get to uncover the hidden tomb of an ancient king."

"You're ridiculous," she said with a smirk.

"I'll take that as a compliment."

"Take it however you may. However, I need some sleep. Would you be terribly opposed to joining me for brunch?"

Richard glanced at his watch. It was just past 3:00 a.m. "I have some things I need to do in the morning."

"Are you mad? I'm about to fall over from exhaustion."

"So am I, but there are some things that I must do first. Perhaps we can reconvene for dinner."

"I'm afraid I already have plans," she said.

"We'll find the time again. Don't worry," he said.

"I certainly hope so," Elizabeth said before kissing Richard on the cheek and then dashing up the steps.

He smiled and waved as she glanced over her shoulder for one final look. Lingering for a moment outside, Richard gazed at the majestic ridgeline in the distance, lit up by the bright moon.

Grandpa, you would've loved Egypt.

* * *

RICHARD SLEPT HARD UNTIL 6:30 A.M. WHEN HIS ALARM

startled him awake. He staggered to his feet and got dressed in a set of fresh clothes before hustling back down to the dock. The 7:00 a.m. ferry was preparing to depart when he boarded. Paying the attendant, he was the last passenger allowed on before the vessel shoved off across the Nile.

Richard clutched his satchel, keeping it close to his body and trying to hide just how much the object weighed him down. He didn't look out of place among the dozens of other workers attempting to get a few hours of digging in before the blazing sun inflicted misery upon them for the majority of the day. But he was certain he was the only one carrying an artifact, the kind they all might kill for— some figuratively, others quite literally.

He rented a horse and joined the caravan for the Valley of the Kings, peeling off when they reached the site. As most everyone else scurried off to their assigned site, Richard tied off his steed near the entrance to the area and stole off into the tomb of Ramses VI.

Richard only needed an hour to slither his way back down the tunnel into the burial chamber for King Tutankhamun. He inched his way through the tight quarters, placing his bag along with his flashlight in front of him. Though the trip was unpleasant in its nature, Richard looked forward to returning to the ultimate destination and getting an opportunity to investigate it without a lunatic threatening others just a room away.

Once inside, he crept up to the sarcophagus and replaced the mask, hoping that he didn't set off another geological event that would shake the foundations of the valley. Leaning over the mummified body, Richard eased the artifact back into place and released it before moving his hands slowly away.

Nothing happened.

Richard sighed in relief. He waved his flashlight around the room, gawking as he took the scene in. The ornate nature of every item housed in the burial chamber arrested his attention. From everyday objects to the royal treasure, they were all meticulously crafted with undoubtedly what were the most expensive materials of that time.

I could spend days in here.

Richard took fifteen minutes to inspect all the fine details before deciding to return. He did his best to ensure that every item was left just as he'd found it. Satisfied that the room looked relatively untouched, he sat down and embarked upon his journey back to the Ramses VI tomb.

Instead of traveling headfirst down the tunnel, Richard led with his feet so he could reseal the portal. He dragged his flashlight and satchel with him. However, when he reached the end, his feet ran into a solid wall. He pushed at it, but it wouldn't budge.

Just stay calm.

While the tombs fascinated Richard, he certainly didn't want to die in one, not like this. He wasn't sure if he felt the oxygen growing thinner because he knew he was in a sealed compartment or if breathable air actually was vanishing. Either way, he couldn't panic, knowing that any form of hyperventilation would reduce the amount of time he had to get out.

Richard decided to ease closer to the tunnel entrance from the Ramses VI tomb and try again. After drawing his knees as high up as he could, he forced them downward. Three times he pushed without any movement. However, on the fourth shove, the stone slid, though no more than an inch.

Convinced that he discovered a blueprint for escaping, Richard remained determined and hopeful. He repeated the process many times, incrementally moving the rock with each kick. After five minutes, the door skidded out into the tomb as oxygen rushed into the tunnel.

Richard filled his lungs with the fresh air before shimmying out. Elated that he escaped, he hopped to his feet and started brushing off all the dirt he'd accumulated. He was so relieved to get out that he hadn't even noticed the trio of Medjay agents who'd surrounded him.

Richard swallowed hard as the end of a scimitar blade lifted up his head so he could see the three men surrounding him.

CHAPTER 41

RICHARD THREW HIS HANDS IN THE AIR AS HE SCANNED the faces of the Medjay guards around him. They all scowled as they glared at him. While he wasn't prepared to come up with an explanation, he knew he needed one.

"Gentlemen," Richard began as he forced a smile, "nice day for a little exploration of the tombs, don't you think?"

"What were you doing in that tunnel?" asked the man who was still holding his sword beneath Richard's chin.

He cocked his head to one side. "Would you believe me if I told you that I was replacing a precious artifact?"

"Search him," the soldier said.

The other two guards sprang into action, ripping Richard's bag off his shoulder and rifling through all the papers inside. One of the men pulled out the map that Jabari had drawn for Richard. The guard handed it to the man in charge.

"What's this?" he asked, waving the sketch in front of Richard's face.

"It's a map."

"To what?"

"A tomb," Richard said.

"Which tomb?"

"Would it make any difference what I told you?"

The man narrowed his eyes, repeating his question in a measured tone. "Which tomb?"

"King Tutankhamun's," Richard said.

The three men all broke into laughter. "King Tutankhamun," the man said as he pointed at Richard while glancing at his colleagues. "He thinks he's going to find it."

Richard's jaw went slack as he watched the men enjoy a good chuckle at his expense.

If only they knew.

"Did you think you were going to find it in that tunnel?" one of the men asked.

"I don't know. I just—"

"He found nothing," one of the other guards said after completing his search of Richard.

The leader nodded knowingly. "That tunnel leads nowhere. I've been down it several times. It comes to a dead end after a long way. You're lucky that you made it out alive."

"We noticed the stone ajar here," another agent said. "So, we sealed it back with some mortar. Fortunately for you, it hadn't fully dried yet."

"You're very lucky—and foolish," the leader said. "Whoever sold you this map did so at your expense. The legend of King Tutankhamun's tomb is nothing more than a fanciful tale."

One of the other agents shoved Richard's bag into his chest. "I suggest you stop wasting your time and get out of here."

Richard wanted to tell the men what he'd found, especially since they were tasked with being the guardians of the tombs. But if they thought he was a fool and were ready to release him without further incident, Richard figured he'd keep his mouth shut and let them assume whatever they wanted.

Less than a half hour later, he was racing across the valley on his horse back toward the ferry.

***

LATER THAT EVENING, RICHARD WAS HEADING DOWNSTAIRS for dinner when he ran into Vincent Vance.

"Mr. Francois, I had another satisfied client gush about your abilities as a tour guide."

"Miss Corbett?" Richard asked.

Vincent nodded. "I think we need to consider appointing you to this post on a permanent basis."

"While I appreciate the kind words and the gesture, I'm not sure I want to stay here."

"Why not? I've never heard of anyone unearthing such adventure in only a week in Luxor. You have an extraordinary gift that's only going to result in a stampede of future clients if you're here. And these clients are all quite wealthy."

Richard shook his head. "I've always wanted to see Egypt, but there are other places I'd like to explore. My wanderlust won't be quenched by a permanent post escorting wealthy English noblemen and their wives to the Valley of the Kings."

"Are you declining my offer?"

"In no uncertain terms do I want to stay here, though I have appreciated my time with Thomas Cook & Son, even if we got off to a bit of a bumpy start."

Vincent smiled. "Well, it wasn't all smooth sailing, but I will respect your decision. However, if you ever change your mind, please let me know."

"I will, sir."

"Where will you head next?"

"I'm not sure, though I'm hoping to relax and take a slow ride up the Nile to Cairo. Do you think you can make that happen for me?"

"Consider it a parting gift for all you've done," Vincent said before slapping Richard on the chest with an envelope. "And here's what I owe you for your work."

"Thank you, sir," Richard said, offering his hand. "It's been quite an experience."

Richard tipped his hat to Vincent before continuing downstairs and scanning the room for Elizabeth. She wasn't here. However, he noticed Dr. Howard Carter sitting alone at a table against the back wall with a glass and a half-empty bottle of port on the table.

"Is anyone sitting here?" Richard asked.

Dr. Carter shrugged and gestured to the seat. "I'm not sure I'd be the best company right now, Mr. Francois, but if you insist."

Richard sat down and leaned forward on the table. "Why do you look so glum? More trouble with the Egyptian Antiquities Society?"

"They've informed me that I'm free to resume my work, but it's my patron who is the problem now."

"Funding issues?"

Dr. Carter nodded. "Yes, as in he doesn't want to invest any more money in the project."

"So, where does that leave you?"

"On a slow boat back to England," he said as he shook his head and then took another long pull on his glass of port. "I really thought I was going to find it this time."

"Find what?" Richard asked.

"King Tutankhamun's tomb. I know it's out there, despite what people say. There's too much evidence."

"What if I told you where to find it?"

Dr. Carter laughed. "I'd say you have no idea what you're talking about."

Richard reached into his coat pocket and produced the

map Jabari had given him. "When you get back to England, have a chat with your patron and then show him this."

He pushed it across the table toward Dr. Carter, who hesitated to touch the document.

"Go ahead," Richard said. "It's not going to bite you."

Dr. Carter unfolded it, smoothing it out on the table. "Where did you get this?"

"That's really not important," Richard said. "However, what is important is the fact that this will lead you right to King Tutankhamun's tomb and all its glorious riches."

"You say that as if you've been there."

"Perhaps I have," Richard said with a wink. "But you have done such great work here. You deserve to be the one to discover it and handle it with the care necessary to preserve such a historic find."

Dr. Carter cocked his head and eyed Richard carefully. "You're serious about this, aren't you?"

Richard nodded. "I wouldn't joke about such a matter."

Dr. Carter folded the map and then stuffed it into his pocket. A smile spread across his face.

"If you're right about this, I'm going to owe you in a big way," he said.

"I'd rather you not mention me," Richard said. "Seeing you unearth the site so others can experience the grandeur of the tomb for themselves will be satisfaction enough for me."

"You must want something then. What is it? Money? Credit?"

Richard shook his head. "Do me a favor and hire a couple of men to help with your dig—and pay them handsomely. The names of these local guides are Sherif Nazari and Jabari Gamal."

"I'm acquainted with them both."

"Good," Richard said. "They deserve an opportunity like this."

Dr. Carter nodded and then leaned in close. "What's it like?"

"What's what like?"

"The tomb—what's in there?"

Richard leaned back and wagged his index finger at the doctor. "You need to discover it for yourself. But I can promise you won't be disappointed."

"Would you like a glass of port?" Dr. Carter asked as his countenance lifted.

"You enjoy the rest of that bottle," Richard said. "I need to get some sleep before my journey tomorrow."

"Where are you going?"

"Back to Cairo."

"And then where?"

Richard shrugged. "I'm not sure just yet. Maybe I'll send you a postcard."

Dr. Carter poured another glass and raised it toward Richard. "To you, Mr. Francois."

"Actually, that's just my tour guide name."

"Oh?"

"Yes, I'm Richard Halliburton, from Memphis—Memphis, Tennessee, that is."

"Well, Mr. Halliburton, it's been a pleasure to make your acquaintance."

"Good luck, Dr. Carter."

Richard got up and hustled down the street to Sherif's mercantile. He was locking up the store as Richard arrived.

"I'm sorry, but we're closed," Sherif said before he recognized Richard.

"Sherif!"

Sherif unlocked the door and waved Richard inside. "I

heard you had quite the night last night."

"I doubt you've heard half of it," Richard said.

Jabari strode through the door leading to the supply room. He was holding his arm.

"How are you, Jabari?" Richard asked.

Jabari shrugged. "I've been better, but I'm alive. And I see you somehow made it, too. I was beginning to get worried."

"I managed," Richard said as he produced the envelope Vincent had given him. After removing twenty dollars, he handed the rest to Sherif.

"What's this for?" Sherif asked.

"It's not much, but it's a portion of what I owe you for all your help. Divide it among yourselves."

"You need this more than I do," Sherif said.

"Perhaps, but I want to make good on all my debts. And on that note, I wanted to let you know that Dr. Howard Carter will be hiring you both to help him on his new dig site—the tomb of King Tutankhamun."

"Should be simple enough," Jabari said with a wry grin.

"I appreciate all you did, and I'm sorry you got caught up in all of this."

"It's not your fault," Sherif said. "If anyone's to blame, it's Jabari. He's the one who got me into this mess."

Richard looked at Jabari. "How's your family?"

"Safe and far away from where the Germans will be able to find us. Thank you for asking."

"I doubt the Germans will be bothering you again," Richard said. "If anyone is going to draw their ire, I'm certain that will be me."

"Did you get the golden mask back?" Jabari asked.

Richard nodded as Jabari's eyes widened.

"How on Earth did you—"

"It's a long story."

"And where is it now?" Jabari asked.

"They won't be finding it any time soon," Richard said as he grinned.

"You need to worry more about the Medjay than the Germans," Sherif said.

"I already handled them, too." Richard glanced at his watch. "I'd love to stay and chat, but I need to get going. I'm leaving in the morning, and I need to gather all my things."

Both men approached Richard and gave him a hug.

"You are forever our brother," Sherif said. "If you need anything ever again, you know how to find us."

"I'm going to miss you both," Richard said before he turned and walked out that back exit.

CHAPTER 42

THE JOURNEY ON THE STEAMSHIP BACK TO CAIRO TOOK five days, most of which Richard spent either sleeping or gazing upon the exotic wildlife roaming around the banks of the Nile. He consumed plenty of free drinks given to him by grateful Thomas Cook & Son tourists. While he had related numerous stories to return home with, he didn't mind giving them a few more about his previous ventures around Europe, which may or may not have included a few embellishments. However, the rest of his time was spent conversing with Elizabeth Corbett.

On the final night of their voyage, he dined alone with her before inviting her to join him on the dance floor. While Elizabeth was considerably cultured, she hadn't fully embraced the American dancing styles. When Richard asked the band if they knew any jazz, the leader said they had recently learned one. And as they began to play, Richard introduced Elizabeth to the Foxtrot.

After the song ended, Elizabeth clapped her hands before bending over and resting her hands on her knees.

"That was quite different," she said.

Richard glanced up to see that their performance had gathered a small crowd of onlookers who were also applauding.

"Bet you didn't think you were going to be on display, did you?" he asked.

She shook her head and smiled. "Though I'm beginning to expect the unexpected when I'm with you."

He chuckled and led her back to their table where they both sat down.

"So, where's our globetrotting explorer off to next?" Elizabeth asked.

Richard shrugged. "I'm not quite sure, to be honest. I have some business to attend to in Cairo. But after that—who knows."

She reached across the table and took both of his hands. "Come back with me to England then. There are plenty of places I'd love to take you, places that won't require your acrobatic, aquatic, or antiquity skills."

"Sounds rather dull, don't you think?" Richard said with a wink.

"Oh, don't be so daft. You'll be amazed by some of the sites I can show you—and likely in a way that not many others can."

"You do remember that I've already been to England, don't you?"

"Maybe you mentioned it, but I'm offering you the opportunity to see it in a new light."

Richard withdrew, pulling his hands away from Elizabeth. "I've really enjoyed our time together, but I'd hate for you to get the wrong idea."

"The wrong idea about what?"

Richard's eyebrows shot upward as he cocked his head to one side. "Oh, Elizabeth, perhaps I've misread your intentions. I just thought—"

Her face fell as she threw her hands in the air and set her jaw. "Say no more. I'm the one who's been the fool."

Richard could tell she was fighting back tears. "There's no denying that we have a special connection after what we went through," he said. "However, as much as I adore you, I'm afraid I could never be faithful to you."

She eyed him closely as she knit her brow. "What kind of man are you?"

"A good one, I hope," he said. "What I mean is that adventure will always be my mistress—and I'm certain that you nor anyone else will be able to compete with her. She's quite demanding in that way."

Elizabeth leaned on the table and looked down. "I knew you were too good to be true. Why did I ever—"

"Stop," he said. "I never meant to give you the wrong impression."

"I know, I know. You've been nothing but a perfect gentleman. And I just—"

He reached across the table and grabbed her hands. "You're a courageous woman. Don't ever change. You'll find a man who will appreciate your spirit and be ready to explore the world with you. And to be quite frank, I'm not that man—though it has nothing to do with you and everything to do with me. If there's one thing I know about myself, it's that I'll never settle down."

She sighed as a faint smile crept across her lips. "Don't ever change, Richard."

"I don't plan on it."

"And good luck," she said before she stood.

Richard stood with her, and they exchanged cordial kisses on the sides of their cheeks before exiting the dining room together and retiring for the evening in their respective quarters.

* * *

ONCE THE SHIP MADE PORT THE NEXT MORNING, RICHARD searched for a place to send a telegraph to Hank Foster. Richard composed a brief report using Foster's cipher.

Treasure safe. Germans departed region.
Please respond.

Richard grabbed a bite to eat from a street vendor before returning to the store to wait for a note from Foster. To pass the time, Richard strolled around the streets of Cairo. The sphinx souvenir was still in his pocket, and he couldn't help but smile when he considered how he had fulfilled a dream for his grandfather.

Three hours later, Richard returned to the telegraph outpost to see if he had received a response. He was excited to receive a coded note.

Thank you. Money wired to you.
Danger in India. Interested?

Richard re-read the message several times. He was excited about getting paid for what he did. But another assignment off gallivanting around the globe and risking his life to stop the Germans?

How can I resist?

THE END

ACKNOWLEDGMENTS

This project has been incredibly exciting and fun to embark upon, mixing fiction with fact. And quite frankly, none of it would've ever come about without my wife's introduction of Richard Halliburton to me through his timeless Book of Marvels. My children also played a huge role in convincing me to write something about Halliburton after they read his books and would regale me with his stories everyday until I finally decided I needed to read them for myself.

I'd like to thank Rhodes College and Bill Short for allowing me access to Richard Halliburton's archived journals and other material that helped fill in the blanks about what kind of man Richard really was and where he really went. Bill was an incredible help in gathering the information for me and graciously allowing me to plod my way through the material I requested. Without Bill's assistance, I'm not sure this project would've ever become a reality—at least in my lifetime.

Sir Richard J. Evans also enthusiastically aided the creation of this story in giving me plausible creative ways to weave the storyline of the Reichswehr into this fictionalized tale. I'm so grateful that when I reached out to him that he was more than gracious in supplying me with ample fodder— material that will be used in future novels in this series.

And as always, this book wouldn't be what it is without Krystal Wade's skillful editorial direction. She made this book much better than when I originally conceived it.

Dwight Kuhlman has been incredible to partner with in creating the audio version of this book, and I look forward to his voice being the one that shares many more Richard Halliburton tales in the future.

And last but certainly not least, I'm most grateful for you, the reader, who decided to invest your time with one of my stories. I hope you had as much fun reading this book as I did writing it.

Made in United States
Troutdale, OR
08/04/2023